—THE—
MISSION

WARNER BROS., GOLDCREST and KINGSMERE Present
An ENIGMA PRODUCTION In Association With FERNANDO GHIA
ROBERT DE NIRO   JEREMY IRONS   In "THE MISSION"
Music by ENNIO MORRICONE   Written by ROBERT BOLT
Produced by FERNANDO GHIA AND DAVID PUTTNAM   Directed by ROLAND JOFFÉ

DISTRIBUTED BY **WARNER BROS.**
A WARNER COMMUNICATIONS COMPANY

—THE—
MISSION
ROBERT BOLT

A JOVE BOOK

THE MISSION

A Jove Book/published by arrangement with
Muse Publishing Corporation APS

PRINTING HISTORY
Jove edition/November 1986

ISBN: 0–515–08877–3

Jove Books are published by The Berkley Publishing Group,
200 Madison Avenue, New York, N.Y. 10016.
The words "A JOVE BOOK" and the "J" with sunburst
are trademarks belonging to Jove Publications, Inc.

PRINTED IN THE UNITED STATES OF AMERICA

Part
One

RODRIGO MENDOZA WAS fourteen in 1725 when the rowing boat of his father Alvaro was found floating in the harbor of Cadiz at dawn. One oar was jammed between the keel and the thwarts and an empty wine flask was stuck in the bottom. Alvaro had fallen into the slack waters of the harbor in the course of a lighterage job. A few sacks of grain were still waiting to be ferried out, so Cesare Matius, the lighterage boss, loaded them onto his own boat and rowed them to the waiting *Grosso*. In answer to the enquiry where Alvaro was, he shrugged and indicated the waters of the harbor.

He went and knocked on the door of Mendoza's house and took off his hat as he told Rodrigo that his father was dead. The orphan went indoors and came out carrying his younger brother Philippo, age three. Then he went down to his father's boat and carefully inspected it. He set his brother playing, accepted a cheroot from Cesare and listened to him.

"I offer my condolences on the death of your father."

"I thank you."

"The boat is yours," Cesare went on, with a wave of his cheroot.

"True," said the boy.

"You, of course, cannot handle it yourself."

"I can try."

"Who will look after Philippo?"

"I will."

"Listen, I have decided to give you ten dineros for the boat with license."

"It is worth twenty."

"No, no. Say, twelve."

Mendoza looked down into the boat and then up at the

three-masted aviso *Grosso* in the harbor. "Had he delivered all the corn before he fell?"

Cesare said, "I finished it for him."

"All of it?"

"The last part."

"Thank you," replied Mendoza. "It is good to know that when a boatman is claimed by the waters of the harbor, he is not forgotten," and looked away. So, he decided, Cesare would have to give him the full payment.

Mendoza lifted his brother off the pebbles. "I must have time to turn over in my mind my father's death."

"Naturally."

Mendoza bought a piece of cheese, some bread, a flask of milk, and some wine. When he had shuttered the heat out of the cavernous house, which his father had paid for by the week, he gave all of the milk and half of the bread and cheese to Philippo. He said a prayer for the dead and then settled himself at the foot of the wall looking up at the window while Philippo ate his meal and then turned over on his side to sleep. While the walls of the place became dark and the window became bright with stars, Mendoza passed his thoughts across his mind.

He had not liked his father. His mother, Catherine, had been different, but death had come for her while she was giving birth to Philippo. Thenceforward his father had taken no notice of his two sons, but found his solace in the bottle. Mendoza's affection was all turned to his little brother, enfolding the child, while Philippo regarded him as the ultimate authority and adored him.

Now that his father was dead, Rodrigo could remain with Philippo and earn a living by lighterage, but this would mean that his brother would grow up into an untaught man, as he was himself. The alternative was to leave the child with the Sisters of San Fernando and chance his own arm overseas. He decided to go and see the Mother Superior the following day.

He took the wine flask and snuggled down into the rock-hard bed, pulling the woven sacks about him, overwhelmed. Maybe it would be best to be a lighterman. It would provide a respectable living for them both. But next morning he went to the Hospice of San Fernando.

"The question is, can you afford it? We make a charge here, alas," the Mother Superior told him. "What is your trade?"

Why not say he was the son of an aristocrat from up in the hills? he thought. It would not matter a whit then, not being able to read. But his mother had told him it was wrong to lie; that way perdition lay. He said, "I am a lighterman."

The Mother Superior inclined her head. A lighterman! she thought. Ah, me! "We charge fifteen dineros a year," she said.

Mendoza's face grew stiff. He counted on getting twenty dineros for the boat. This would leave him with five dineros to start his life abroad. He inclined his head. "That is all included?"

"Did you not hear me? Fifteen dineros."

"I will place it in your hand tomorrow."

"How?"

"I will do it."

"Where can we put Philippo if you cannot keep up with the fifteen dineros a year?"

"There will be nobody to protect him; you can make him your gardener."

The Mother Superior tried not to smile. The young! she thought. All the world seems a straight path to them. She leaned forward. "What are you going to do yourself?"

"I intend to go abroad."

Ah, abroad! she thought, That might be different. "You have prospects?" she enquired.

Mendoza nodded; his boat provided him with prospects.

Later that day, after he had returned to the village, he sought out Cesare, who offered him fourteen dineros for the boat.

"No," said Mendoza, "twenty."

Having seen Mendoza's determined expression, Cesare said, "Sixteen."

Mendoza shook his head. "Twenty."

Cesare threw up his hands and walked away. But in the evening he returned and said, "Look, I have thought long about this; you are an orphan, and with nowhere to turn your head; my price is now seventeen; put your hand there."

Mendoza ignored the outstretched hand. "The price is twenty."

Cesare swore a fistful of oaths and went away to his house, slamming the door. The next morning, before anyone else was awake, he went once again to speak to Mendoza. "Look, this is my final offer. If you do not take this, I retract all other offers. Eighteen."

Mendoza said, "Twenty."

Cesare gave in.

Mendoza collected the payment, placed five dineros in a strip of canvas and tied this tightly around his stomach, and then took the fifteen dineros and Philippo to the orphanage. "God be with you, Philippo," he said, and he kissed his brother farewell. Philippo understood, and the ancient stones of the nunnery were rent by a whole day and night of the child's weeping and banging his head on the walls.

Mendoza collected a small roll of clothes from his home, looked around it, and shut the door. He went down to the harbor. There were three three-masted avisos just about to sail for South America: The *Grosso* for Havana, the *Nuestra Señora de Pilar* for Caracas, the *Concepcion* for Buenos Aires.

He sat down against the jetty and watched the boats that came in and out to them.

At three o'clock came a large coach. A gentleman, two ladies, and a young man came from it and climbed with much assistance into a ship's boat. The coachman and a sailor lifted two big trunks in after them, and the sailors, under the command of a bosun, rowed out to the *Concepcion*. In the afternoon the adults returned, without the young man. With one of the women in tears and the gentleman comforting her, they piled back into the coach and drove away. Mendoza wrapped up his hunk of bread and waited.

At seven a long boat from the *Concepcion* brought the young man back to the quayside, and Mendoza followed him. The youth walked into town with a sullen air and sat at an open-air eating place where he knocked his cup of coffee onto the ground; he was close to tears.

"Please," said Mendoza and fetched another.

"Thank you," said the youth.

"The *Concepcion* is it, *señor?*"

"Yes."

"A wholesome boat, they tell me."

"Deplorable. Filthy."

"Truly?"

"This is my first voyage."

"Ah, *señor,* I understand."

"You, I suppose, have been on many such trips?"

"Not on board the *Concepcion, señor.* Many others." That was not a lie. He had been on trips to the other side of the Gulf of Cadiz.

"You have been to Buenos Aires?"

"No, *señor.*"

"I am to be a business partner with my great uncle in Buenos Aires."

"Ah, *señor,* you have a long head for figures."

"Alas, no. And two other persons will be sharing my cabin with me."

"That is to be expected, *señor.*"

"Yes."

"Would you like another cup?"

"Thank you." The youth was gratified at having someone to wait on him. He said, "You have a family in Cadiz?"

"A brother, *señor.* He is being taken care of."

"I have no servant for this trip."

"No, *señor?*"

"You could not be persuaded to take the trip with me, as my servant?"

"No, *señor.*"

"Why not?"

"How could I pay for my passage back home?"

"I will pay for the trip back home."

"I see. But pardon me, how much?"

"I would pay you two months' wages."

"You make it very attractive, *señor.*"

"Four dineros, plus two dineros for the two months' wages."

"But the captain may not have room for a service man, *señor.*"

"I, in my grandfather's name, will tell him."

Two days later they sailed from Cadiz harbor. Mendoza's last sights were of the bell tower of the Hospice of San Fernando and of Cesare rowing his dead father's boat.

The slow pitch and roll of the ship made Mendoza ill, but he obeyed the orders of the captain, the officers, the bosun, the yeomen, the seamen, and his young master and never complained. He watched the pilot closely and cast his own eyes after his at the fluttering luff of the sails or at the stray currents of the ocean. Silent and withdrawn, the pilot alone knew where they were.

Week after week, Mendoza waited until all the sailors had finished their food before receiving his helping of salt pork and biscuits. He slept in the night alone among the foul-smelling anchor cables.

As the days passed, the sailors began to look emaciated.

At the Canaries a ship's boy named Salvador came on board. He was about fifteen years old, with a slovenly face. Looking about, he saw that no one but Mendoza was beneath him, and so whenever he had a foul job to do, he called Mendoza and made him do it.

When they entered the tropics, the captain allowed the two boys to sleep on deck in the bows. One hot night Mendoza opened his eyes to the slowly gyrating stars and caught the surprised face of Salvador a foot from his. Salvador grinned foolishly and took his hand away from Mendoza's waist where he kept his money.

Mendoza coiled his hands around the neck of Salvador and threw himself on top of him. The night watch came and watched, for a fight between two boys was better than nothing. They were writhing about the deck. Salvador was roaring and blaspheming, but Mendoza fought with his mouth drawn back. He pressed his face near to the throat of his enemy, who went quiet and then screamed. Snatched into the burly arms of the watchman, Mendoza fought him. "Jesus Christ!" the watchman growled, and threw him from him. So he was up and after Salvador again. The sailors gripped him and poured buckets of salt water over him. Only when he was two parts drowned did he give over.

The sailors laughed uneasily. "Holy mother, who would have thought he had such a devil in him?" Salvador gave Mendoza a wide berth after that. Mendoza was not molested. He was not befriended either.

The pilot announced that Montevideo was just ahead, and the crewmen were all in the rigging when at last Mendoza saw the pale mountains loom out of the gray sea. Then Buenos Aires lay before them. They pulled right alongside the harbor wall, and a wide gangplank was run ashore.

The young master paid Mendoza, with a nod and a smile, and went ashore where he disappeared with his two trunks, in the company of his great uncle and a pretty cousin. They all got into a coach, and that was the last Mendoza saw of them.

Turning seaward he saw strange vessels passing slowly in the distance, making stealthily for the far side of the bay. He could make out a harbor there, with four or five ships at anchor.

"What's that?" he asked a sailor.

"Colonia del Sacramento."

"What kind of ships are those?"

"Slavers."

At the end of the day when the officers and crew had all been paid and allowed ashore, Mendoza, too, was permitted to walk down the gangplank and make his way into town.

Wandering, he found himself in a public square that offered the shade of some overhanging trees and a stall that sold flapjacks stuffed with pork. He bought some and ate, seated near the fountain.

He was impressed by the streets of modern houses, delicately ornamented public buildings, and imposing churches. They struck a familiar note. But there were also strange, shrieking birds with garish plumage, and the sun was too hot, and a fine white dust rose from the roads to hang a pall over everything.

The Spanish citizens seemed half smothered. Yawning, they entered upon gestures that they lacked the energy to fin-

ish, sitting there in the square in loose waistcoats and unbuck-
led pantaloons.

There was also a group of natives—olive brown, muscular, and dressed in ragged garments—dozing in the shadow of
a church. He peered at them narrowly, but they looked back at
him uninquisitively.

Mendoza rose to his feet and went up to a little knot of
Spaniards. "Good afternoon, *señores*. D'you want a boy to
work for you?"

"No."

"Do you chance to know anyone who does, *señores?*"

"No." Briefly they looked him up and down and then
turned away.

Twilight began to gather in the twittering trees. Someone
nearby was playing a guitar. Mendoza sat on near the fountain.

An officer from the ship came by, together with a man of
about forty with a seamed face. Seeing Mendoza sitting there,
he said, "Here is a boy, if a boy will do."

"Yes, a boy will do."

The officer beckoned Mendoza across. "This is my friend,
Palacio."

"Good evening, Señor Palacio."

"How old are you?"

"Fourteen."

"You can handle a boat?"

"He can handle a boat," said the officer.

"I want a boy to come on a barge to Asunción."

"Asunción," said Mendoza. "I see."

"It is two hundred leagues up the river. I am offering half a
dinero."

"One dinero, *señor,*" said Mendoza.

The man laughed. "One, then! The barge is the *Flores*. Cut
along to the port now and tell the captain I sent you."

The captain proved a dour old man who only grunted when
Mendoza made himself known. From start to finish of the
ensuing voyage he never spoke a needless word. The barge
was a ninety-footer with a huge sprit sail and four long sweeps
on either side, laden with ironware from Madrid. There were a

dozen natives to raise the sail and, when the wind veered around, to lower it.

When they were under way, Mendoza took the helm. The captain watched him for a little and then, satisfied the new hand could steer, sat down to peer myopically over the meandering waters. Mendoza had never seen such a broad river. Both banks were covered with tangled forest. He gestured at the muddy river: "Big."

"Yes."

He nodded at the muddy water flowing past: "A slow current."

"Yes."

He looked at the native crew. They were sunk in lethargy. "What kind of men are they?"

"Guarani."

"Guarani?" No response. At home in Spain nobody cared whether the captain was alive or dead. He was waiting to finish his days there.

One or two words floated back to them from the main deck.

"What language is that?"

"Guarani."

"Are they from these parts?"

The captain pointed to the huge and silent forest that trespassed into the river.

"From there?"

"Up there." He gestured far away up the river.

Mendoza watched them. "They are stupid."

"Yes."

Each night they put in to the shore, at some place where the forest was cut back for about a mile and a village of three or four houses and a church presented itself, surrounded by big farms with mansions and fields of cattle, maize, and orchards. The Guarani would build a fire and serve them maize gruel and fruits, which they washed down with cheap red wine.

Mendoza saw three of these small towns on the journey, and then the vast forest would close back in, creeping stealthily into the water. In one quiet stretch their course took them near the trees. The Guarani crew peered into the trees and exchanged a guttural word in an undertone, but then they saw Mendoza looking and resumed their blank expressions.

After five weeks, a marked increase in the number of fishing boats and farms announced the approach of Asunción. At last, around a headland, the capital of the la Plata region hove into view.

They worked their way through a crowd of barges to the harbor wall, and the captain tied up and disappeared ashore. Mendoza looked at the Guarani, and they looked listlessly back, so he sat down with them to wait. The captain reappeared, ordering the Guarani to work at clearing the boat, and disappeared again. At length Palacio, who had journeyed to Asunción overland, appeared.

"Why are you hanging about here? You have arrived, is it not so?" he said.

"*Si, señor,* but my dinero."

"What dinero?"

"The dinero you promised me."

"I never promised you a dinero."

"*Señor,* you gave me your word on it."

"You have a paper?"

"A paper? No."

Palacio wagged a finger, shook his head, said, "There. You see?" and went off into the town again, but Mendoza followed and persisted.

"*Señor,* you have not paid me my wages." He followed him through the cathedral square, across the two or three fashionable streets, and down the dark alleyways into the old part of town.

"*Señor,* you have not paid me my wages. Excuse me, *señor . . .*"

Palacio turned and looked up and down the alleyway. Then he dragged Mendoza into a courtyard and beat him soundly with the horn handle of his whip till he was semiconscious.

"There. You see?" he said, breathless. "You see? Huh? You see? See? See?" He went off.

Mendoza limped to a fountain and bathed his cuts. Then he

searched the streets. In the evening he found Palacio dining in a restaurant, sitting below a high window. He went around behind the window and called: *"Señor,* you have not paid me my wages. Excuse me, *señor,* one dinero." A short break in the conversation ensued, there was silence from the eating place, and he called again, *"Señor,* you have not paid me my wages. One dinero, *señor.* One dinero." He heard the sound of a chair being pushed back and voices raised in laughter.

Mendoza went quickly and hid across the street. He watched Palacio search for him. Then Palacio paused and finally went back inside. He was greeted by laughter and a burst of foot stamping. Then gradually conversation was resumed. Mendoza approached the window again and said: "I will return for my dinero, *señor."* Then he sprinted off.

The following morning Mendoza, asleep in the square, was roused by the fluttering and bouncing of the birds and Guarani arriving with pitchers of water to prepare for the coming day. They said not a word at finding him stretched out there. A little later, however, the Spanish proprietor of a bakehouse appeared and began staring at him, so he made his way back to the harbor.

Dock workers were clambering sleepily upon the sides of a careened merchant ship. Someone was cooking tortillas and fish. Mendoza bought some and enjoyed it.

Then he noticed an exotic group of men dressed in an assortment of garments, rags, and strange quilted pants. One sported grotesque finery, with soiled ruffles and an earth-stained embroidered coat; he looked as though he had arrived from some dilapidated court. There were also two blacks among them. They were armed with swords and pistols and a musket.

Mendoza asked the vendor of tortillas, "What kind of men are those?" One of the dock workers, who was leisurely eating a tortilla, looked up.

"Mercenaries," he said. "Have nothing to do with that lot. They take no notice of the law."

Mendoza tidied himself and then went around the city of Asunción knocking at the back doors of houses in search of work. The householders and their majordomos liked the look

of him. At one place he was offered a job as a houseboy, at
another a job as a gardener's boy, but when he enquired the
wage, he learned that it was only one dinero a month. He
figured out with a stick how many dineros this would come to
in a year, and it was not enough to pay Philippo's orphanage
fee. He frowned thoughtfully and slept in the square again,
surrounded by the distant barking of dogs and the roar of frogs
from the river.

The next morning a voice awoke him. He looked up and
saw, standing over him, the man who seemed to have come
from the courts of old Madrid.

"You want a place?"

"Yes, *señor.*" Mendoza scrambled to his feet.

"Then work for me."

"Yes, *señor.*"

"Come."

Mendoza followed. "How much, *señor?*"

"Two dineros."

"For how much time, *señor?*"

"Four months. Who knows?"

Supposing it was twelve months' work? *"Señor,* four dineros for four months' work. And then, *señor,* the same for
any time I work for you."

"Dios, you strike a hard bargain."

"Yes, *señor.* And a half now and half when I have finished."

The man stopped, and his narrow eyes flickered as though
someone behind the lids were suddenly peering out.

"No," he said.

"Señor, in that case maybe you will perhaps sign a paper?"

"What?" And then the man laughed. "Why not?"

"What shall I call you, *señor?*"

"Victorio Paramin Tinjare Lopez Lusavida y Jermano," he
replied with pride. "Now come."

Mendoza picked up the man's muskets, pistols, traveling
bag, and his own small roll, and followed him to a quiet
warehouse where some fifteen mercenaries, including the
black men, were assembled. Their voices rose into the high
roof where birds were darting.

"Good morning, beloved," said one of the black men.

"Greetings, Gaspachio."

"Who is that?" asked Gaspachio.

"My boy."

A laugh came from the group. "Victorio's got a boy."

The leader, Tiberio, entered—a middle-aged man, a trifle fat, with a face swollen by a suppurating disease. He looked at the men and then turned to Victorio. "Are these all the men you could find?"

"Where can I get more?"

"You, nowhere. Who is this boy?"

"Señor," answered Mendoza, "Mendoza Jorge."

"Call me sir."

"Sir."

"We are collecting slaves."

"Yes, sir."

"It is against the law."

Mendoza could only think of the fifteen dineros a year, so he just said, "Yes, sir."

Tiberio shrugged. "Come, then."

Mendoza begged a pencil and a sheet of paper from one of the men. Victorio made out a paper, which Gaspachio read aloud. It seemed to match what Victorio had promised, so he stowed it away in the strip of cloth where he kept his dineros from the voyage and, carrying his new master's bags and weapons, followed the others to the riverside. He noticed that all the townspeople nearby drew markedly away from them and turned their backs.

They embarked in ten forty-foot canoes, each crewed by two Guarani, and shoved off in dead silence. Looking back, he saw that none of the townspeople had turned toward them to watch them go.

"Why are they like that?" he asked the black man, who was in the same canoe. "Why don't they wish us godspeed?"

"They wish it, but they don't want to be heard wishing it."

"I do not understand."

"You will. My name is Gaspachio."

"My name is Mendoza."

"I know."

So, with a slow murmur from the paddles, they set out on their long journey upriver from the capital city of Asunción.

The black slave trader told them a tale of the life he was leaving behind there. Mendoza had heard many such stories but none as carnal as this one, delivered in a cheerful tone. And yet the men laughed!

Victorio sang a song, full of mournful trees and a suffering maiden and a heartbroken man. When he came to the end, they applauded him, with cries of *"Formidable!"* and *"Elegant!"*

Gaspachio said, "Alas. He will go back to his pavements in Madrid when he has made enough money. But I? What can I do?"

"You can go back between the legs of the little Madelaine," said a man.

"She is dead."

"Hey, Madelaine is dead! How did that happen?"

"I did not stop it."

"Then you can tickle the bum of her son."

"I have done," said the black man. "It is a nice bum, too, but not as nice as Madelaine's. I have only her son and the Guarani now to ease my aching."

Mendoza asked, "Are the Guarani servants or slaves, Gaspachio?"

"Better ask Tiberio."

"Not slaves, but a special kind of servant," said Tiberio.

Farther up the river, where the forest had been cleared, they passed a moored fishing boat. A Jesuit priest and a trio of Guarani were sitting in it and, as they approached, Tiberio called out, "Good evening, Father." Neither the father nor the Guarani seemed to have heard. They behaved as though there were no canoes going by. Looking back, Mendoza saw them still sitting without a movement in their motionless boat.

Then came the mission. Mendoza caught his breath at the size of it. There was a long quayside with Guarani children playing on it, two large barges, and a host of canoes. As they went past, the children stopped playing and watched. There was a large cross in the center of the wide square of the mission and, on two sides of the square, row upon row, the dormitories of the Guarani. Dominating everything towered an astounding church, much bigger than any in Asunción. It was crowned by a grotesque carving, half angel and half eagle, with an expression both threatening and righteous. To one side of this were spacious storehouses and workrooms, and to the other the house of the Jesuits, two-storied and built of stone.

A Jesuit came down to the water's edge and shepherded the children away.

Enormous fields pushed the forest far back into the distance, with hundreds of Guarani placidly at work in them. They looked up as the mercenaries passed in midstream, and then down again.

When the forest had closed back upon the river, Gaspachio said, "Did you ever see anything like that before?"

"No," said Mendoza, "they must be very holy men."

"Very. Under them, all people are free. Even the Guarani."

"The Guarani?"

"Yes. They own the land and the mission. But they like the Jesuits to rule over them."

"Tiberio said we go to collect slaves."

"A slip of the tongue. In the Portuguese territories they have slaves, but here we just have special servants called encomiendaros."

"I see."

"Do you? Explain it to me, then. For example, the encomiendaros are paid no wages."

"They are slaves, then."

"No, as I told you, they are encomiendaros. It is very important to remember there is a difference. They are paid no wages all the same. We go now to pick some up."

"Where?"

"On the Portuguese side of the mountains, where they are slaves. But when we bring them back with us over the mountains, they'll become encomiendaros."

"Where is the boundary?"

"Ah, who can say? Who knows from which side of the mountains Guarani come?"

That evening Mendoza said in a low voice, "Gaspachio?"

"Yes."

"Who pays us for the Guarani we bring back?"

A long pause, then: "The captain general."

"The captain general?"

"He is the chief of the planters. Hush now, I want to go to sleep."

Early in the morning, Gaspachio took Mendoza aside.

"You have no knife, I see."

"No," said Mendoza.

"You need one like this." Gaspachio pulled a rondelle dagger from its leather sheath. Mendoza bent over it.

"Next time, perhaps."

"No, now. Four reales."

"The sheath is faulty."

"I know."

"Three reales."

"Three, agreed."

Gaspachio also sold him, for one real, a belt with which to sling the dagger across his chest. Mendoza felt like a man now.

They reached a funnel where the river was broken by colossal square boulders and the trees hung down. Here they got out and, leaving two mercenaries and six Guarani to keep watch over the canoes, set out on the climb.

"How far is the Portuguese territory, sir?"

"Over there." Tiberio pointed to the distant hills shrouded in mist.

"You, boy," said Victorio, "carry that." He pointed to a jug of wine. "Take care of it. It's very special."

Toward the end of a day of climbing, the bottle weighed like lead. But Mendoza was also carrying a dagger.

2

IT TOOK THEM a full month to scale the mountains. The Guarani carried the muskets, pots, and bedrolls. At the end of each day, when everyone had settled to sleep, Victorio would call Mendoza and demand a cup of wine or maté. This was something like tea or coffee made from the dried yerba maté plant, which made a stimulating brew. Mendoza would prepare the fire and mix a cup and take it to him. Each morning he would find it by Victorio's bed, untouched. He would set his face hard, remembering how he had mixed it in the night. Then he would fold the bedding tightly and take it to the Guarani. Picking up the wine jar, he would commence his uphill journey.

"Do you like Victorio now?" asked Gaspachio.

Mendoza maintained his silence.

"Hey, you, I am talking to you."

"I don't hear," replied Mendoza.

"You are a prudent man."

It was the first time he had been called a man. He was filled with a peculiar mixture of fear and exultation. He was fifteen.

The next day they came upon a trampled patch of earth with many prints of bare human feet. The men sat down and put on high boots, hide suits reaching along to the ground, padded cotton armor, and broad-brimmed hats.

"For the arrows," Gaspachio explained.

Victorio was left in charge of the camp. He was excited, and set the Guarani to work building a round, high fence of thornbushes to keep the Guarani captives in.

Nothing happened during the first four days, but on the evening of the fifth, Tiberio and his party returned with four-

teen Guarani—twelve men and two women. They were thrust
inside the fence. They paced around the enclosure, came together to exchange a few words in a whisper, and then separated again, sat down, and would not speak. One of the
Guarani servants gave them a pot of maize, but was careful to
avert his eyes.

Well pleased, the men drank, and when dark came two of
them pulled the prettier of the two women out of the enclosure. Tiberio took her with oaths and grunts, calling forth
hissing groans and laughs from those waiting their turn. Mendoza went and hid in the undergrowth. When they shouted for
him, he did not reply. The night sky had begun to flush by the
time the woman rejoined the other captives. She went and hid
in a corner of the enclosure. Two Spaniards stood guard over
the prisoners, and peace descended on the little camp. Mendoza came out of the jungle.

"Hey, that was good," said one of the sentries, and
yawned.

Tiberio and his men went into the bush on three more expeditions, returning first with nine captives, then with five,
and finally with none. The last time they returned, a mercenary named Mandu had been pierced through the arm with a
long, sharp arrow; it was broken off front and rear.

Mendoza asked Gaspachio in a hushed voice, "Will he
die?"

"Probably."

"Do many fall like that?"

"Naturally."

"It hurts him?"

And then Gaspachio, angered, called, "Hey, Mandu, does
it hurt?"

"Yes, like hell, it hurts."

"You see, it hurts." Then he fell silent.

Tiberio sent Victorio this time, and six other men, to buy
more slaves at the Portuguese town of Cuzerio de Oeste, ten
days away. They all reveled like schoolboys in the trek.

Cuzerio de Oeste itself was a little town in a fold in the
mountains down among the trees. The men lodged there at an
inn, but Mendoza was sent to sleep among the horses. The

next day Victorio bought a parasol and gave it to him to carry over him, to give the Portuguese an impression that he was an hidalgo.

He inspected the slaves and then opened negotiations. It took all day to bargain for the twenty-five he wanted—seventeen men and eight women, all very young. When he had struck a bargain, he called for a bottle of wine, toasted his clients, and signed his full aristocratic name: Victorio Paramin Tinjare Lopez Lusavida y Jermano.

"Behold the Don of Lopez," said one of his men.

Victorio laid down his pen and looked at him. Everything went very quiet. "You are a servile pig, Alendras."

"I am a servile pig?"

"Yes."

Alendras looked at everybody, but nobody would look at him. "Very well," he said.

"An abject pig."

"No doubt."

"No, no, you must of necessity say it."

"If you say so."

"Let me hear you say it."

"I am a pig."

"A servile pig."

"A servile pig."

"Now go. Take care I do not catch you in the evening."

So Alendras left, and Victorio continued writing out his name. The silence was broken by a little embarrassed conversation among the Portuguese.

When they were alone, Mendoza asked Gaspachio: "What's a servile pig."

"I don't know, but Alendras has left."

"It was just a joke."

"But taken in *espirito malo*."

"Should he have fought him?"

"Of course."

"Victorio would have won."

"Oh, yes. He knows where to pick his quarrels. He would not have tried that on Tiberio."

They stocked up with maize and mutton, loaded it onto the

Guarani slaves, and set off on their way back to the camp. The
Guarani made slow work of it, but stumbled along without a
word, urged on by an occasional blow from a rope's end.

A fortnight had gone by before they saw Tiberio again. In
the meantime, Mandu, the man with the arrow wound, had
died. It took them another month to reach their boats and
another five weeks to get back at last to Asunción.

Tiberio left them at the quayside to return in the late evening dressed in new clothes. He had four men with him. They
carried muskets and wore the captain general's badge on their
sleeves. They had come to take delivery of the slaves.

Tiberio pulled out a bag and paid the mercenaries off on
the quayside. They said good night in turn and drifted off in
twos and threes into the town.

When Victorio had been paid, he said to Mendoza,
"Come." The rest watched Mendoza labor his way up into
town, laden with Victorio's baggage and parasol. Then they
looked at Tiberio, but he pretended not to notice. His business
finished, he, too, went off.

In the back court of his inn Victorio said, "Here," and
threw Mendoza one dinero. The blood drained away beneath
Mendoza's mahogany tan.

"You owe me five dineros, *señor,* for five months of
work."

"No, one dinero. You are a useful boy. I may have work
for you again. *Adios.*"

"I need the five dineros."

"Now you—you make me angry."

"See, you signed." Mendoza produced his paper, and Victorio leaned across and took it.

"I see no paper." He went in and shut the door.

Mendoza sought out Gaspachio, who said, "But where is
your paper?"

"Victorio has it."

"Fool. You should have taken it to the officials tomorrow."

"Will you not help me?"

"No. This a bloodletting matter between men. Try Tiberio.
You'll find him at Marcia's."

Mendoza went to Marcia's. Tiberio emerged from an inner
room.

"Do you remember, sir, a paper that Victorio signed for
me?"

"Yes. Has he taken it?"

"Yes. Will you help me?"

"No help is possible."

"Why not?"

"The paper was all. *Adios.*"

Mendoza went down to the harbor and stared at the water.
They all knew that Victorio had taken the paper and kept the
money that was his by right, yet none of them would help
him. It was a matter between the two of them. He looked
down at the webbed image of the moon in the harbor waters,
and then up at the peaceful sky, and said a prayer to the
Blessed Virgin. Hiding his bedding near a pile of rubble, he
took off his shoes and went silently to Victorio's inn.

He spied him alone, asleep in a bedraggled bed, and
slipped into the room through the open room. Drawing his
dagger from its sheath, he knelt by Victorio's bed. Then he
placed the dagger against his enemy's neck and pressed gently.
Victorio awoke with a start. The dagger went in farther, and
Victorio froze.

"Who is that?" he asked in a soft voice.

"Me," replied Mendoza.

Victorio laughed quietly. "What do you want?"

"My five dineros."

"Of course. I see you are a man to be reckoned with. I will
get it for you," and he was halfway out of bed when, in wrath
and panic, Mendoza struck, driving the blade home. Reaching
repeatedly for the dagger which he had knocked out of Mendoza's hand, Victorio fell without making a sound.

Mendoza was dumbfounded. It had been so easy. His
enemy lay there without a sound. Blood had started seeping
from the wound. The rest of the building was undisturbed.

He must get the paper, he reminded himself. No, the
money, not the paper. The paper was no use now. Under the
pillow, he found a wallet with thirty-seven dineros in it. He

would take just five. No, not five. He would take the lot. That
was what a casual thief would have done. He took the money,
slipped out of the window and walked back to the harbor.

Nothing had altered since he left the quayside. The reflection of the moon was just the same. He stared at the money. It
was nearly two years' payment, but if he kept it all, he would
be a thief, so counting out his five, he threw the remaining
coins into the water and lay down to sleep. A few moments
later he got up again and took his dagger down to the water's
edge to wash it. Then he lay down to sleep again. Five minutes later, he got up once more, this time to wash himself
thoroughly, standing naked on the harbor bottom. When he lay
down this time, he was feverish. Sleep would not come.

He was relieved when dawn broke, with Guaranis, dock
laborers, and shipwrights arriving to start a new day. Nobody
seemed to have heard about what had happened in the night.
A passing laborer wished him good day.

At ten o'clock, however, a group of people from the town
came looking for him. They crowded around him—the
watchman, Tiberio, and a bunch of townspeople. He should
have eaten breakfast, he thought, as he stood up.

Tiberio asked, "Have you heard what happened to Victorio?"

"Victorio? No, sir, what?"

"Somebody killed him."

"Last night," added the watchman.

"Did you have anything to do with it?" Tibero continued.

"Me, sir? No."

"Let us see your money," the watchman ordered.

Mendoza showed it to him.

"There are eight dineros here," said the watchman.

"Yes, *señor,* what of that?"

"Where did you get them?"

"In Spain."

"Victorio had more than thirty dineros on him when he was
killed," Tiberio said.

The watchman said: "Now show me your knife."

"My knife? Certainly." He held it out.

"This has recently been washed."

"I always wash it at the end of every day."

The watchman thought this over. "I see no reason to suppose this boy is guilty," he declared.

"Neither do I," said Tiberio.

"But *señores,*" Mendoza protested, "he owed me five dineros. What shall I do?"

Said Tiberio, "You can say good-bye to that," and he led them all back into town. There was a small smile on his lips.

He knows, thought Mendoza, looking after him. He knows, and I have gone up in his esteem. He is the confidant of the captain general. This is a strange world. He shook his head. His mother, too, knew what he had done. What would it do to her love for him? He went to the Church of Santa Anna, in the shadows of the trees. It was blessedly cool within. There was a priest. Mendoza approached and asked to make a confession.

When he had heard Mendoza's confession, the priest wiped his forehead with a handkerchief and asked, "Have you told me all?"

"Yes, Father," said Mendoza.

"What manner of man was it you killed?"

"Victorio, Father."

Victorio! thought the priest. It must have been a lucky blow! Good riddance to him! Aloud he said, "You have been engaged in an affair of honor. Do you know what that means?"

"Does it mean I am not guilty of murder, Father?"

"In the eyes of the Heavenly Father you are guilty, but not in the eyes of men."

"Thank you, Father. Now, Father, I have a worse sin to confess."

Dios! said the priest to himself. "What is it, my son?"

"I lied."

"You did what?"

"Lied."

The priest, upon reflection, decided that the penitent was not insane. "I see," he said. "Well, do not lie again."

"No, Father."

Imposing a lengthy penance, the priest dismissed Mendoza

and watched him retreat the length of the nave, where he knelt to pray.

His mother had been a saint, Mendoza thought, kneeling there in the church. That was why she had been able to live a life acceptable to Christ. Her soul was always ready for the transcendent vision. But she knew her son was not like that. She had not expected him to be a saint. She had only told him to be no more guilty than other men were. Well, he was guiltless in the eyes of men. The priest had said so. But he must be careful not to lie. Resolved in his mind, he started on the Hail Marys the priest had allotted him.

The priest left through the curtains, thankful to be a priest.

When Mendoza left the church, he found Gaspachio waiting for him, chuckling conspiratorially.

"My dagger, you see?" Gaspachio said.

"What do you mean?"

"You did it with my dagger."

"I did what?"

"Killed Victorio."

"Excuse me," Mendoza said and walked away. He saw what his mother had meant when she said lying was the pathway to perdition.

Gaspachio caught up with him. "Pardon, somehow I thought you had done it."

"No."

"I see now that I was mistaken. Come and have supper."

"Tonight?"

"Yes, yes, tonight."

"I thank you. Tonight, then." Turning toward the harbor, he thought, It is so easy.

Gaspachio said at supper that night: "There's a new encomienda in a fortnight. They need men."

"I am only fifteen."

"You are seventeen."

"I am?"

"Aren't you?"

"I am seventeen."

"You must get a sword."

"I cannot afford one."

"You can spend some of your thirty-seven dineros."

"I haven't got thirty-seven dineros."

"Dios! You can spend some of however much you have, then, on a sword."

"How much?"

"About five reales. It is important. Listen, a man without a sword is like a man without a *cojón.*"

Gaspachio led Mendoza in the pitch dark night to a high wall with a gate, on which he hammered. A man arrived with a candle. He recognized Gaspachio and took them to a low-ceilinged room where he lit more candles on a table. Through flickering shadows Mendoza saw rows of rapiers, muskets, and pistols, and he felt a quickening of his blood.

Said Gaspachio softly, "Aye, see."

Now Mendoza had been taught the evil of weapons by his mother. Moreover, he had not enough money to buy any of the swords. Looking past them, he saw a weapon with a thick, short blade.

"What's that?"

"A baselard," said the swordsmith, "for use while riding a horse." He drew it out of its scabbard. It was one and a half inches wide, two feet long, and had a stabbing point. "It was made a hundred years ago in Basel. A chopping blade."

Mendoza took it and felt its solid weight. "How much?"

"No, no." Gaspachio laughed. "You cannot fence with that."

"It feels good in my hand."

"No. Listen, Mendoza, you mustn't take that."

"You said I must have a sword; this is a sword."

"But for use while on horseback," said the swordsmith.

"I understand. How much?"

"I do not know; say, six reales."

"You will regret it," said Gaspachio. "And how much for me?" he said to the swordsmith.

"For you, five reales."

"Five reales is reasonable. But you will be discontented, Mendoza."

The next day Gaspachio brought Mendoza to the new head

of the mercenaries, Alexandro. "This is a friend of mine."

Alexandro asked how old he was.

"I don't know," replied Gaspachio. "How old are you?"

"Seventeen," said Mendoza.

"I would have said as much. Seventeen," he told Alexandro. Alexandro grunted and undertook to pay him two dineros a month.

When Mendoza was outside again, he said, "I lack the means to recompense you."

"I will remind you of it. Now we must get your cotton armor."

"I have no money for that."

"There is no need for you to keep this up with me," Gaspachio said, offended. "The cotton armor will be useful."

"Not this time. *Adios.*"

He found a letter writer in the marketplace, a Jew, to whom he dictated a letter to the Mother Superior in Cadiz.

> *Reverenced Holy Mother,*
>
> *I am sending you one half of the sum I owe you. Please accept it in the faith that more will come. I beg you to do this as Christ shall have mercy. I will be going away on a trading trip, and when I return I shall send you the rest. In four or five months. I implore you to have belief in this. Forever and ever, amen. I hope that Philippo is a satisfactory pupil. Teach him to read and write. If he is not good, beat him. And anything else you think necessary. I go to confession in the Church of Santa Anna here in Asunción. There are birds in the trees. I hope that you, sanctified Mother in God, are in good health. Amen. And give Philippo my brotherly love. I am your most obedient, true, and pious servant in Christ,*
>
> > *Rodrigo Mendoza*

He went, without his sword and dagger, to a priest who was going to Cadiz. He gave the priest his money, explained who the recipient was, and thanked him.

"What makes you believe I will deliver it?" asked the Franciscan.

"You are a priest," replied Mendoza.

The friar grimaced. "Ah, would all priests were as honest as you believe them to be, my son."

Five months later, when the Mother Superior received the letter and the money, she got down on her knees and gave thanks. Philippo was a high-spirited boy full of natural charm and, behold, he had a strong brother.

3

IN PREPARATION FOR the next encomienda, Mendoza went to a French fencing master. Upon seeing the baselard, the master shook his head. "That sword is not correct; get another."

"Here is my money."

The master held out his hand for it, shrugged, and taught Mendoza to thrust and parry. When the evening came, Mendoza continued his thrust and parry outside in the open, and then went to sleep. He practiced this daily up against a tree until he set off with Alexandro's mercenaries.

When they found the tracks of Guarani in the ninth week, Mendoza was one of the party Alexandro led in pursuit of them. On the second day they came across a fire still burning, and Alexandro went off with some of the men. Four hours passed, and Mendoza was half asleep when suddenly there was a bedlam of brown bodies tearing through the undergrowth, and the forest was shaken with roars. A Guarani, his spear arm drawn back, appeared above Mendoza, only to plunge down a moment later on the leveled baselard sword. When the blade came out through his back, the Guarani's face was very close to Mendoza's.

Gaspachio clapped Mendoza on the shoulder and said, "Now pull your sword out of his chest."

Mendoza did so and watched while the man died, finding the sight even less disturbing than Victorio's death had been.

I am a killer, Mendoza thought.

They thrust their captives inside the thorn hedge, and darkness fell. Gaspachio drew Mendoza to one side. "Some say you have; others say you have not. Have you?"

"Been with women?"

"Assuredly."

31

"No."

"It is easy and pleasurable."

"I will consider it."

"No, do not consider it; do it."

Mendoza went over to the Guarani captives and chose the youngest of the girls. He led her into a dark part of the jungle, looked around, and said, "Strip." When she did so, he became excited and said, "Lie down." For her part, the girl was glad this one was so defenseless. His penis grew stiff, and he began to move it toward her, but could not find his way. "Help me," he said. Her hand came down. He came.

Liking him, she lay still under him for a while, and his penis began to stiffen again. This time he thrust and she began to whine, and he came again.

Then she got down and made him stand and, placing her lips around his penis, began to draw it in, when all at once he heard the laughter of others. Bellowing, he snatched his sword and hunted them, trembling with rage and shame, but they got away. Treading on a thorn, he was forced to sit down and take it out of his foot.

When he limped back to the girl, Gaspachio was standing over her, and asked, "Do you want her?"

Mendoza shook his head. He returned to the fire and wrapped a blanket around himself, sitting there crestfallen. All night he sat there, and all the while Gaspachio was astir upon the girl.

They went on two more missions and captured five more slaves, but after that, nothing. The next day, they set off for the Portuguese village of Bonito. It was seven days' journey. They bought forty more slaves to add to those they had captured, and transported the whole lot back to Asunción.

For this trip, Mendoza received ten dineros. He returned to the writer and sent a letter.

Reverenced Holy Mother,

I have returned from the trading expedition. Here is the money which I owe you. That is, nine dineros for the tuition past. I shall send you more when I have finished another trading enterprise about to start. This will be

under my first trade officer, Tiberio, who is the single
most promising trader here. Be confident that I shall
send the rest. The trading here is good. Thanks be to
God. I hope very much, Holy Mother, to receive a letter
from you as your time permits. And also one from Phi-
lippo. I hope that all is well with Philippo, my brother.
Convey to him my kind regards. That is, if he deserves
them. I have a sword, a baselard. I am your most obe-
dient, true, and pious servant in Christ,

Rodrigo Mendoza

The Jesuit missionary who took the letter gave Mendoza a
long, severe look.

"Are you a soldier of fortune?"

"Yes, Father."

"What you are doing is against the law."

"I only do what Tiberio tells me to do, Father."

"It is against the law. Well, I will take the money to
Cadiz." Six months later, when the Mother Superior received
Mendoza's letter, she said to the Jesuit: "I did send him a
letter; he has not received it. Is he well?"

"Mother, he is a mercenary."

"I see. I shall write him about that; he does not understand.
See, he sends me this money."

"Blood money."

"Thank you." She rang her little bell to show the Jesuit out.

Mendoza went to the fencing master once a day. He
thought because his weapon was not a rapier, it was not evil,
and he liked the solid weight of it in his hands. The fencing
master was provoked by this new pupil who had no respect for
the rapier. He must not be allowed to cling onto that club of a
sword. He demonstrated how the rapier could sweep aside his
baselard.

"You see?" he said. "You see? Again. You comprehend?"

"I see," his pupil said, "but I will stick to the baselard."

The fencing master struck a bargain with him. "Listen, we
will fence. If you can parry my attack, I will pay for all the
fencing lessons you have had. But if you cannot, you will give

up the baselard and adopt the rapier. Agreed, or are you afraid?"

They fought. Mendoza could not force his way through the glittering guard. The master smiled. Mendoza knew the one way was to rush it. Like a Roman executioner, he swung his face to one side, taking a small cut on the side of his neck, and then was at his opponent's throat with the point of his sword. They both froze, motionless.

There was a moment's silence. The fencing master stared. Then he said, "Do not come here again." He fetched the money. "I will not teach a murderer."

With Gaspachio to help him, Mendoza went to buy a musket and a pistol. He also bought hide boots and cotton armor. Once he had put them all on, Gaspachio said, *"Madre de Dios!"*

"What?"

"You look like a real warrior."

Mendoza was sixteen when he embarked on his next expedition with Tiberio. He was seventeen when he returned.

There were two letters waiting for him. Gaspachio read them aloud for him as they sat in the square.

"'To our dearly beloved Mendoza, greetings. I did send you a letter in answer to your first one. I do not know where it can have gone. It came by the ship *Navidad* in May of last year.' The *Navidad* went down," said Gaspachio.

"I see. Go on."

"'Philippo is at the top of his groups.' Who is Philippo?"

"My brother."

"I did not know you had one."

"He is not like me. Read on."

"'I send a letter to you written by him.'"

"Read it."

"'Dearest brother Mendoza. I am well. I hope that you are well. This is the first letter that Sister Angela has permitted me to write. I hope you are pleased with it. I try hard with my lessons. Mother Julia will also say this, because she has promised. When can I come and stay with you? There are many ships sailing from Cadiz. There is a new game called Sabande. I cannot explain it to you in this letter. It has a club and a ball and there is a wall. This letter comes to you from your most respectful brother Philippo.'"

"That letter is not a bad one," Mendoza observed.

"Very good."

"But maybe Sister Angela helped him."

"I see that you are proud of your Philippo. Shall I continue?"

"Please. I truly think it is by him."

"'I have a word of warning to you. It is about the slave trade. I hear that you partake in this. It is against the law of Holy Church, and of the land also. Consider how you would feel yourself if you were the merchandise. Therefore, choose some other business.'"

Gaspachio laughed, but Mendoza said soberly, "Read that again." When Gaspachio had done so, he was silent. The rest of the Mother Superior's letter was concerned with holy practices. He went to the church and sought out the priest who had received his previous confession.

"Father, I earn my living as a slave trader."

"As an encomienda trader, you mean."

"We take the Guarani without their consent, Father, and oftentimes against resistance."

Said the priest, casting about in vain for help: "Well, that is wrong."

"But we do it for the captain general."

"You do not take them as slaves, only as encomiendaros."

Mendoza peered at him. "Father, shall I go and tell the captain general?"

The priest saw his quiet little benefice disappearing. "The captain general would tell you the encomienda is acceptable."

"You would absolve me, then?"

"Yes."

"Even if I am planning another voyage?"

The priest considered. "If you were so foolish as to express it so, then I would not absolve you."

"Thank you, Father."

Mendoza knew that he must pay for his brother's education. Let the Mother Superior say it was all one whether Philippo became a gentleman or a lighterman. She did not know; she had no experience of life. Thereafter, he never went to confession or to church, nor did he pray to his mother.

He signed on for another expedition, at three dineros a month this time. When they had captured the first fifteen slaves, he said to Fernandez, the leader: "Why go to the Portuguese side to find Guarani? Why don't we push on till we come up with more captives in Spanish territory?"

"This way is easier."

"Of course, but we would get more money the other way."

"Go, if you will," said Fernandez with a shrug, "and God go with you." The others smiled. Mendoza stayed.

When he was nineteen he saw Palacio, who had just returned from Barcelona. He waited until nightfall and found Palacio in a lamplit yard chatting with a group of ladies and gentlemen. Mendoza went up to him and stood there until he was recognized and the conversation gradually ceased. The only sound was the flutter of the moths.

"Palacio, you recognize me?"

"But of course."

"You owe me one dinero."

Palacio said, "Do I? Well, then, so be it," and he took a coin from his pocket.

"You have owed it to me five years."

"I see. What, then?"

"Today that makes five thousand dineros."

"Five thousand?"

"And I am here to collect it."

"Go, while you still have time."

"Palacio," said Mendoza, "you are a servile pig. It is I who say so."

They went to a place by the river attended by a throng of people with lanterns, which they set up in the trees.

A person who had appointed himself master of ceremonies said, "Now, gentlemen, are you ready?"

"Ready," asserted Palacio.

"Commence, then!"

Mendoza moved in directly and struck Palacio through the

chest with his baselard. The dying man stared into Mendoza's face and fell against him. It was over. Mendoza wiped his blade.

A Spaniard said, "You were lucky."

Mendoza turned around. "It was not luck."

"Would you care to prove it?"

"No."

"Luck."

Another fight then, only this time his opponent's footsteps were sure and menacing. Mendoza was borne back. Then suddenly he turned his head to one side and thrust.

"My God," gasped an elderly man.

Mendoza left the two prone bodies in the lamplight and walked away. A crowd of Asunción ladies and gentlemen, and tradesmen and servants, and poor whites and wealthy adventurers and Guarani gazed after him.

Wrapping himself in his cloak that night, he thought first, I am a murderer. And then, So be it. And finally, That thrust with the baselard, it is good. He settled himself and yawned and went to sleep. He slept like a man without hope.

"So," said Tiberio, "you are a fencing master?"

"No. Is there another expedition?"

"Yes. Do you wish to come on it?"

"Yes."

Tiberio glanced at the other men, who looked uneasy. "Well, then, come."

Mendoza found the Jew and dictated another letter for the Mother Superior.

Reverenced Mother in God,

I read your last letter with attention. Thanks to your instruction, I am giving up slave trading and will enter the yerba maté trade instead. Thank Philippo for his letter. It is a great joy to me. Is there a hospice similar to yours in these parts? I mean in Montevideo, in Buenos Aires, or in Asunción? I have asked the priests, and they think not, but if there is, I could bring Philippo here. As usual I enclose fifteen dineros for his upkeep.

*This is a cruel place, particularly at night. I will send
for him only if there is a quiet place likes yours out
here. I hope that you, Holy Mother, continue to enjoy
good health. Your most obedient, true, and pious servant in Christ,*

                                        Rodrigo Mendoza

He joined the little convoy of canoes under Tiberio, and
they traveled up the river as usual, then left the canoes and
walked.

All the time he was aware of Tiberio's eyes following him.

"Look out!" he would say. "Here comes the fencing master! On your guard!" Tiberio smiled, without revealing
whether he said this in jest or not. He was an old man, forty,
and saw this new young man as a challenge to his position as
leader. Mendoza and Gaspachio could see the others beginning to take sides. Finally, Mendoza approached Tiberio by
the fire, in front of all of them.

"Tiberio, you are the leader, I am just a soldier."

"Indeed. What else?" replied Tiberio, smoking his cheroot.

"I am happy it is so."

"Very well, then. Good night."

When the other men went after the Guarani, Mendoza was
left to guard the camp. There came a sudden rushing through
bushes and trampling down of grass. Four braves came hurtling at him, yelling. He felled the first with his short sword,
he struck the second with his dagger, but the third dealt him a
blow in the throat with his spear before Mendoza shot him with
his pistol. He chased the fourth, for he was a huge fellow who
would fetch a high price, and threw him down.

The Spanish soldiers ran up, congratulating him. "Well
done, *hombre*, well done!"

That evening at the campfire, Tiberio called him over.

"Let me look at that throat. I will stitch it up for you." He
stitched up the raw wound with curious gentleness. "Well
done, *hombre*, well done."

For the next few days Mendoza was left at the camp to
recuperate while the rest went hunting for more slaves. They
caught only three. Tiberio, in an evil temper, went to the

Portuguese town of Uguiriana to buy the rest, whom he drove back to the camp.

Gaspachio warned, "Tiberio is in a funny mood. Keep out of his way."

Later that night, Tiberio was drunk but did not show it. "Hey, Mendoza, it is time those stitches came out," he called.

"You can do it tomorrow."

"No, now."

After a pause, Mendoza replied: "Very well then—now." He got up and went across to sit by Tiberio.

"Tiberio, wait till tomorrow," Gaspachio said.

"Keep quiet, Negro," growled Tiberio. "Mendoza, does this hurt?"

"A bit."

There was silence all around as Tiberio nicked away with his knife. "Now for the last one."

"Gracias."

Tiberio jerked his knife and made a gash. A runnel of blood started down Mendoza's cheek. He got up silently and walked back to his place. Tiberio asked: "Aren't you going to thank me?"

"No."

"But you must thank me: mustn't he?" Nobody answered.

"I will thank you tomorrow," responded Mendoza and pulled the blankets over his head.

In the morning he went over to Tiberio and woke him.

"I am ready to thank you," he said, "for, do you see, I think you were drunk."

Tiberio sat up rubbing his eyes and said, "Not drunk. I did it on purpose."

"I see. Then how shall we settle it?"

"I settle all things by the sword." Tiberio threw off his blankets, but delayed to pull on a pair of shoes. "I do not sleep shod," he said. "Do you?"

"Yes."

"You have bad manners, then. That is bad manners." Tiberio got to his feet and made a swinging pass with his rapier, from which the men backed off.

"Here?" Mendoza asked.

"Agreed."

"That is good, you have—"

Unexpectedly, Tiberio lunged, forcing Mendoza to back off. Then again he lunged, and again Mendoza was forced to withdraw.

"What's the matter? Aren't you ready?" Tiberio asked.

"It is a pity that you—" Mendoza felt a burning pain in his right cheekbone as he smashed his short blade into Tiberio's chest. The force of the blow carried Tiberio backwards until the point of the baselard was buried in a tree. His victim looked at him, opening his mouth as if to say something, and then died standing upright.

A deep wound had uncovered Mendoza's cheekbone. Gaspachio came and stitched it up. "Listen," he said, "you could take command now."

Looking around, Mendoza saw that the others were waiting to be told what to do. He ordered four of them to bury Tiberio, and then said, "Now we go."

4

BACK IN ASUNCIÓN nine weeks later, Mendoza left the others on the dockside and went to report to Don Cabeza, the captain general. He went up through the evening air to where the very best houses were. The captain general lived in the most imposing residence of all. Mendoza passed between two sentries, lolling at their posts, found his way through the outer garden where Guarani servants dozed, and mounted a short flight of stairs underneath the portico to fetch up before a Spanish sergeant at a gilded table in the hall. The sergeant looked at the ragged figure and demanded his business. Mendoza answered that he carried a message from Señor Tiberio.

A secretary, coming to the head of the stairs, saw a mercenary who was very young and had an ugly wound on his face. Nevertheless, he beckoned Mendoza forward, told him to wait, and went to tell Don Cabeza.

Mendoza gazed around. He looked at the candlesticks and the Guarani servants squatting against one of the doors. Below where the sergeant sat, a bright shaft of light came in from outside. Everything else was dim. This was where the ecclesiastics and other diplomats held their consultations when they discussed Asunción's affairs.

A door was suddenly thrust open, and Don Cabeza himself stood there, dressed in a loose cotton gown. He was fifty years old, fat and ungainly, particularly when, as now, without his wig, but still remarkably surefooted on his short, thick legs. He was fourth-generation South American–born. His great-grandfather had been a weaver and his grandfather an exporter of hides, but his father was an hildago appointed by the Casa de South America, interested in the ownership of haciendas, while he, Don Cabeza, was at the center of the internal politics of the Río de la Plata region.

"Where is Tiberio?" the captain general asked.

"I killed him, Excellency."

"Why?"

"He picked a quarrel. There are many who can testify to this, Your Excellency."

Don Cabeza looked at this young adventurer.

"What's your name?"

"Mendoza Jorge, Excellency."

"What about the encomiendaros?"

"I have them. Forty-eight."

Cabeza called his secretary and instructed him to send six of the Spanish guards down to the harbor. Then he sat down. "What made Tiberio pick a quarrel with you?"

"I do not know, Excellency."

"Who has taken his place?"

"I have, Excellency."

"How old are you?"

"Twenty-four, Excellency."

A liar, thought Cabeza, and hard to see through. He said, "Very well, I will pay you what I would have given to Tiberio, minus Tibero's share."

"His share is mine now."

"You did not organize the expedition."

"Then who will get the leader's share?"

Sharp, thought Don Cabeza, and greedy. He said, "I will give it to you if you organize another expedition."

"How much is the leader's share, Your Excellency?" There was a pause. "I can ask the other leaders."

Don Cabeza frowned. The boy was insolent. "One dinero per head for each slave you bring in."

"That is forty-eight dineros for the present lot, and the same for the next lot?"

"Correct."

Mendoza left with his head spinning. That made nearly a hundred dineros, two hundred for the year. He saw a way of raising it to three hundred or even four. Philippo was safe now. Nothing else mattered. Where else was he to place his burden of love?

He went to the most fashionable tailor in Asunción to order a suit. The cutters gave him sideways supercilious smiles, but he returned a steady stare that made them cringe. The suit was black, the color he had noticed the men of the upper classes most often wore. He asked for it to be ready within five months.

Down at the quayside the other men gathered about him and, standing with his back against a pile of sacks, he told them, "Come with me. You will earn a third more than you did before."

"Truly?"

"Truly."

"But what must we do?"

"Follow me."

"Where?"

"Who knows?"

"Into Portuguese territory?"

"Perhaps."

"To commandeer slaves?"

"Not to buy them."

"Things are all right the way they are."

"*Adios.*"

"I am with you," said a young adventurer.

"And I," said an old one.

It was the middle-aged who hung back; they were too old to dream of windfalls and too young to feel the need of a lump sum.

The Spanish officials had no intention of enquiring where he meant to go. Officially they frowned on any incursion into Portuguese territory, but they were happy to pay good prices for encomiendaros with no questions asked, once the captives had arrived safely in Asunción.

Mendoza's men, therefore, were tolerated but not accepted.

Cabeza watched them from a thoughtful distance. There was a fine profit to be made out of Mendoza, and officially the captain general knew nothing about him. Meanwhile, sticking to Mendoza's side like a shadow, Gaspachio shook his head and smiled.

In three months they had captured as many Guarani as could be rounded up, but there were only six; they were getting scarce. Mendoza sent Gaspachio and a small party of men back to the river with the slaves, to wait with the boats.

Gaspachio said, "Are you going west?"

"I will see what Guarani there are there."

"Then you will assuredly trespass into the territory of the Portuguese."

"Is that so? Nobody knows the boundary."

"Nobody, but it is there. Godspeed." And Gaspachio left on the long trek back to the river.

Mendoza led his men west. After four weeks they encountered a tribe of Guarani who had seldom seen the white men before, though they had heard of them. They fought tenaciously. Mendoza lost five men in a three-day battle, but he captured eighty-six Guarani before the rest suddenly disappeared. They had cost him no money.

Then he struck due south, back to the river. One evening he came to the head of a rise and saw, in the far distance to the west, a tongue of rose-colored smoke rising a thousand feet from the forest into the blue air.

"Look," he said. "Look."

"The Falls of Iguaçú," said an elderly soldier.

"The Falls of Iguaçú?" Mendoza repeated, looking at the distant column, which was like an illuminated cloud. "Have you ever been there?"

"I do not know of anyone who has, except the Jesuits. They have a mission called Santa Croce there." The old man pointed far away over the jungle. "That is the last mission of all."

"They have Guarani?"

"On this side of the falls they have. On the far side, who can say?"

"I wish to see the Falls of Iguaçú," said Mendoza, looking under his hand at the far jet of mist. "There must be a fat profit to be made there," and he stayed looking at the tongue of spume while the night fell.

At last they reached the river and followed it down to their camp. They could not find Gaspachio or the boats or the six captives, though they searched for them all the next day. At the end of the second day, Mendoza sat on the banks of the river and realized what all the others had known the instant they arrived: Gaspachio had betrayed him.

Mendoza was sitting there when darkness fell. He could trust no one. In the morning, he and his men started off on rafts big enough to carry them and all their captives downriver to Asunción.

An old dockside worker who was smoking his pipe on the quayside in Asunción told him: "Gaspachio has left."

"For where?"

"For Montevideo."

"And the company with him?"

"Gone, too."

"They had six slaves with them."

"Gaspachio sold them to Don Cabeza."

Mendoza shrugged and turned to his men. *"Tanto de los cojones.* I owed him that. It was he who equipped me for my first trek for the encomienda."

"He has gone nonetheless." The old man grinned.

"If you come across him, tell him I call it quits."

He looked at the rafts loaded with Guarani and the mercenaries standing on the jetty. "I go now to bargain with the captain general. There are eighty-six captives here and fourteen men; be sure they stay so."

He went to the tailor's shop, washed himself from head to foot, pulled his hair back into a club, and dressed himself in his new clothes. Then, a dark figure with a scar, he donned his dagger and sword and went to see Don Cabeza. He was admitted without difficulty, and Cabeza was impressed.

He said, "Sit down, Mendoza."

"Thank you, Excellency."

"A glass of wine?"

"No, Excellency."

"I have had Gaspachio through here with six slaves. Did you know that?"

"Yes. And he said of me?"

"He said that you were dead."

"I am here."

"Where have you been?"

"I have eighty-six for sale, Excellency."

"Eighty-six?"

"Yes, Excellency." Cabeza called for his secretary and gave orders for six of his soldiers to fetch the Indians, but Mendoza said, "Send twelve, Your Excellency."

"Twelve, then." When the secretary had gone, Don Cabeza asked, "Did you buy them?"

"Naturally, Your Excellency."

"At what town?"

"I forget, Your Excellency."

"Let me see them."

"Of course, Your Excellency."

"Will you take a glass of wine now?"

"No, Excellency."

"I will."

When the Guarani were herded into the back courtyard, Cabeza saw, delighted, that they were an outstanding lot.

"How many men did you lose?"

"Five. From disease, Your Excellency."

"I shall pay you three-quarters of a dinero for each. Come along with me."

When they got back to the room, Mendoza said, "Forty-eight for the last lot, and two dineros a head for this one."

Cabeza turned on Mendoza and said furiously, "Call me Excellency."

"That makes," replied Mendoza, "two hundred and twenty dineros."

Cabeza struck the table. *"Cara de pijo.* Call me Excellency."

"If you do not want them, I will take them elsewhere."

Cabeza sat down at his chair, undid the collar of his shirt, and drank his wine. He laughed shortly. "Where did you come from?"

"Cadiz."

"When do you go back?"

"I do not know."

"You will make your next foray for me."

"I will make it for the one who pays the most."

"I shall pay you the two hundred and twenty dineros for this lot." He counted out the money. Mendoza counted it again and dropped it into his coat pocket.

"My thanks to you, Your Excellency. I shall make my next expedition for you." And he went out.

Cabeza sat and thought. Mendoza was taking all the risks, but he was also a free agent. The captain general was not altogether sure this arrangement pleased him. After a while, however, he decided it did.

After leaving Cabeza, Mendoza went to see the Jew and found that a letter from the Mother Superior had arrived for him. He sat down among the Jew's books to give it his full attention.

Dear Mendoza,

Praised be Jesus Christ, you are a good brother, and your brother Philippo is well. And to say truth, more than well; he is the chosen one of all the ladies in the town of Cadiz, and my dearly loved one. But he is now ten and must leave us. I was thinking of sending him to the Colegio de Loreto de Huérfanos, where the sons of the servants of the king are brought up, at the partial expense of the king, God befriend him. But now your letter has come and I have made enquiries. There is in Montevideo an orphanage founded by lay and church money. It is run by the lay brotherhood. As well as the languages and mathematics, they engage special teachers of dancing, fencing, and deportment. Or so I hear. Go and see them and let me know what you think. If you are satisfied with it, I shall send Philippo out to you.

The rest of the letter was full of shrewd comments about his soul, from which he withdrew his attention, looking at the Jew's books. Mendoza had nothing to do with his soul.

The letter from Philippo, which the mother Superior had sent, along with her own message, was full of his doings with the relatives of a classmate of his called Alfonso de Vicent. Mendoza had this read out to him three times. Then he went by boat to Buenos Aires and then to Montevideo and the orphanage of the Hospital of the Passion. The school contained only twelve boys, eight of whom had parents. Each boy paid thirty dineros a year to the Brotherhood of Refugio, who ran the school. This brotherhood had fallen in stature since the days when it was first founded. The brothers were now servants of the hidalgos. At first they regarded Mendoza doubtfully, but when he produced the thirty dineros, their manner changed. He was not offended by their skepticism; he understood it and approved of it. His letter to the Mother Superior was full of praise.

At Buenos Aires, on the return trip, while waiting for a ship to Asunción, his eye was caught by the slavers across at Colonia del Sacramento. He hired a boat and was rowed out past the English, Dutch, and French ships to land there. The Portuguese standard flew above all. Two walks around the harbor told him that there was nothing there for him. They were all slavers and pirates, gathered around the bollards. Because of his scars and his sober suiting and the sword and dagger at his side, he was not molested. Before getting back into his boat, he spoke to a Spanish sailor and asked if he knew Gaspachio from Asunción.

"I know everything that happens here, *señor,*" said the Spanish sailor, taking off his hat. "Gaspachio? He went off to the West Indies months ago, *señor*. In the *Esmeralda.*"

"A pity," Mendoza said, "because now he cannot know how I regard everything as fair between us."

"I see."

"Tell him that, if you ever meet him." Mendoza slipped a coin into the man's palm, telling him his name.

After three more expeditions he rented himself a house. It was small, but in the aristocratic quarter of the town. He also bought a small farm on the outskirts.

After the third trip he found three letters from Montevideo waiting for him. One was from the brothers to notify him that Philippo had been received under the care of a Franciscan priest, and the second was a stylish letter from Philippo himself, who also enclosed a letter from the Mother Superior in Cadiz.

From the last of these, he learned that Philippo was a good and charming boy, blessed in possessing so benevolent a brother, and that she hoped she would hear from him. The message from the brothers said that they allowed their charges to go home three months each year, or if it so pleased him Philippo could remain with them for that period, at an extra charge. Mendoza dictated a short note saying that he would, of course, come and pick up Philippo when the holidays started in three months' time.

Philippo's own letter was full of amusing accounts of the new school and his longing to see his brother. Mendoza wrote the Mother Superior in Cadiz a formal letter of thanks and then dismissed her from his mind. She was sure of her place in paradise.

5

WHEN THE THREE months were up, he went to Montevideo to collect his brother. Philippo, waiting in the courtyard of the school, saw a man approaching him. The man looked to be in his thirties. Surely his brother was only twenty-three? The man had a set face, deep eyes, and a scar. He was dressed in a linen suit of black and carried a sword and dagger. Philippo, awestruck, was on his best behavior instantly. The man gave him a long and searching stare, but said nothing. Philippo smiled and said, "Rodrigo?"

Then suddenly the man embraced him passionately. Philippo wept. Proudly he showed a letter from the Mother Superior in Cadiz. "I will read it to you, for it is all about me," he said.

Mendoza listened to the letter and then said, "It appears you are not good at Latin; that is a pity. Latin is what priests speak."

"Some of them do," said Philippo.

"No, all."

"Some of them only pretend to."

Mendoza looked at him. "Is that true?"

"You didn't know?"

"No. That is very bad."

"Why? You read no language, but you are not bad."

Mendoza looked away. "Listen to me. I live by the encomienda."

"I see. What is it?"

"Slave-collecting."

"But the mother said you did not."

"I lied to her."

"I see. It is so bad, then?"

"It is not a trade for *caballeros*."

"I see."

"I have told you this because it is a fact that you must know."

"Do the *caballeros* speak to you?"

"When it suits them."

"Do they malign you?"

"No."

"I understand." Philippo thought for a minute, then said, "The Mother Superior is far away from here."

"Let me not hear you say so again. She is innocent."

Philippo wondered at his formidable brother. "May I introduce you to my friends?"

"Who are they?" Mendoza asked.

"Martim, Joachim, and Sebastião. There," Philippo said, pointing toward the house.

Mendoza looked up and saw a trio of Philippo's fellow pupils on the third floor. "Yes, of course," he answered. Philippo signaled to them to come down. "What are their parents?"

"Martim and Joachim have no parents; they have inherited haciendas. Sebastião's father is a minister."

"I see," said Mendoza. Good, he thought, very good.

He shook hands with the three boys while Philippo made the introductions. Mendoza then stood with his hands clasped behind his back. A stretch of silence in the closed courtyard followed, and Philippo said, "I will go and fetch a porter to take my things, shall I?"

The four boys scampered up the stairs.

"Hey, what a man your brother is!" Sebastião said.

"I think so," said Philippo.

"Tiene cojones," remarked Sebastião.

"Very much so," said Joachim.

"My father was much the same kind of man," said Martim.

"Yes? I am glad you like him," said Philippo.

"Did you see his sword?" Joachim asked.

"I think that has seen much use."

Arrived in Asunción, Philippo was taken to Mendoza's little house and invited to explore it. Mendoza waited while his brother went into every room, including the ones housing the three servants, who made bows, to which Philippo returned a friendly shake of his hand and a nod of the head, and then the kitchens, wash house, stables, and the tiny outer courtyard. Mendoza waited without moving.

Philippo said, walking back, "Brother, you have elevated your position in the world."

"Thanks. Now let me see you make some use of it."

"But how?"

"Haven't they taught you?"

Philippo blushed.

Every evening Mendoza took Philippo to the square. They sat and ordered drinks, and he looked at his most forbidding. Philippo was full of respect for him. He noticed that Mendoza bowed to people and they bowed back, but he had no other social interaction. Then, on the fourth day, a middle-aged man came over to them with a welcoming smile.

"Good evening, Señor Mendoza."

"Good evening, Señor Quiroda. It is a most charming evening."

"It is."

"May I present my brother, Philippo."

"Your brother. Good evening."

Philippo was on his feet. "Good evening, Señor Quiroda. It is a magnificent sunset, is it not?"

"It is, it is," agreed the older man, laughing. "Señor Mendoza, come across to our table. I must introduce your brother to my nephew."

Mendoza looked across at the little family group on the opposite side of the square. They bowed. He shook his head. "No, thank you, we will not incommode you and Señora Quiroda with our presence."

"But I should like it. You see, our nephew has no companions."

"I see. It is bad to be alone."

"It is, it is."

"Then, thank you."

So they crossed the square and sat down with the Quiroda family. Philippo charmed them all with his dry humor, good manners, and stories of Cadiz. The next day Mendoza had a note requesting him to let his young brother go to the Quirodas' house.

Señor Quiroda came from Madrid. By trade he was a haberdasher, but he had prospered in Asunción. Moreover, he always knew how to take the next step up. Taken in stages, it was easy. Philippo, too, went on a formal round of visits, first to the middle, then to the upper circles of Asunción society, and made all their acquaintance with becoming etiquette and humor.

One day he said to Mendoza, "These invitations are always for me, never for you."

"Invitations come also for me—this one from Señorita Vignola, for example."

"But you never accept," replied Philippo.

"No."

"Because you take part in the encomienda?"

"Perhaps." Mendoza shrugged.

"Then I, too, shall not go."

"That would be a pity."

"Why?"

"It gives me pleasure to see you enjoy yourself."

Philippo searched his face. "So, then, I shall go."

Philippo touched everything that was tender in Mendoza's heart, for he was all his brother had ever found to love. Mendoza moved his younger brother both to pity and to hero worship, for Philippo was still a child.

After three months, however, the time came for him to return to Montevideo and his school friends. Mendoza went down to the harbor to see him off, watching Philippo's boat as long as he could, until it disappeared beyond a curve in the river.

On their last night together, Philippo had said: "The encomienda is a dangerous trade."

"No, no."

"Yes. I have heard. If you fall, what shall I do?"

"I will try not to. If I do fall, then accept what God sends."

* * *

The next time Mendoza went on an expedition, however, he took four times as many soldiers as usual and directed them from behind. He lost seven men, and one adventurer made a sneering reference to his caution. In a fit of rage, Mendoza challenged the man and killed him.

This time they had captured two hundred and twenty-eight Guarani.

Back in the city Mendoza shut his ears, but nobody dared to slight his honor. He was a man to treat with utmost politeness, one whom, if they saw him coming, the townsfolk turned down alleyways to avoid or, if it was too late for that, treated with punctilious civility.

He bought a larger farm and a bigger house, for Philippo, whose three months' vacation was the hinge on which his year revolved. He taught him musketry, swordsmanship, and riding, and watched Philippo sweep all before him socially. By the time he was seventeen, many ladies were in love with him, or claimed to be. He charmed them all with his dry wit and the way he had of linking any subject to the people he was with.

When Philippo turned eighteen, his brother said, "Now is the time for you to go to Europe."

"What? Why?"

"To learn."

"To learn what?"

"Whatever it is that young men learn in Europe."

So, with a Swiss tutor, he was sent on a tour of London, Paris, Rome, Augsburg, and Madrid. Mendoza saw them off at Buenos Aires. There were many tears from Philippo, and he stood by the afterrail until he could no longer distinguish his brother among the crowd. Then he dried his tears, smiled a melancholy smile at his tutor to ask forgiveness, climbed the topmost tree of the foremast, and dreamed over the sea.

Mendoza stayed until the ship was out of sight and then turned back to his solitary existence.

Part
Two

6

ON THE VERGE of the jungle that lay beyond the barrier of the Iguaçú Falls, a tribe of Guarani were making their way to the bank of a river that fed into the main stream of the waterfall. Some were dressed in strips of cloth and others in animal skins. The flesh of the shaman who led them was painted to look like the markings of some jungle creature. He was smoking a long cheroot, and his face was creased in thought. Behind him came the braves, followed by the women and children. They were all silent.

They carried a cross raised high, so that the lower branches of the trees they passed struck at the face of Father Julien Lanzotti, who was tied onto it, naked, with ropes of twisted fiber. His face was expressionless, his eyes were closed, and he looked dead.

The murmur of the river rose above the occasional whispers of the women and children. The trees thinned out, and the Guarani stood on the riverbank. All together, with an upward swing, they flung the cross far out into the stream. It splashed, sank, and then rose again. The children ran along the bank, screaming, as it began to float away, then stopped to throw handfuls of mud after it as it disappeared into the distance.

It was not going fast as yet. A clump of water flowers caught it—irises, taller than a man—and leaned tenderly above the river's human burden. Then, turning around, the cross found its way back into the current. A butterfly came to perch on it, opening and closing its delicate wings. Beneath benevolent trees the cross sailed on. It was going faster. The river widened, and the trees drew back. The cross's pathway was decided. There was only one way now. The main stream held it.

Though the falls were still five miles away, the sky was already misted over with vapor rising from the rocks where the cataract crashed down, far away below. On the banks of the jungle, leaves were drenched with spray, and the roar of water, muted but not obliterated by the distance, sounded a continuous undertone.

The cross gathered more speed. Father Lanzotti, not yet dead, opened his eyes as, with his face full of terror, he was carried over the edge. Somersaulting over and over, the cross rode down three hundred feet of tumbling water to be lost in the wet fog that rose from the churned surface at the bottom. Three hundred yards farther on, it reappeared to be snatched out of sight again by the frenzy of the current until at last, a mile farther down, the river resumed its normal course. Behind it the tower of spume still hung aloft above the falls.

Far downstream, gazing from his perch beside the quiet river, Father Sebastian Larrantozo noticed something lurching in the water and recognized its shape. He stood up, shading his eyes, and then scrambled down the sloping rock.

"It is a cross," he said.

He and the other two Jesuits pushed out their raft. The cross was floating with its burden underneath, but when they reached it they saw the fiber bound around the crossbars. Sebastian managed to tilt the floating bulk of it and peer underneath. The look on his face told the others what he had seen. He looked like what he once had been, a sergeant in the Royal Troop. They hitched the cross to the raft and poled back to the bank.

As soon as they got there, the other two Jesuits waded out and dragged the cross ashore, where they turned it over. Father Sebastian cursed and cut the body free and was about to lift it when Father Antonio stayed his hand and said: "Let him lie there." They had a spade with them, and made a deep pit there in the bank, and buried Julien wrapped in Sebastian's habit.

Sebastian said, "Let us also set the cross here." When the cross was upright, Antonio led them in the burial service. The next day they set out on their journey back to the Santa Croce Mission, poling into the quiet darkness of the forest.

They arrived, after a fortnight of journeying through the forest by land and water, to find a small crowd awaiting them; the Guarani always knew when someone was coming. Sebastian took Brother Itapua, a Guarani and deputy chief of the mission, aside and said a few words to him. Itapua went to the practice hall.

Father Gabriel O'Donnell was totally absorbed in the music of a Guarani consort of viols when Itapua quietly came and told him the news. He sat for several minutes in silence before dismissing the musicians. Then he went with Itapua to his cell where he found Sebastian waiting. Father Sebastian reported in a steady voice, watching to see how Gabriel would take it. For Julien had been one of the youngest and most amiable of priests.

"Is he well buried?"

"Yes."

Gabriel looked at the floor. "I shall go and see him."

Sebastian and Itapua looked at each other, for Gabriel was aging. Sebastian said, "Why go? There is nothing to see."

"Then I shall go and see nothing."

Once they were both outside, Sebastian said to Itapua, "He will try to go where Julien went. He will try to pass the falls."

"That is evident."

"Will you dissuade him?"

"No, I will not."

Itapua told Tapu to pull the great church bell. It had been cast in Barcelona. It tolled out over the church square and the meeting house, and rows of stone houses with pantiled roofs and workshops set around with moats, out over the fields and into the forests beyond the Mission of Santa Croce. Hearing the summons, the Guarani ceased their labors and looked at one another, lifting their hoes. Then quietly, unexcitedly, as one man, they started to troop back.

Gabriel sat on his bed with his knees drawn up, confronted by the fact that he had sent Julien to an awesome death. Then he shot to his feet and began striding up and down his tiny cell, dogged by a thought he could not shake off. He had done wrong in sending Julien to approach the Guarani above the falls. The objectors had been right. If only he had listened to them, he would not have lost Julien.

Suddenly he stopped short. But what would Julien himself say? Julien would urge him onward. There could be no doubt. He was as sure as if he could hear the dead man speaking. He resumed his pacing. Come what may, the Guarani above the falls could not be abandoned to their ignorance. The work Julien had undertaken must be done. His sacrifice would not be wasted then. But what a death! Gabriel shuddered, and knew he could not send another Jesuit to face such a martyrdom.

He sat on his bed again, peering at one of the hard slivers of light that slipped through the pantiled roof, without knowing what it was, for his thoughts had taken him back to his childhood on the coast of Kerry.

A marvelous, overblown, strange, stormy place that had been, the tides racing to catch up with the boy and the girl he now remembered, and then ebbing out so slowly. And the hills that had seemed so high to him then, in Ireland, with the sheep, and the bits of fields his father tended when he had finished his day's work for Mr. Butler. Maureen O'Neill, that was the girl's name! He wondered what had become of her and of Siamus Kavanagh, the scared priest, forever looking over his shoulder for Protestants and ducking into the little Catholic school he taught in the barn of Butler's homestead. It was Father Kavanagh who had picked Gabriel out to be a priest, all on account of his Latin.

One night the priest had come to the drafty stone-built cottage and stood there in the light of a crackling fire, trying to persuade Gabriel's father and mother to let him go for a priest. The whole family had been there to hear it, his grandfather as well as his parents, and also his aunts and nine other children.

His grandfather, wise in the ways of this world said, "No, Father, he shall stay here and learn to fish and look after the stupid sheep, which is what he was born to. Look you, he shall be a Catholic all his life; on that you have our promise. But a priest!" He shook his head. "Look you, here's a question now I've never asked before, but, counting everything in, now, how much do you get in a year?"

"It's not for the stipend the boy must be a priest, so I shan't be telling you what mine is."

"Then let *me* tell *you.*" The old man leaned forward to look closely into the priest's face, which was even more worn and lined than his own. "Eleven pounds," he said.

Siamus looked askance at this. "Eleven pounds!" he scoffed. "Why, even if you bate your own shilling, I get plenty more than that." He laughed, inviting the family to join him, but no one did.

"Eleven pounds is what I said, and I stick to it," the old man answered. "And for the present year I shall bate that shilling you mention, too. Where would I be getting a shilling, the way things are?"

"A penny at a time you could put it by if you had the wish," the priest said sternly, "but you have not."

"The wish, is it?" the old man asked. "I've got the wish all right. We all have the wish, Father—Pat Leary, the Halloran, the O'Connor, the Fitzpatrick—all of us. We have the wish, but we haven't the shillings. I say eleven pounds. You're a good man, there's no denying it, and you'll see heaven, that's sure, but don't take Gabriel, our boy, to be one like you."

"I tell you, it's not eleven. Fourteen is what it is, and last year no less than that is what it came to."

"Then I beg your pardon for underrating you, but I'd still like to know what good that sum does you, a man with the blades of his shoulders sticking out through his shirt and his skin as dead as paper. See here, Father Siamus, tonight you sup with us, and tomorrow night you sup with the Mountjoys. We all take thought, you see, for your empty bowl, but that doesn't say we want this lad to join you in it."

"He is a clever boy. Now, I'm not saying that he will, mind, but what if he advances to be a bishop?"

"No, excuse me, Father, but if it comes to bishops, now you raise the subject, let me say that if he came to be a bishop of the eastern parts, there'd be great harm done to the lad, for he'd be little better than a Protestant. Here in the West, I grant you, bishops suffer with the faithful people, but of the many thousand priests there are in Ireland, Father, how many get to be bishops, will you tell me that?"

"Not many, I grant you. What does Pegeen say?"

Gabriel's mother said, "I say my father has said true, though God forgive him for saying that much to a priest. Leave the child be, Father Siamus, for the love of Christ."

Gabriel's father was whittling a lobster basket with his knife, letting the peelings fall into the turf fire. So far he had not said a word. Siamus turned to him. "Michael," he asked, "what's your opinion?"

Michael inquired, "What does the big lad think himself?"

They all turned to Gabriel. He was an obedient son of Holy Church, but he did not know what to answer. To be sure, it was a fine thing to be chosen for a priest out of all the children in the school, but he knew the kind of life that Father Siamus lived, always looking over his shoulder in case somebody had given the word that would set the soldiers after him, for the English law said he had no right to be there. He lived in the shadows, giving a wide berth to the English Protestant gentry, doffing his headpiece swiftly if they chanced upon him somewhere. Of course, his flock hailed Father Siamus as the bringer of the mass, and honored the priest at births, deaths, and marriages in their low cottages, but everyone also knew how he lived alone in his drafty place, never knowing where his next meal might be coming from. Gabriel said, "I do not know, Father."

"Let us leave it there, then," said Siamus. "In a year's time I will ask again."

"I suppose," said his mother sorrowfully, "that if the boy did go for the priesthood it would be many years before we saw him."

"He would go and study at the French Academy. Then he'd come back to Ireland, and who knows but that he might be sent back here?"

"And he might not," said Michael.

"He might not," Siamus agreed. "Do I smell a stew of onions and potatoes and mutton, can it be?"

"No, not mutton," Michael answered with a wink.

So they all sat down at the board table and after the father had said grace they ate, and it was obvious to Gabriel that the priest hadn't eaten mutton for several days.

When it was time for him to go out into the starry darkness, Siamus said, "Good night and God be with you," to Michael and then, exercising the authority all priests had, he said to Gabriel, "Come with me to the end of the path." Gabriel remembered how the starlight danced on the air above the hills and the sea, for it was the turn of the year into autumn. The priest was silent until they reached the place, switched by a cutting wind, where the moors began. His cottage lay beyond three hills. He stopped and said, "It is a great honor I have done you this night, Gabriel. Do you know that?"

"Yes, Father," Gabriel said.

"A great honor," the priest repeated, and added, casting about for an explanation the boy could pride himself on: "It is because you are good at Latin."

"Yes, I know. My Latin is excellent," Gabriel remembered saying. "Is that all that is required to be a priest?"

Siamus had laughed. Gabriel knew now what he must have been thinking. "No, not that only," he had said with a sigh, "though the Latin is a good beginning. What do you most like doing, Gabriel?"

"Playing my flute," Gabriel answered, and he showed his companion the whistle that his father had bought at the local fair and that he had always by him, wrapped in a piece of cloth.

"Play," Siamus had invited him, and Gabriel did not need to be invited twice. Even now he seemed to recall that, inspired by the silence of the night, he had played well. The notes had seemed precious to him, like pearls in the dark.

"Very good," said Siamus when he had finished. "Well, they can teach you the flute at the college, and many more things about music besides."

He remembered thinking, Now that would be a thing, wouldn't it? "I suppose they can teach anything," he had answered, and returned to the cottage much impressed.

Siamus's offer to take him for a priest was known over the lands and sea next day, and his mother got used to that special respect which was shown to the parents of a priest. Secretly she began to urge him to accept. But his father said that if God wanted him to be a priest, he would surely make it known to Gabriel. Already, however, the other boys and girls were treating him with the deference due the boy who would be leaving the hills for the college across the sea.

He knew it all went to show what great power the Church had. If he went, he would become one of the Wild Geese, as they were called, the Catholics who could not bear to stay at home in slavery but flew to France. Sometimes their families paid for their flight, but only a hundred families or so could afford the expense. The rest went at the Church's cost. If he went, he would be one of them. There were times when, alone, playing his whistle over the sad land, he felt himself a marked man already.

When the year was through, he asked what he was to say.

"No," said his grandfather.

His mother said, "Yes."

What his father said had stayed with him ever since: "Do as God counsels you."

With this instruction, one evening he went off alone where he could look over the sea. He played his whistle and, not knowing what might come of it, asked Christ directly, "What should I do?"

It was the first of many times. A tranquillity he had never known before descended upon him and upon the cottage, the fields and the sea as well. "Why," Christ said to him very simply, "do this."

He went back down to the cottage, ducking under the humble lintel, and said yes to the waiting priest.

The Jesuits took special note of the boy with the clear blue eyes who had come from Kerry to the upper Loire, in the heart of France, for alone among the learners, while he said his prayers with a simple heart, unquestioningly, he reasoned subtly. Finding him enamored of music, they asked him, "Did you know that our founder, Saint Ignatius Loyola, was in love with music, too?" and told him the story of how the saint, a Spaniard, although a dutiful Christian had at first devoted

himself to courtliness and the disciplines of war. As a soldier
he had performed many notable feats of arms, until at last,
crippled by wounds received in a siege against the French, he
had found himself at the gate of death. Then he had seen all
things for certain, as a child might see them, and hung up his
sword and dagger by the statue of the Blessed Virgin Mary.
From then on, going daily to mass, he lived as a beggar, but
followers came to him, attracted by his saintliness. It had been
for them that Saint Ignatius wrote the *Spiritual Exercises,* a
book that Gabriel could borrow when he had been at the
school a little longer. That book would teach him how to be a
soldier in Christ's keeping.

Then the saint took Holy Orders, and at this point Gabriel
was instructed to attend carefully. Seeing how the saint had
collected a large following, certain parties in the Holy City
launched charges of heresy against him and he was imprisoned. May God pardon their foolish souls, and, blessed be His
Holiness Pope Paul III who clearly saw the charges were ridic-
ulous! So when he was released, the founder added a vow of
obedience to the Pope to his other vows, and the Vicar of
Christ, seeing his servant's worth, commissioned him to found
an order. That was how the Society of Jesus, known as the
Jesuits, was founded, the Soldiers in Christ, among whom his
present instructors were numbered. It was not for them in their
humility to make a claim, but many certainly did say that in
this present time of trouble the Order was the Church's trust-
iest shield—a circumstance for him to bear in mind as the
time of his ordination approached.

As for music, they told him with a smile, certain people
called them the Operatic Society of Jesus. But in truth, as he
must know himself, enthusiasm for music blended easily with
a passion for Christ. There were many missionaries who made
exquisite music. For instance, Father Joseph taught the oboe
and the flute. Lessons could be arranged for Gabriel. And he
must read the biography of their blessed founder.

So, as he passed though the college he learned to play the
oboe and the organ like a master. As for other studies, he
passed out exactly in the middle of his class, and when he
went on to the Jesuit College in Rome, he was neither ap-

palled nor puzzled by what he found there. Nor did he ever
seek out a courtesan to satisfy his lusts even though one or two
of the instructors were prepared to look the other way, thinking this was part of his mind that a man ought to know about
before he took his vows. When at last he became a member of
the Order, his instructors found in him a source of puzzlement
that was half admiration, for although there was no denying he
had understood everything he had been taught and had a grasp
of metaphysical fundamentals that nothing could shake, he
had somehow still emerged with the mind of a peasant.

Perhaps that was why the chief instructor in theology, a
burly German with the blank eyes of a boiled fish, approached
him privately the day after he entered the Order and poured
out an account of his doings with the girls who hung about the
Papal City. He had gone down on his knees to do it and, when
he finished, had squinted up at the young man with a laugh,
waiting for absolution.

Gabriel said, "What is tormenting your soul has nothing to
do with any of that. All of that matters very little. Your tor-
ment is not having been consulted by the head of our Order, in
perfecting the conclusions he is putting to the Pope. I suggest
you pray he will not need the assistance of your sophistry.
Shall I pronounce the absolution now."

The German was astounded. Then he gave a little smile
and accepted absolution with a roar of laughter. That night he
slept better than usual.

Gabriel returned to Ireland and saw his family. His grandfather was already dead, and Father Siamus looked very near
his end, but although none of them knew it, this was the last
time he would see any of them. His father, mother, brother,
and sisters joined with all the neighbors to persuade him to
address them in French and Italian, and were duly impressed
when he did so, but he could see that, despite their admiration
for his learning, they were anxious on his account. They
thought of him as a helpless innocent. "You mustn't worry
about me," he tried to reassure his mother. "I am no longer a
child."

Then he set out for Tipperary, where he had been posted as
curate. His mother came to see him on his way and stayed

there, even after he had waved to her from the turning, still watching him as far as she could see.

The priest he had come to assist in Tipperary was even closer to death than Father Siamus. After a month of watching at his bedside, Gabriel closed the priest's eyes. Then in the ground of a chapel that was hardly more than a cottage by a lake, he buried the old curate with proper ceremony in the presence of thousands of mourners.

Before he died, the old priest had tried to tell Gabriel how things were in the parish, but he had only been able to say, "Terrible, my son, and pitiful. I will introduce you to John O'Burke, and he, God save his soul, will tell you more of it than I can, so close to death as I am. Why have I lived? I don't see why, no, I don't, I don't." He turned over and remained all that day staring at the limestone wall in which were wedged segments of gorse roots from the plants outside, fretted even here by the wind blowing in.

John O'Burke had introduced himself while the old priest was still alive. After the funeral he summoned Gabriel to his big dank house. It stood, surrounded by his dwindling estates, backing onto the lake. All that emerged from its crowd of chimneys was a couple of spires of smoke from the two hearths that remained alive—one in the kitchen where his entire hangdog household spent the day, and one from the hallway, where he lived himself. It was over that fire that he had hung the sword he was no longer allowed to wear like the gentleman he was. A big-made man, as old as Gabriel's father, O'Burke sat there by the fireplace, handing out instructions and advice to the peasants who still came to him when they were in trouble.

"I am not the local landlord, you must understand," O'Burke told Gabriel. "That's Mr. Edwardes, J. P., a Protestant. He owns more than half this county, and·is a member of the Dublin Parliament as well, although, do you see, he lives in London, and that despite the fact he is now the owner of Crowell Castle that is here by, and belonged to the O'Burke, in living memory. Now it belongs to the J. P., M. P., and so will this house, too, belong to him when I am dead. Isn't that so, Charles?" He turned to a slim young man who had been fondling the dogs at the fireside but now straightened himself and approached Gabriel to shake his hand with a friendly smile.

"So it will, Father, the more's the pity. Charles O'Burke is the name. I keep explaining to my father that it doesn't matter who the property belongs to."

"It doesn't matter?"

"No, in good faith it doesn't." He pointed a finger at his senior. "I will not even try to claim my inheritance when he is gone. If you want me then, seek me among the Wild Geese. I'll be joining the flight." He struck a pose and smiled.

"The fellow is in love with those lunatics over there in France," the old man said proudly, glowering with warmth at his son.

7

THE PARISHIONERS OF Durraine in County Kerry were only destitute, whereas those of Mamegoff near Tipperary were starving. The law was in the hands of Mr. Edwardes, the local justice of the peace, except for serious cases, which went to Mr. Martin and Mr. Howarth, who, acting jointly, were empowered to punish serious breaches of the law with a long terms of imprisonment.

Although nine-tenths of the peasantry were Catholic, Catholic gentlemen were debarred from being justices of the peace, nor could they sit in Parliament. A Catholic was not even permitted to purchase a piece of land, no matter how long he had farmed it, if a Protestant also happened to want it. If a Catholic presumed to buy a horse, it had to be worth less than five pounds. A Catholic could neither vote nor be a schoolmaster nor hold office under the Crown, nor marry a Protestant. Acts of the Dublin Parliament became law only after being authenticated by the Parliament at Westminster. On the other hand, any act passed in Westminster ipso facto became the law of Ireland. In any case, most members of the Dublin Parliament were nominees of English aristocrats. Mamegoff, for example, was represented in Dublin by Mr. Edwardes as a result of a wager with the Earl of Berkshire, whom nobody in Mamegoff had ever seen.

The laws were one thing; their enforcement was another. In Mamegoff the magistrate, a Protestant surrounded by Catholics, was happy to let sleeping dogs lie. The J.P.s, too, were an idle lot with little interest in persecution as an official duty. Persecution as a source of profit, however, was another matter. They were intent on converting arable land into pasture, and this meant turning their tenants off their lands, and the anti-Catholic laws gave them a way of doing this. When a Protestant landowner was minded to turn his estate over to pasture, he had only to enforce the law with energy to squeeze his tenants onto scraps of land not big enough to feed a goat. He could even dispossess them entirely, leaving them to wander homeless over the hills. The peasants did not take this oppression lying down, of course. Troops were brought in, and then the law began to lay about it with a vengeance.

When Gabriel arrived in Mamegoff, he was soon recognized as a priest who knew the fruits of harvest did not last all year and there were times when a hardworking man and his family had to live on gorse. He never looked to a parishioner for a bite to eat, and if he was offered one, he was not embarrassingly grateful either. Late and early he was to be seen on his way over the moors with a hunk of bread, and maybe more, to some sick cottage, and if he chanced to cross the path of another man who perhaps was out to deal with Mr. Edwardes's sheep, he averted his eyes.

Not everyone in the locality was poor, however. Some lived comfortably in stone-built mansions. But these—the Martins, the Howarths, and the Greensides—although neighbors, were Protestants, not in the cure of Gabriel. Nevertheless, when Christmas was approaching, he did not scruple to warn them that their mansions were built on foundations of sand because their brothers and sisters were starving around them in hovels. He also informed them that their silks and velvets had been torn from the naked backs they had only to look out of their fine windows to catch sight of—or even around at the back in their own servants' quarters. Nor was Gabriel satisfied with just having his say. He stood fasting in the cold, where all could see, and refused to talk anymore with them when they invited him to come and eat with them and discuss the matter further. "I have nothing more to say," he declared.

In the end, Mr. Cox, the rector of the Established Church of Ireland, visited each of these mansions in turn, and as a result the Martins, the Howarths, and the Greensides dipped cautiously into their pockets and a not inconsiderable sum was applied to the cottagers' needs. The donors felt some self-satisfaction when it was over and done with, and Mr. Cox had thanked and congratulated them in an appropriately gratifying way. Gabriel, however, had received their charity ungraciously, they all agreed. All he had said was "Well, I shall go now and do what I can with this, which is less than justice would bestow on them." He was not the only Jesuit in Ireland at that time to make leveling remarks, a fact that contributed not a little to their sinister reputation with the Establishment.

Yet Mr. Cox, although he lived in a fine brick rectory that was almost as grand as Mr. Howarth's mansion nearby, respected Gabriel greatly and enjoyed nothing more than to walk along with him discussing questions of theology. In the end, however, he, too, was disappointed. The day came when Gabriel said, "I have had enough of this talking. I am no good at arguing, and I don't want to be. I believe the Blessed Virgin was seen ascending into heaven because I have the Pope's account of it. I should be glad if you could believe it, too, Mr. Cox, but you inform me you cannot and I accept your word, so there's an end of it. In conclusion I have to observe to you that, as a priest cannot live with women, then either your wife really is your wife—which I think is the case—and therefore you are not a priest at all; or else she is not your wife, in which case you must be a bad priest." And he said all this with a lowering expression he sometimes had that made him an oppressive companion, but there were other times when, although he never obliged a gathering with a jig, the lilt of his oboe lightened a gloom that seemed to have settled on Mamegoff forever.

John O'Burke was well pleased with the new priest but cautioned him to keep his head down. "For you know yourself, the law says you've no right to be in Ireland. Bide more still. Let the Protestants be, at least."

But when any wrong came to his notice, Gabriel could not let anyone rest easy who had power to right it, and the sight of him trudging up to their doorways became so wearisome to the Martins, the Howarths, and the Greensides that the time came when they informed their servants, who were Catholics, that they were no longer at home to the priest.

When John O'Burke died, the bishop of the eastern parts

who came to bury him, in addition to the comforting words he bestowed on the hundreds of peasants who had turned out to pay their last respects to their protector, also had a few sage words for Gabriel in private. "A light rein," he said. "That's my advice to you, a light rein." Then he drove away in his own carriage.

A week later, Gabriel went to pay his respects to the new O'Burke and to commiserate with him on the loss of the family house, remembering what the dead man had said about the law affecting inheritances by Catholics. It was an uncomfortable interview. Young Charles O'Burke seemed to brush Gabriel's remarks aside.

Two months later, however, Gabriel was passing the rectory when Mr. Cox came dashing out to invite him in. To his surprise he found Charles O'Burke there, sitting in awkward silence in the rector's study.

Cox said, "The time has come for you to know that Mr. O'Burke has decided to become a member of the Established Church of Ireland."

"Look," said Charles, "sit down. I do wish you would sit down, Father." He smiled charmingly. "Well, anyway, it's true. Mr. Cox and I have been having long talks."

"I have cleared up certain points for him," Cox put in.

"You, Mr. Cox, cannot clear up anything. O'Burke, is this true?"

"I've already told you. Next Sunday I will receive the mass from Mr. Cox."

"Call it Communion," said Cox with a nervous laugh. "Communion is what we call it." He turned to Gabriel. "I thought it best to tell you in advance."

"I've given it a lot of thought, you know," Charles assured him. "Theology is not one-sided."

Gabriel's answer was an impatient gesture. "You never saw fit to discuss your doubts with me. Why not?"

"I thought it best to wrestle with them alone."

"Quite so," murmured Cox.

Gabriel rose, white-faced. "This has nothing to do with doubts," he said. "What has happened is that you have turned your back on Christ entirely. In your present opinion, being

true to your Savior matters less than being a country gentleman, and no doubt a justice of the peace into the bargain. You
haven't changed your faith, my lad. You've decided you can
do without it. Well, you don't feel the need of it now, may be,
but the time will come when you will feel the need of it,
believe me."

"You see?" said Charles, turning to his new guide. "I told
you."

"Can't you at least wish him well in his new faith?" Mr.
Cox asked.

"What nonsense is that for a priest to be saying?"

"Well, Charles, we priests are as weak as other men are,"
Cox pointed out smoothly. "May God forgive us!"

"Amen!" quoth Charles.

"You disgust me, both of you," Gabriel said. "He put on
his cap and strode out.

Many of Charles's dependents peered through the church
windows to see him take the Protestants' bread and wine.
When they dropped down from the sills, they knew that they
had lost their last protection against the full force of the law.

As Gabriel had foreseen, the debonair young man was
welcomed into the ranks of the local gentry, and it did not take
him long to become a J.P. His manner was so easy and oblig-
ing when he was with them. To his house servants and tenants, however, he was a different man. Most of them had
known him since he was a baby, but now he could no longer
be on intimate terms with them. Ashamed of his betrayal, he
turned against them. In the space of a year he became a rabid
persecutor of his old co-religionists. His new friends, the gentlemen of the Protestant Ascendancy, confined their excesses
to gambling and the hunting field. They had too much confidence in themselves to run to denominational excess. Secretly
smiling at the zeal of the recent convert, they advised him to
take it easy, but he would not listen.

On his own estate—securely his now—sheep were soon
grazing where his father's Catholic kinsmen had tilled the soil.
He did not go so far as to evict them, allowing them to remain
in their cottages but making no provision for their subsistence.
After the Catholic tenants had scraped out a living for two

years, Gabriel led a ragged collection of men, women, and children up to the house. Hearing they were there, Charles came to the door backed by three outsiders, strangers to the place, whom he had taken on and armed with guns. He asked the peasants what they wanted.

Gabriel answered, "See!" Then he turned to his followers. "Kneel," he told them.

The women got down on their knees, and so did the children. The men did not.

Charles O'Burke was infuriated. "It's no use!" he shouted. "Your priest has misled you. You'll get nothing from me. Be off, before I tell my men to shoot."

Gabriel replied gently, "When they told me they were starving, I counseled them to come to you and ask for bread. I cannot believe I was misleading them in that."

"Bread!" one woman repeated.

"Bread!" echoed another.

"Bread, bread, bread!" the entire crowd began to chant in unison. "Bread, bread, bread!"

Trembling, Charles signaled his men back inside, followed them, and slammed the door.

His housekeeper, who had also served his father, heard the cry outside. She came up to O'Burke and told him that by the mercy of God there was a full batch of loaves all ready for the oven.

He stared at her for half a minute and then told her to go ahead. "You're a good woman," he added, which encouraged her to make some broth while the loaves were baking.

Outside at the doorway the men surged around Gabriel. "We've given him his chance," growled one of them, "and we've seen what he thinks of it. Now it's our turn. Come on, lads. There's only three of them!" He had brought a cudgel with him, which he now flourished. The younger men cheered. The older ones looked pensive. The speaker turned to Gabriel. "Father," he appealed, and he did not smile to use the word to someone young enough to be his son. "What do you say? If we're going to get anything, we've got to attack, and we want you to lead."

"If you do want to attack, then, yes, I will lead if you wish it. We've seen they have guns, however. Before we break in, quite a few of us will be wounded or dead. You realize that, don't you? When the rest of us get inside, what will happen? Have you thought of that?"

"We'll kill them," a younger man answered in a low voice.

"Very well. And then what?"

"You tell us," answered a third voice, an old woman's this time.

"After that it won't make. much difference what we do," Gabriel said.

"We could wait here for the soldiers to take us all together, or go back to our homes and let them arrest us one by one, or we might scatter and force them to hunt us in the open."

The young man who had spoken of killing said bitterly, "I know your sort, Father Gabriel. You'll go far and no further. That's the way of it with men of your cloth. You see?" he remarked to the others. "Already he's got us talking instead of doing." And there were sounds of agreement.

At this stage, however, the servants of the house came out and set up the long trestle tables that had not been seen since the old O'Burke's death. The servants told them they had softened the young master's heart. Maybe he had changed his mind about being a Protestant. Smiling all over their faces, they said there would be bread for everyone in a couple of hours, and a bowl of good broth to go with it, so the whole crowd sat down—the men, too, this time—and waited. Some women went back to the village to collect any children who had been left behind.

The men told one another what a good thing it was the priest had held them up with his talking. After a time, Charles O'Burke himself came out again and confessed he was most impressed by their orderly behavior. If they had grievances, he said, he was prepared to hear them, and invited them to select six spokesmen to come and see him after their meal, to which they were most welcome.

The spokesman were chosen, with Gabriel as their leader, and, after noting their names, their host retired into the house to await developments. For what the crowd did not know was that he had secretly dispatched one of his new men to Tipperary to fetch the military.

The dragoons appeared over the hill on their horses before the feast was well begun, and at the sight of their drawn sabers, everyone scattered. There was no escape for the six men whose names Charles O'Burke had noted down, however, and he took special care to tell the sergeant not to forget "the Catholic priest," as he had now for some time been referring to his father's old friend.

Only one outcome was possible. Five of the six ringleaders were sentenced to ten years' imprisonment. Gabriel was to be imprisoned for life by a regretful judge who had never quite succeeded in reconciling himself to those occasional cases where justice required the ill-treatment of just men. It was obvious, however, that as long as this impressive young priest was loose in Ireland, he would be a source of unrest. He belonged to an Ireland that was dead and buried, or very soon would be.

Out of sight in the squalid, gloomy, and disease-ridden prison of Glenmarie, Gabriel was soon forgotten by everyone except Charles O'Burke, who never tired of regaling his bored guests with the story of how he had foiled the Jesuit's plot to raise a rebellion. As for the prison itself, it was in a state of utter neglect, and nobody capable of doing anything to improve it ever came near it. It was left entirely at the mercy of a jailer whose sole interest in its inmates was the perquisites he could extract from them. In other words, his solicitude—for which he charged heavily—was confined to prisoners who could pay extra for better board and lodging. Debtors were the object of his peculiar care.

Catholics, footpads, and murderers fared badly. Atrociously housed and fed, in cells that were murky by day and pitch-dark at night—for how could the prisoners pay for candles when they could not even afford a blanket?—the only money the jailer was able to make out of them came from tips donated by ladies and gentlemen who visited Glenmarie for the curious amusement the sight of its inmates offered.

When Gabriel's personal funds were exhausted, his imme-

diate reacton was one of relief. Now his money was finished
he could no longer buy food or blankets for the needier prisoners as he had been doing, but it was nonetheless a blessing
to be at one with them, all alike, at the same level, in the
presence of their Savior.

The actual experience of this lowly condition, however,
affected him like a stunning blow. One of the most shocking
discoveries he had made was that all of the gashes and bruises
he found on the stinking, half-naked bodies had not been in-
flicted by the warders. Some were the handiwork of their fellow sufferers. The realization that humanity could sink to such
degradation shook his belief in the possibility of redemption.

He had never shirked the duty of rebuke, however, and
whenever inhumanity, whether committed by warder or prisoner, presented an occasion for it, he administered reprimands
as liberally as he had administered food and medicine when he
could buy it. After his funds were exhausted, he saw no reason to discontinue admonishing the warders. But, the next
time he remonstrated with a warder he was knocked down, the
other two were called, and Gabriel was kicked and beaten
senseless. The last perception he registered before he fell unconscious was the sight of the faces of a crowd of fellow
prisoners—men, women, and children—who had gathered to
watch the unusual sport with lively interest.

After that, he looked in another direction when a beating
was being administered, and in general kept his face to the
wall. At first he tried at least to offer the victims his assistance
when their persecutors had gone. To his chagrin, however, he
discovered that such ministrations were not welcome. On the
contrary, the great satisfaction he now gave the other prisoners
was an opportunity to vent their hatred. Priests, in their experience, were in league with the rich and comfortable and com-
placent. The prisoners knew of no cause to love or even
respect them.

These were the blackest days Gabriel ever knew. Gradually
he stopped praying. He put his breviary aside and, when he
looked for it, found that it had disappeared. He did not care.
What mattered was making sure he got his fair share of the
soup. Then one night he cried out in his sleep, protesting that

there was no justice, and seemed to hear the mocking laughter of the Creator he used to worship, and awoke with his cheeks wet with tears. There came a night when he had a dream in which Christ spoke to him: "What ails you?" he asked. "Has what is good ceased to be good just because you suffer? What I promised you at the beginning is still true. You are in trouble, that is true, but nothing has altered. I am still the same, and always will be."

Gabriel was surprised and delighted. "I had forgotten!" he exclaimed, and awoke laughing. Then he fell asleep a second time, and slept as he had never slept in that place before.

The next morning he found his dream remained with him. Later he tried to intervene with the warders in defense of a very old and frail prisoner, and the warders again dragged him into a corner to beat him, and a crowd of prisoners gathered to watch as before. He was becoming one of them, they thought, but something told them that it was not so. Later in the day, the children made friends with him. Their mothers, though they still jeered at him, addressed him as Father once again. Some of the men came and sat near him, and when they found he was no longer disposed to find fault with them, they began to talk freely. He was at one with them, not one of them. It was they who asked him to offer a prayer.

One day the jailer himself came and kicked him where he lay. Gabriel opened his eyes and said, "Tell me if you want me to do something, but why kick me? I am not a stone; neither is any creature of flesh and blood a stone."

The jailer made a show of bafflement. "This one's gone mad now," he remarked, and walked away. After that incident, however, all the prisoners were treated more leniently when Gabriel was by, and Gabriel himself was never beaten again.

Meanwhile Charles O'Burke was putting on weight, and his handsome face was growing heavy with drink. His hospitality had become notorious, and his oft-told tale of how he foiled a Jesuit's plot became a standing joke. One day, in the course of a shooting party, the guest standing beside him waiting for the next flight of pheasants inquired, "How is the Jesuit these days?"

The question came out of the blue, but Charles replied, "How should I know? He's in Glenmarie jail."

"I bet fifty guineas he doesn't exist and never did," another guest offered. "Why not show us the creature, if you want us to believe in him?"

"My faith," said Charles, "but I will at that."

Two coachloads of ladies and gentlemen, including O'Burke, arrived at Glenmarie two mornings later. They fell silent as soon as they entered the prison and perceived the stench of the half-naked wretches on display.

"The air may be pestilential," a lady said through her handkerchief. "We mustn't stay too long. Which one is the Jesuit?"

"Here I am," said Gabriel. He was squatting in a corner with a child in his arms. They all stared at him, and then at Charles, for Gabriel's gaze was fixed on the man who had put him where he was, not malevolently but with serious attention, as if confirming certain truths.

Charles made a valiant effort to return this scrutiny. Then, gasping, he turned around and rushed out. His guests were more than ready to follow him. Undeniably, the jaunt had been a failure, best quickly forgotten. Charles had enjoyed it least of all. In answer to a question from the lady, he replied that he'd be damned if he'd lift a finger to get the traitor out. He was where he belonged.

In many a night that followed, however, Charles O'Burke's dreams were haunted by a pair of unusually clear light blue eyes that followed him in judgment everywhere he went, and a little more than twelve months later, Gabriel was released from prison in response to a statement deposed by Charles O'Burke, J.P., saying that the Jesuit had seen the error of his ways and recommending accordingly that upon giving a promise to leave Ireland and never return, he should be released.

The said Jesuit was unwilling to give such an undertaking, but upon the deposit of such a promise by the bishop of the eastern parts on his behalf, was released nevertheless. The same bishop drove in his coach to collect Gabriel from the jail and, although the day was a raw one, found it necessary to open the windows when his passenger got in.

So it came about that Gabriel found himself back at the Jesuit College in Rome. The German teacher of theology found that his old pupil—and, as he reminded him, confessor—had turned into just the intimidating figure he had expected. He had brought along with him a present of a dozen bottles of red wine and was delighted when his host immediately opened one of them.

"Do you remember the truth you handed out to me that time?" the German said.

"Yes I do. Does the head of our Order do you the honor of consulting you now?"

"All the time. It is very boring." The German priest opened the second bottle himself. "And where are we going to send you now, do you suppose?"

"Wherever I am wanted."

"That could be anywhere. The father I secretly call Calvin will make the decision. Shall I narrow it down for you? India, the Congo, or South America. How do they strike you? I mean, supposing we were talking about someone else, not about you?"

"It would seem fitting."

"Then let us hope it fits." He raised his glass.

8

EIGHT MONTHS LATER, after braving stormy seas and pirates, Gabriel had come to rest in the Santa Croce Mission below the Falls of Iguaçú, far into the interior. He was regarded there as a model priest. His regard for order and discipline was meticulous and unremitting. So was his love for the Guarani residents on the mission lands, whose language he quickly mastered.

Four years later, when he became superior of the mission, nobody thought of questioning the appointment. No more did he. As far as he was concerned, he was simply carrying on the work they all believed in. That the others thought of him as a leader was a notion that never crossed his mind, but it was so. Even his bouts of temper were welcome to his subordinates. They loved him too much to wish him to be perfect, although they believed he walked with Christ.

This last was true. Gabriel argued, expostulated, and pleaded with his Savior all day and every day. In this, however, he found nothing notable because he believed that every Christian did the same. Now, alone in his hut, he laid before his Divine Confidant the question of Julien's martyrdom.

When evening fell, Brother Itapua knocked at the door to tell him all was ready for the mass. Gabriel invited the Guarani to make himself comfortable while he robed himself. He regarded his vestments as an encumbrance, but as they were prescribed he kept them carefully laundered and pressed. When he emerged, robed, with his gray hair flying and his mouth set in a straight line, he looked the picture of the priesthood. No words were spoken. He immediately set off behind the procession of Guarani altar boys and priests in the direction of the mission church.

As he went along, every Guarani he passed knelt, and those who were near enough reached out to kiss his hand. At first, scenting idolatry, he had requested them not to do this, but he had submitted in the end. He passed through the Church's wide double doors into its candlelit interior, and the organ burst into harmony with guitars, violins, and flutes, and the choir began a deep plainsong.

Father Julien, he thought, we mourn for you. Pray for us sinners. Yet, looking over the crowded congregation of Guarani, whom he knew so well, he wondered whether they were not mourning some different loss from his. He raised his eyes to the Guarani altar and looked, as he so often had, at the strange winged beast, half an angel and half a threatening hooded bird, that a Guarani had carved.

The Psalm soared out from the church into the night. When silence had fallen, Gabriel said, "Almighty and most merciful Father, we commend to your special care the soul of our brother Julien who, we doubt not, will make intercession for your ignorant children, the Guarani of the Upper Paraná."

The next morning, thousands of Guarani stood silent on the bank of the river while Gabriel and four other Jesuits cast off their two canoes. After they had vanished, the Guarani returned to their labors. Many were sure that they would never see him again.

The five Jesuits neared the falls of Iguaçú and heard their thunder. Turning a bend in the river, they saw the gaunt, lonely cross that marked the grave of Julien Lanzotti. Raising his eyes to the top of the falls, Gabriel could see the smoking spray that mounted from below.

They ran their craft up on the beach and surrounded the cross with flowers from the jungle and the backwaters. Gabriel would have it so. They then conducted a lengthy service. After that, they built a fire, ate their meal, and fell asleep. The air about them shook ceaselessly from the falls.

That same evening, five miles above the falls, Julien's killers were starting to feast and get drunk around a blazing fire. The women had spat maté seeds into a murky mixture of brown liquid in a hollow log, and now this was tested. The shaman rolled his eyes, smote his stomach, and pronounced it ready. He took it to half a dozen mature warriors, and they confirmed his judgment. He then turned to the rest of the tribe and told them to begin.

Two hours later they were all happily drunk. Men, women, and children ate the flesh of deer, and the grease ran down their own flesh. A father offered his cup to a sticky-faced five-year-old, who drank thirstily. An old man and an old woman with humorless faces exchanged time-honored tribal witticisms to howls of laughter. A young buck leaped to his feet and pranced straddle-legged before a line of seated girls, brandishing the treat he had to offer. A girl looked straight into his eyes invitingly, and he flung her down with half the tribe getting up to watch. The oldest and the youngest, however, just went on eating and drinking.

By the time first light of the morning filtered through the dense foliage, they had all fallen asleep. By early afternoon they were all awake. They had vanished by nightfall.

Camping below the falls, Father Gabriel sat with his companions by the fire. He said, "I have decided to go and preach to the Guarani up there."

Said Father Antonio, "You, Father Gabriel, are old. Let one of us do it."

"No. It was I who sent Julien."

"So let us all go, then," Father Sebastian said.

"Yes," said Gabriel sarcastically, "and let us also take a troop of warriors and a train of artillery. They will take us for slave traders if we come upon them all together."

"Supposing that you get to the head of the falls, what will you do?" Antonio asked.

"I shall pray."

"I mean, what will you offer them?"

"Music."

"Music!" Sebastian threw up his hands.

"You don't believe in music, Sebastian?"

"It does nothing for me."

"I speak of more tractable people, the Guarani. You know

what Minoria said: 'Give me an orchestra and I will conquer South America. I shall try it."

"Splendid. When you reach the head of the falls, you will play them something."

"The slave traders brought them firearms." Father Gabriel took an oboe out of his roll and extracted it from its sleeve of wool. "We bring them music." He fitted the reed into the oboe.

"They are not ready," stated Father Ferdinand.

Gabriel stopped fitting the reed and asked, "Oh? How do you know?"

"It is no good reasoning with you," Sebastian complained. "The death of Julien was the will of God, but you yourself assume responsibility for it."

"Ah, yes. Yes, perhaps I do," said Gabriel. "I shall think about that."

"You can't turn an argument inside out by pretending to accept it," Sebastian told him.

Gabriel answered with a smile. "It seemed a reasonable thing to do." Lifting the oboe to his mouth, he played a simple melody that was drowned in the roar of the falls.

The next morning the others said, "God be with you," and only Sebastian accompanied Gabriel to the foot of the falls. The ceaseless thunder of the water made it impossible for them to speak to each other. They could only embrace. Gabriel smiled a smile of pure benevolence. Sebastian scowled. Back in camp, he climbed onto a rock and refused to speak to anyone.

Meanwhile, Gabriel had found a fissure and was following it uphill. The sides grew together, and the trees closed in. Then it petered out against the face of the matted cliff. He was forced to turn around and go back to the start. This time he found a narrow aperture to his right, which brought him through a narrow chimney to the edge of the falling cliff of water.

"Christ, tell me why I am doing this?" said Gabriel, appalled.

He struck off to his left again through the dripping leaves. When the time came, he leaned himself back and said Vespers in a loud voice that was derided by the surrounding din. Then he went on.

It was dusk when he emerged from the undergrowth that covered the head of the falls, and knew he had succeeded. Awestruck, he stood, like Adam, gazing at the landslide of water as it vanished over the edge. While he stood there, the sky above became night and was pierced by stars, but he continued upriver in the darkness. The noise of the falls came more gently, and the river, too, was growing less disturbed. A moon came up, glinting through the foliage. He struck inland. A dead branch cracked.

In the camp below, where the others waited, Sebastian lay motionless, looking up at the moon.

Antonio asked, "Do you think he's found them?"

"I don't know."

"He may never find them."

"True."

"What will he do if—"

"I don't know!" Sebastian shouted.

At that same moment, Gabriel was bending to examine the smoldering remains of a fire. How long since it had been burning? He could not tell. The forest was all around him; the falls were far away. He straightened up and asked Christ a question: "Did you, in the Garden of Gethsemane, feel the onset of death as clearly as I do here? If so, you were a man. If not, you were a god. What help can you give me?"

He sat down and took out the oboe. Sweat poured down his face, and he looked again at the opaque forest. He raised the oboe to his lips, cleared his throat, and began to play. The melody was a favorite of his, the oboe obbligato from the Fifth Trio by Albino Masaschio.

In the forest a pair of monkeys, catching the tremulous notes on the night air, stopped combing each other's hair and listened.

A score of blue and purple birds, half asleep, raised their suddenly alert heads and heard.

A hog came to the opening of its burrow with four little ones, and with the bright moon reflecting in their eyes, they attended.

A jaguar, prowling stealthily over the rocks, paused and drew back its mouth into a silent snarl.

Gabriel caught sight of a brave's face peering at him steadily from the undergrowth, and stopped playing. Their eyes met, and they caught each other's fleeting message of fear. The savage's face withdrew, and Gabriel resumed his playing hastily. The brave reappeared. Then, with a lifting of the scalp, Gabriel realized there was another standing behind him, so close that he could smell him. Then a third one came a little way out of the brushwood about forty yards away and cocked his head, peering slantwise at Gabriel. The first savage now pushed out of the undergrowth and stood about twenty feet from Gabriel, with his spear held high, but seeing the musician was unarmed, he drew closer and squatted down on his heels. More Guarani emerged from the jungle. They stood bemused.

Then they began to discuss his music in an undertone.

"It does not come from his mouth."

"No, it comes from that whistle."

"It is pleasing."

"Yes. It is like the first call of the birds."

"Like the first call, yes. It is new."

"Like the first breath of the morning breeze."

"Yes."

The shaman entered the glade in a rush. He yelled, "Fools. Can't you see? Behold." And he dashed up to Gabriel, seized the oboe, and broke it over his knee.

At first no one spoke. Then one of the first comers said, "You have broken the whistle that made it."

"Yes, the whistle, not the man who blew it."

"Now mend it."

"I do not know how."

The braves nodded, took the broken halves of the oboe from the shaman's hand, and offered them to Gabriel.

"You mend it."

Gabriel took the instrument; it was smashed beyond repair. "I cannot do it here. Perhaps at your village I might do better."

The brave looked wary. "You speak our language?"

"Yes."

"Kill him," said the shaman. "Throw him in the river."

"Yes," many agreed, "kill him."

"Eat him," urged the shaman.

A brave with white hair asked the one who had spoken first, "What do you say?"

"Let us see if he can mend the whistle."

"If he cannot mend it, we will throw him in the river," the white-haired brave told the shaman. "There is plenty of time to decide."

"Yes. Later we can decide," the majority agreed.

The warrior who had spoken first held out his hand to Gabriel and led him alongside the narrow stream. The rest of the braves followed while the shaman fulminated to himself. Gabriel turned his attention to the man who had him by the hand; his grip was amicable. So as they walked, Gabriel said, "My name is Gabriel."

The brave looked at him hard, then said, "Mine is Hacugh."

"You are the chief?"

"We are not at war."

"You make the decisions?"

"That one," he pointed to the shaman, "is the wise man."

"Is he wise?"

"Yes, very wise."

"Kill him," the shaman said. "Do not listen to him."

They arrived at the village; it consisted of three huge huts whose papaya-leaf thatches brushed the ground. A fire was burning. Water came from the stream. Watching their arrival gravely were the women and children.

Hacugh said to him, "Now, you sleep."

With all the tribe as spectators, Gabriel said his prayers and, rolling over, pretended to sleep.

In the morning he was given a thick gruel and then set before the entire tribe. The women in front sat with children in their laps while the braves behind remained standing. He asked for a clean white sheet of their cloth on which to lay the two halves of his oboe. He screwed up his eyes and pretended to examine the two halves of the oboe very closely. Then he said, "What is the name of your shaman?"

"Tanretopra. Why?"

"He is a man of great potency."

"Why?"

"He has destroyed the whistle."

"You cannot mend it?"

"I fear not."

"Kill him, kill him," said Tanretopra.

A woman, who had been watching Gabriel closely, disappeared into her hut and returned with a sheaf of fine reeds. He bound together the two halves of the oboe with reeds and then blew on the instrument and was rewarded by a hoot. He heard the whole tribe suck in its breath with satisfaction and then break into a murmur. He operated the keys, and the oboe uttered a series of groans and then one high, magically lovely note. They laughed at it and then were quiet.

Gabriel, thinking hard, said, "Perhaps, given time, I can mend it."

"How much time?" queried Hacugh.

"That is in the hands"—a pause for breath—"of Jesus Christ."

Hacugh looked at his tribesmen and then said, "We have heard of him."

"Of course, Julien told you of him before you cast him onto the river."

The shaman said, "Now we will cast you there."

Gabriel said steadily, and his steadiness impressed them, "That will be as Christ wills."

The woman said, "What more would you say of him?"

Gabriel told them that Jesus Christ was the greatest of friends; for example, he guided his friends through the dark places and across the open spaces of life, and at their death he opened his kingdom to them, where they lived forever.

The brave with white hair, whose name was Unulu, asked, "Does he do this for you?"

Gabriel thought. Then he laughed softly. "He does."

"Why do you laugh?"

"I have never been asked that before, but it is true, he does."

"This Jesus Christ must be a warrior of gigantic size."

"He was born a baby."

"A baby?" the woman asked.

"Born of a woman. Look," and he brought from his pocket a cheap, sentimental picture of the infant Christ sitting upright in Mary's arms.

"He looks unforgiving," she said, peering at him.

"That is the fault of the painter," he explained. "Have you ever seen a child look unforgiving?"

"Lots of times," she answered.

What a convert she would be! "Yes, you are right. Perhaps he looks like that because he has just seen the devil."

"The devil is one of our gods," Hacugh said.

"Are you sure he really is the devil?"

"Kill him, kill him. There is still time," urged the shaman.

"What harm do I do to you?" asked Gabriel.

"I do not know, therefore I say, kill him."

"I do not think that you will kill me, but if you do, you will find me ready. Look at the Christ Child. Is that a God who harms people?"

The woman passed the crude picture around, each group studying it carefully, women, men, and children. Then she looked at Gabriel. "It would be nice if he was ruler of the world," she said.

"He is."

"Then he will help you mend your whistle," argued Hacugh.

"Of course," Gabriel agreed, "but it will take time."

As the days went by, Gabriel came to marvel at the Indians' silent passage through the jungle, the accuracy with which they hurled their spears, and the power of their humming bows. Gratified, he watched the women returning with wild vegetables for the tribe and observed their benevolence with the babies.

He also brooded on their polygamy, their drunkenness, and their sloth. When they had culled and caught all they needed for one day, they were content to sit and talk, or sleep.

The Guarani discovered him, when he thought he was unobserved, praying and communicating with Christ in the forest, and this impressed them greatly.

Tanretopra, the shaman, detested Gabriel from his heart. Each night he would come to him and say, with a kick of his foot toward the oboe: "Is it mended yet?"

Gabriel replied, "Not yet." The shaman would laugh and turn, each day with increasing mockery, to the others who were watching, and then walk off.

At length, Gabriel took his courage in both hands and said, "Christ does not want me to mend this here."

The shaman said triumphantly, "Did I not say so? He is a false prophet."

"Not so. I could mend it at my mission."

Tanretopra leaped to his feet. "Did I not tell you? Behold, he would take you back with him to his mission. Now, while there is yet time, kill him!"

"Aye," said a very old man, "kill him!"

Gabriel asked, "What have I done to hurt you? Tell me."

"That is true. He has done nothing," Hacugh said.

"Listen to me very carefully," Gabriel told them, "and think of what I say. I have four brothers waiting at the bottom of the falls. They will take the oboe back to the mission and get it mended, then return with two others who can all make music on their instruments. We will play to you."

Hacugh said, "I would like to hear the oboe and these other instruments."

"Thereafter if we so desire," said the white-haired Unulu, "we can cast them all in the river. Tanretopra, we thank you for your counsel, but now we have heard you. Be silent, if it please you." And most of the Guarani agreed.

Then they piled into their canoes—men, women, and children—and made for the head of the falls.

Squinting over the river at the forest below the cannonade of water, Gabriel said, "I cannot see my brothers."

"Could you from there?" Hacugh asked, pointing to an islet at the very edge of the falls.

"Yes," said Gabriel, "but that island is impossible to reach."

"No, no, it is easy to get there."

They went out to the islet in the canoes, with Gabriel marveling at the gentle current just before the final drop. He clapped his hands and said, "Marvelous, marvelous." Once there, they collected a fire and set it alight and fed it with wet grass so that black smoke poured out.

Within ten minutes Sebastian had seen it down below, and within an hour he was standing just below them, tiny, looking up toward them. Gabriel signaled joyfully for him to come up, and Sebastian disappeared into the forest.

"See, he is coming up," said Gabriel, and then they paddled back to the bank to wait until at last Sebastian stood at the head of the falls, filthy from his climb, and embraced Gabriel. Then he took in the wild Guarani and asked in a low voice, "Holy God! Gabriel, you are all right?"

"I am all right, but I do not know whether we shall be all right for very long."

"What shall I do?"

"Just wait."

"Can you mend this?" Hacugh asked, displaying the two halves of the oboe.

"Tell him yes," said Gabriel.

"Yes."

"Where?"

"At the mission," said Gabriel.

Gabriel said to Hacugh, "Let him take the oboe and bring it back made good."

"And if he does not come back?" asked the shaman.

Said Hacugh, pointing to Gabriel, "Then we shall crucify this one."

"And if he returns with slave traders?" the shaman asked.

"I am the enemy of all slave traders," Sebastian said.

"Ha, hear him," said Tanretopra. "Who believes what he says?"

"If they come," said Hacugh, "they will come. I do not think they will come quicker because of that one."

The shaman made a last appeal. "Come! Let us cast them both into the river and be done with them."

Hacugh said, "I have placed my word. Who agrees with me?"

Some said one thing and some another. The argument went

on into the evening. "I think we have won," Gabriel said at last. "Saints be praised."

"Amen."

Hacugh announced, "He can go, and you shall stay."

Sebastian said, "It will take three weeks."

"Three weeks."

"Possibly five."

"Five weeks. Then we shall kill him."

Gabriel gave Sebastian these orders: "You and the others go back to the mission and get this instrument repaired. This one and no other. Then bring it back with you. Bring also Mateo and Pedrarias with their instruments. No one else."

"I understand."

"Let me tell you, Sebastian, music does work miracles with these people. They are passing spiritual, you see."

"Father, you are profoundly mad and holy."

Then Sebastian climbed back down the overhanging cliffs with the two halves of the fissured oboe, and explained the situation to the other Jesuits. They struck camp and made their way downstream, along the middle of the river. Gabriel went back up river with the tribe.

9

FROM A DISTANCE, Mendoza had seen the smoke from the fire at the top of the falls. He was working his way upstream on a raft with a group of his men. He called a halt, and they paddled slowly to one side of the river. After watching for a little, he decided that the smoke was coming from the Guarani fire, but could not guess what it was for. All that he and the other settlers knew about the unexplored territory above the falls was that it was inhabited by Guaranis. He did not know of Father Gabriel's expedition, just as the Jesuits at the mission knew nothing of Mendoza's raid, for he had stolen past them in the night. Each party deemed itself to be the first thrust from the Old World to the New World beyond the falls.

The captain general had given Mendoza the nod. Cabeza planned to extend his territory at the expense of the Portuguese. That did not concern Mendoza. Ever since he had first seen the falls from far off, it had seemed to him the gateway to El Dorado.

He ordered his men to stay silent, and they set out again on their slow passage up the river. During the journey, from the deep cover at the river's edge, Mendoza watched Sebastian and the other three Jesuits strike camp and head back toward the Santa Croce Mission.

When the priests were gone, Mendoza looked up at the falls. "There may be more of them up there."

"We have the captain general's permission," said one of his men.

Mendoza answered, "We have Cabeza's permission to bring back any Guarani we find beyond those cliffs, but not to tangle with the Jesuits."

He urged his men forward, and when they reached the top of the cliffs, the tranquillity that closed about them as the night fell made them uneasy.

The next day they set off as usual into the jungle, and in the middle of the day came upon the prints of many bare feet in the ground. Mendoza looked at them and said, "They are close." They cocked their muskets and pistols quietly, and pressed noiselessly through the undergrowth among the massive trees. The Guarani were there.

Hacugh was standing in a glade; he raised a hand for silence. There was a moment of stillness, and then Mendoza fired his pistol and his followers rushed in. The Guarani hurled their spears and made off through the thick tangle of creepers, leaving the Spaniards with five taken and two fallen, one dead and the other with a long grazing wound.

Suddenly from nowhere Hacugh hurled his spear at Mendoza. It missed and stuck, quivering, in a tree. Mendoza went charging after him, but only heard the sound of footsteps getting rapidly fainter until there was silence.

He stopped, crouched, went forward, and stopped again. Listening, he heard only the steady drone of insects and the whispering of leaves. Then the whiz of an arrow. It lodged, vibrating, close to him.

Hacugh quickly fitted another, but from behind him, Gabriel cried, "Stop!"

The Jesuit came forward to within fifteen feet of where Mendoza was crouching and said, "You in there."

Mendoza, whose eyes never left Hacugh, said, "Yes, Father."

"I can get a score of these men here."

"I have a musket and a pistol, Father."

"How many have you captured?"

"I do not know, Father."

"Let them go."

"No, Father."

"Do you think it makes a difference to me whether you 'Father' me?" Gabriel thrust his way through to Mendoza's hiding place but found nobody there. "Let the braves go," he cried. And then, in a strident voice: "Tell Don Cabeza you have found me here. Tell him these people are outside his authority. Tell him we will make Christians of these people."

He turned and warned the Guarani: "Do not go after them. They have muskets and will shoot you down."

Hacugh said, "We would have done better to heed the shaman."

When they were back in the village, the shaman said in a deep tone, "Did I not tell you? After the men of Jesus come the slave takers."

Gabriel said in agreement, "What you have said has been made good. So kill me."

"What do you counsel, O Shaman?" asked Hacugh. "Is this a bad man?"

Tanretopra came close up to the alien priest and studied him searchingly. At length he moved his head slowly from side to side. "No. It is a good man. Nevertheless, I have told you what to do with him," and he went into the forest.

Gabriel lived, and stayed. Before long, Sebastian, Mateo, and Pedrarias joined him. On the still, sun-soaked, butterfly-laden air, they made the music of Handel and Tallis and Scarlatti, and thereby won the hearts of the Guarani, although not as yet the minds. And all the while, in the world below the falls, the settlers went about their business. Mendoza returned to Asunción and showed Cabeza the five braves he had brought back.

Cabeza said, "They are superb."

"Yes. They will be good for outside work, Don Cabeza."

"Of course. Are there many of them above the falls?"

"I do not know. The priests are also on the ground. They have a place above the falls." Cabeza stared.

"How many priests?"

"I saw only one."

Cabeza took a turn up and down the room, and then came to a stop. "Tell me, how soon can you lead another band up there?"

"In two months, Excellency."

"No, in one month."

"In two months. It needs careful handling, Excellency. For one thing, I shall have to give a wide berth to the land occupied by the Jesuits."

"Well, do it, do it, do it."

However, in less than six weeks Don Cabeza received a formal visit from Father Ribiro, the superior of the Jesuits in the Río de la Plata region, a subtle politician who despised Cabeza and flattered him, of course.

Cabeza knew how Ribiro felt and resented it from the bottom of his heart. Accordingly, he, too, smiled as he requested his visitor to sit. He nodded toward the heavy leather file the Jesuit laid on the table: "Is this a formal visit?"

"Alas, it is."

"Can the business wait until I get you a glass of wine?"

"Is it the same as the barrel you sent us last Easter?"

"Is it?" Cabeza asked the secretary.

"It can be made so," said the secretary, smiling. He bowed himself out, and his soft footsteps echoed on the flagged floor outside. The cheeping of the birds in the carved rafters was clearly audible.

Ribiro glanced up at them, looked down, and said, "I have heard from Father Gabriel at the Mission of Santa Croce."

"A good man."

"He sent a message from above the falls."

Cabeza mimed astonishment. *"Above* the falls? Well, tell me, what did he find there?"

"The Guarani."

"Ah, and they were—"

"Wild. Unfortunately other people have been there, too," the Jesuit said. "Mendoza Jorge went there after slaves."

"Slaves?" Cabeza frowned and formed his fingers into a steeple and examined it carefully. "There is no slave trade in the Río de la Plata region. You know that, Father."

"There is the encomienda."

Cabeza unsteepled his fingers and smiled. "Ah, that is different."

"Father Gabriel's letter says the Guarani have been taken by force."

"Father, that is a serious charge."

Ribiro's sandaled foot started tapping on the floor. "I should like to see Mendoza, now."

Cabeza looked at the careworn, subtle face of his antago-
nist and congratulated himself on having such a ready liar as
Mendoza at his service. "Certainly. I shall make enquiries
when he is expected in the city."

"I saw him on my way here."

Cabeza dispatched a servant. While they waited, they remarked on the birds in the rafters, the maté yield, the sugar-
cane crop, the steady influx of settlers to Asunción.

Mendoza knocked at the door and came in.

Cabeza put on a threatening face. "Attend you to Father
Ribiro."

"Father?"

"You have been above the falls."

"Yes, Father Provincial."

Cabeza protested, "You did not tell me that."

"I wasn't asked, Excellency."

"True."

Ribiro said, "You came back with five slaves."

"Encomiendaros, Father."

"They volunteered?"

"How else?"

"Where did you get rid of them?"

"To a sugar planter."

"What was his name?"

"I forget, Father."

"You forget?"

"Yes, Father."

Cabeza was studying the birds in the rafters. "Do you see
that one?" he pointed. "That one is the boss."

"It makes most fuss," replied Ribiro, and then continued
with Mendoza. "You spoke to Father Gabriel."

"Yes. Excuse me, but I think that priest is too old to be up
there, Father Ribiro."

"He can take care of himself. You told him you would
deliver your Guarani to Don Cabeza."

"What?" said Cabeza, giving up the pretense of watching
the birds.

"No, that is a mistake," said Mendoza. "It was not I who
spoke of the captain general. Father Gabriel did."

Ribiro knew this was correct. He pulled angrily at his chin. "Mendoza, you will not go up there again."

Cabeza shot him a wary look. "I do not understand, Father Ribiro."

Ribiro took hold of his spectacles and, opening the leather file, produced a folded document, which he straightened carefully, for it was old. "I have here the granting of the mission to my order. By His Catholic Majesty, Philip the Third, whom God preserve."

"Amen," said Cabeza, taking it from him. He studied it a minute or two, and then, his breath coming quickly and his finger loosening his collar, he coughed.

Good, thought Ribiro, good, and then went on: "His Catholic Majesty—"

"—whom the saints preserve, assigns the land above the falls to you," Cabeza finished the statement for him.

"Yes."

"But that land was unoccupied then."

"Nevertheless, the rights are clear."

"To all the lands from the falls up to the Portuguese border of the territory?"

"As you see."

"Whereabouts do you place that?" Cabeza asked.

"Who knows. But it is all contained within the grant of land. Is it not?"

"Yes." Cabeza got to his feet and made a short tour of the room; he came to a halt towering over the seated Ribiro. "I must warn you, I will have that altered."

Father Ribiro made a gesture with his open hands. "Possibly. I rather think that may take a long time to do." Then he said inflexibly, looking at Mendoza, "Meanwhile, that land is denied to you, to anyone else like you, and to all members of the government, without permission from myself. Captain General, will you repeat that to Mendoza?"

Cabeza looked at the adventurer.

"You heard that, Mendoza?"

"Yes, Excellency."

"Obey."[1]

"Admirable," said Ribiro with a look of enjoyment on his

face, "that is all I came to say." As he folded the document, bells began to chime throughout the city. On the way out, he turned his attention to the rafters again. "Oh look, Don Cabeza; the other birds have chased the fat one out through the window."

When the door was shut, Mendoza asked Don Cabeza, "Do I take that at face value?"

Cabeza shouted, "You heard him, didn't you?" There was a pause. He caught Mendoza's eyes on him. "Yes, yes, it must be taken at face value."

Mendoza went back to his shadowed house and took some cheese and wine; he lifted one foot above the other onto the shiny table and clasped his hands behind his head. He was smiling, for his thoughts had turned to Carlotta.

Carlotta Maria Herminda Theodosia Antonia de la Cadena de Vilhasante had been born twenty-three years earlier, the only child of the *conde* de Vilhasante and his lackluster wife. It was owing to the drab *condesa* that the family was rich in blood, tracing it back to Fernando and from there back to Otto. It was owing to the formidable *conde* that they were rich in virtue, for he was a stern son of the Church, an honest overlord, and a fair-minded husband and father. Carlotta had been raised in the gloom of the Vilhasante castle in Córdoba, a province famous for the strict piety of its rulers. However, the *conde* was poor, so to the shadow of piety was added the forbidding darkness of heavy debt.

Carlotta was a source of joy to both her parents. Her infectious laugh resounded through the ancient vaults of her home, calling forth a sober smile from her father and the remains of a smile from her mother, which made one see how pretty she had been.

When Carlotta was fourteen, her father died from injuries suffered in a furious riding fall, taken while hawking. Her mother was stricken. The castle became a house of permanent mourning, not to be disturbed by the faintest sound.

Carlotta sank into an unsettled torpor, drifting through the lofty stone corridors of her home, until the family's old Jesuit confessor realized that he hadn't heard her laughter for many months. He went to the *condesa* and spoke to her wisely and sensibly, using words he had gleaned from the yellow shelves of the seminaries where he had been educated, recognizing their wisdom without fully understanding what they meant.

Her mother sighed and agreed, and took Carlotta to the Court at Madrid, where they were made welcome because of that line extending back to Otto.

Carlotta was taken up by the queen as the young *dama de honor*, and saw a great deal that it was not good for her to see. She was held up as the absolute Spanish lady. However, the blood of her father, the *conde*, was hot in her, and when the young sparks of Madrid watched her slight figure emerging from the confessor's box, to be borne away by her mother, she cast them a look out of downcast eyes which set their pulses thudding.

When Carlotta was nineteen, her mother was afflicted by a swelling disease that left her dead, looking like a monstrous rubicund doll, to be placed in an enormous coffin, which lay in the cathedral for three days and then began to stink. Carlotta, kneeling there, realized that she must henceforth take care of herself. There was nobody now who would prepare the awkward passages and make them smooth for her. The revelation left her with a sense of resolution she had lacked before.

When her period of mourning was over, the Conde Marcos Haro y Monteressa informed the ancient Jesuit of his desire to marry Carlotta, and this trusted adviser, seeing a short way out of his responsibilities, earnestly advised her to accept the offer. The *conde* was a good repute and the overlord of a great estate. She refused, however. She objected to something light-minded and skittish she found in him. In reply, the Jesuit reminded her that the castle was all she had.

Carlotta said, "Very well. How much is it worth?"

Hardening himself, he told her, "Three times the cost of a large farm."

"As little as that?" she said, astonished.

"Yes. Think again about the *conde*."

"There can be no question of my marrying him, Father. Make what excuses you think fit." She ushered him out, kissing him to stop the flood of empty words that were beginning to pour from his mouth. Then, shutting herself in her room, she drew the tiny curtains high up in the lofty wall and sat down on the bed. Why had nobody told her she was poor? She lay flat and wept with helplessness.

When Carlotta came out of her room seventy-two hours later, she looked dazzling. Her shining black hair was wrapped around her head in a French coiffeur. Her manner was adroitly poised between gaiety and gravity. She was the talk of the Court.

On her instructions the castle was rented to the bastard son of a local *duque*. The elderly Jesuit was sent to spend the last years of his life elsewhere.

A letter came from a second cousin in Asunción, containing a few conventional words of consolation on her mother's death. The cousin, Blasco de Bigorente, was an official and he promised, in the course of the letter, to call on her when he came to Madrid. Instead of thanks, he received a carefully worded letter asking if she could come and stay with him in Asunción where, of course, she would pay for her keep.

Her cousin thought she was overspent, and he went to consult his wife, who swooned at the prospect of having a *condesa* to stay. At one step she would advance to the front ranks of their little society, let her father be an exporter of hides or not. She begged him to say yes. He, with a glance at the cobwebs that the Guarani servants always left on the dull white ceiling, did so.

When Carlotta received his letter, she was filled with elation. This would show the Court that she could manage her own life her own way.

The king was enthusiastic about her going to Asunción. She would serve as a bond between the Old World and the New. He gave her a gold-covered Bible. Taking her leave, the queen stroked Carlotta's head, smiling secretly to herself, and arranged a special assembly for her. Carlotta made a series of little farewells, and finally drove out of Madrid with a gathering of well-wishers waving hats and hands. Then her existence was forgotten. But she blazed into the view of Asunción like a comet.

She had taken a long time preparing her first appearance

before her cousin Blasco and his wife and other hangers-on who came down to the waterfront to welcome her.

"My God," her cousin exclaimed when he caught sight of the slight figure with the olive skin and coiled black hair. He turned to a Guarani servant: "Go quickly to the house and fetch my parasol."

He was himself a proper-looking man of forty, tall and straight and with a tiny beard. Carlotta stepped ashore in somber black and gave him her hand, which he took with admiration, bending formally to kiss it. His wife, Bernadette, looked like what she was—a trader's daughter—but by adopting a note of humor in his introductions, he pleaded with his cousin not to mock her. Bernadette gave a curtsy, looking up through huge solemn eyes, and Carlotta rewarded her with a languid half-smile.

Sheltering beneath the parasol, she was then introduced to all the citizenry who somehow happened to be there. They were either would-be gentlemen in the government service or, still more distressingly, mere tradesmen. Blasco ushered her into a carriage, and they set off into the narrow, shade-dappled streets. The road drew out into a square with a fountain; but, Carlotta noticed, it was unpaved, raw red earth.

Then the carriage swung around and stopped outside a presentable-looking town house. Carlotta recognized the pride of ownership in the look Bernadette darted at her, so she said, "Cousin, I must felicitate you upon your residence."

"Do you like it? It was my father's."

"Come," said Blasco.

"He died last year."

"Come," Blasco repeated.

"He died of a befuddlement of the heart. What, excuse me, did your blessed mother die of?"

"I don't know."

"This way," said Blasco, "come."

"Nobody knows."

"I am sorry."

They went past half a dozen servants, two of them Span- ish, to the suite of rooms upstairs. Carlotta went to the window and saw opposite her a palatial house with a listless flag dangling over it.

"That's the captain general's residence," said Bernadette. "Next door to it is the home of the colonel of the guard, and next to that is the Hernandez Zungiza residence; on the other side is—"

Blasco said, "You will have plenty of opportunity to show the condesa what elegant neighbors we have after she has taken a rest."

"I am sorry," said Bernadette, flushing. "I do not know how to behave." This drew from Carlotta such a ravishing and wholly spontaneous smile that she had the satisfaction of seeing her hostess fall head over heels in love with her.

She went to the balcony window, and it was not until later that she realized how she had dropped her voice under the rustling of the palms and the gentle splashing of the water from the fountain to ask, "Who is that?"

A man dressed in black, with black hair pulled back from a scarred face, was looking up at her. Blasco said, "Where? Oh, him! That's Mendoza. You won't be troubled with him."

The man, as if he had heard, turned and went across the square to disappear down one of the shadowy side streets.

Mendoza had taken note of Carlotta when she first set foot on shore. He had never seen anything like that Madrid beauty. In the evening he went to one of the mulatto women who plied their trade along the waterfront. For the first time they did not succeed in easing his desire.

Carlotta was automatically invited to the captain general's, to be diverted by Cabeza's uneasy mixture of caution, pomp, and parsimony. Nevertheless, she also noted the rough manner with which he rode over any obstruction that presented itself. He was a man to treat with care, if not respect. He gave a ball in her honor, and through Bernadette she met all the ladies of the city there. They were illiterate. The men, for their part, were even more vainglorious than those she had known at the Court in Madrid. Each man's honor was vested in his sister; every man strove to sully another man's honor. Yet they were only farmers.

Suddenly she saw Mendoza sitting alone at a table. His eyes, still fixed on her, conveyed a glint of something sinister.

When she walked back across the square with Blasco and Bernadette, she said, "Mendoza. There is something terrible about that man."

"He is a soldier of fortune," Bernadette told her. "Did you not notice how no one spoke to him all evening?"

"But the hidalgos bowed in his direction."

"He is Don Cabeza's agent," Blasco said.

"For doing what?"

"He is a slave trader."

The following week a bull running was organized, and Mendoza came upon Carlotta walking the other way with a Guarani servant. He gave no hint of having seen her.

It was she who stopped and said, "I don't believe we have been introduced."

"Rodrigo Mendoza."

My God, she thought, he is formidable. Just like my father! "I am the Condesa Carlotta de la Cadena de Vilhasante. I have come to watch the bulls."

"You can watch them from up there"—he pointed to a bank of seats where all the ladies and gentlemen of the city sat in state beneath an awning—"or from here." He pointed to an evil-smelling crowd who were all pressed in together close to the bulls. As she followed his pointing finger, a bull tossed its head with a flourish of threatening horns. Its eyes seemed to signal danger.

"That's where I want to go."

The arrival of this incongruous pair caused a stir in the crowd. They nudged one another and grimaced as the couple made their way to the front. Carlotta noticed how quickly a path was cleared for them. The arrival of the "Duquesa from Madrid" spurred the young men to fresh feats of athleticism and swordsmanship. She clapped and cried, "Well done, *muchacho*," the common people taking up the applause until there was just one massively horned bull left. Nobody cared to enter the ring with this one. He had already wounded a *muchacho*.

Carlotta said, "Ah, that is a bull."

Doffing his topcoat, Mendoza drew his sword and stepped out. There was a general whisper. Never before had they seen him participate in any festival. Then there was silence, a murmur, a cry, and sucking in of the breath as he drew the bull toward that notorious short sword of his, to dispatch it virtually at Carlotta's feet. The shout that greeted this feat echoed to the edges of the city.

He cut off the ears and handed them to her. Then he stared around at the rabble. A sudden silence fell, in which he collected his coat, bowed, and left.

Of course, Blasco was given the news in no time. Cautiously that evening he tried to hint his disapproval, and was snubbed.

Some days later, there was a *fête champêtre* at the house of the colonel of the army. Carlotta saw Mendoza standing in the shade underneath the pillars, and he gave a bow, stiffly, again. Then he turned away. She sent a servant over to him, watched him approaching her over the flagged pavement, and noticed how all around the conversation was redoubled, while everybody spied on her out of the corners of their eyes.

As he joined her, Mendoza said, with a swift glance around, "Listen, *condesa,* this time there is no sport for the canaille."

"I go riding with my friends tomorrow."

"Indeed?"

Heavens, he made her do everything! "Will you not join us?"

"If your cousin desires it."

"I desire it."

"Then I will come."

The next morning she called him up to the head of the file and saw that his seat on a horse was expert. When the riding was over, she invited him for breakfast at Bernadette's. Here he was asked conventional questions about himself, about his farm, his dogs, and his opinion of the strange things that were coming out of Europe. Around him, meanwhile, whispers were devoted to him and the *condesa.*

As soon as two ladies made their departure, he rose to follow them, but Carlotta whispered, "Please stay, for my sake," so he seated himself once more in his stiff chair. He remained there till all the other guests were gone.

"Asunción bores me," she told him.

He glanced swiftly around the spacious room, now empty save for the Guarani servants slumbering by the door, before replying: "I'm sorry."

"There's nothing here."

"There are one or two things worth seeing."

"Is that so?"

She watched his downward drooping eyes rise slowly to meet hers. "On Sunday there is a wild boar hunt that *señoritas* go to—if they have a mind to it, that is."

"I would have, if some gentleman were kind enough to take me."

"Ask Señor Blasco."

"He is too busy with his receipts and bonds. Won't you be going?"

"I never go."

"A pity. I would have liked it."

He inclined his head. "If Señor Blasco approves, I shall accompany you."

"Blasco!"

He inclined his head gravely.

Bernadette came bustling back and, finding her fashionable guest alone with such a disagreeable companion, seated herself with a look of deep apology in Carlotta's direction. At Mendoza she did not so much as glance. Then Blasco returned from seeing off the captain general. There was alarm in his eyes at finding Mendoza there, at the sight of which the latter took his leave.

The following morning Mendoza went to the Jewish letter writer, to be at once ushered discreetly into the private, shaded room at the back of the premises. Soon afterward a junior clerk delivered a short letter to Blasco's house, seeking the trader's permission to take the *Señora,* his wife, and naturally the *condesa,* whom it might amuse, to the boar hunt—unless, of course, he intended to accompany them himself—and going on to inform its perplexed recipient that the *condesa* had expressed a lively interest in the event at the previous night's festivities.

Blasco knit his brows and pondered. Then he went to inform Bernadette and Carlotta of this unexpected proposal and advise against it. His prudent counsel met first with misunderstanding from Carlotta and then, upon elaboration, with rejection. Certainly she would go. There could be no question of rejecting Señor Mendoza's invitation. It was not courteous of him to take her tedious complaints so seriously.

Blasco went across to the garrison officers' mess and discovered to his great relief that a group of officers were going to join the hunt. Certainly, said the adjutant, who was a major and would be in charge of their party, they would be delighted to keep an eye on Bernadette and the *condesa*. Blasco thanked him, explaining apologetically that his horsemanship was not good enough for him to take part himself, and returned to concede to Carlotta, "Very well, then. You may go with Bernadette. And you, Bernadette," he added for his wife's benefit, "are to mind your manners."

"Bernadette and I will mind each other's manners," his guest assured him.

Early the next morning a collection of hats were swept into the air and magnificently flourished as the two ladies, accompanied by a groom, trotted up to the mounted group of male huntsmen and female spectators who had already assembled.

Mendoza, who had stationed himself at the edge of the brightly chattering party, was dressed in a black linen suit. He bade them a formal good day and then, handing his spears to their groom, dismounted to check their girths, first Bernadette's and then Carlotta's, with unsteady hands. Then he remounted, claimed his weapons, and placing his horse between the two women, escorted them into the forest in the rear of the hunt.

Throughout the day he said little, and what words he did speak were addressed to Bernadette. He took absolutely no part in the hunt. At last, when the sun had begun to fall behind the suddenly dark trees, Carlotta said, "I have seen far better hunting in the valleys of Madrid." At this he requested Bernadette's permission to leave them to join in the last drive of the day.

"But of course," she replied.

The *condesa* said, "Who knows? Perhaps you will change my opinion."

He took his position at the extreme right end of the line, standing out in his black clothing from the others, for by now most of the huntsmen had removed their jackets, which were draped behind them across their mounts' haunches. They rode in their shirtsleeves, a scatter of white-clad figures to his left, many of them half drunk by this time.

Suddenly, from ahead of them where the beaters were lost to view in the forest, there came a trilling cry followed by a stillness, in which the rustle of a leaf could be as distinctly heard as a pistol shot. The darkness now was deepening rapidly.

There came a trumpeting. They could see the bushes moving as something thrust its way through them, and then the speeding hulk of a great bull boar was rushing straight at the horseman on Mendoza's left. Seizing his chance, the hunter spurred down on it with a shout, tearing a strip with his spear along its body from shoulder to rump, but the boar wheeled around on the blow, wrenching the rider's weapon out of his grasp. Spurring his mount more violently than ever, the disarmed hunter made good his escape.

The boar went for Mendoza. He was ready for it. He had already reined in his horse and stayed motionless while the tusker sped at him like a missile, until it was on him. Then the man moved and, as if it had hit a wall, the hurtling brute stopped short. For a long second hunter and hunted stared at each other along the spear. Then the boar was dead.

It was a full five feet in length, and they estimated the weight at two hundred and sixty pounds. In the dusk, when they were gathered around to examine the kill, a drunk man said, "It was a lucky thing you didn't have time to think, Mendoza."

"I had time in plenty, but it was only a boar, no match for a man with a spear," Mendoza answered, fixing his eyes on the speaker, a foolish lieutenant recently arrived from the Old World.

A sudden chill fell. "No, no, no," the major protested weakly. "Bravo, *señor!* Very well done, very well done indeed!" Other voices hastened to join in the congratulations, while Mendoza presented his quarry to Bernadette. This meant the groom had to stay behind to load it onto his horse, so still riding between them, Mendoza escorted Bernadette and Carlotta back to the house in the square.

But when they were almost out of earshot, the major, conscious that he must have seemed too ready to placate Mendoza, passed some remark in a raucous voice that raised a peal of drunken laughter from his junior officers. Mendoza turned his head and stared in his direction in the twilight. Then, turning back, he devoted his attention silently to the two ladies. Throughout the ride he did not utter more than an occasional monosyllable, offered in response to a flow of conversation from Bernadette. Carlotta was as silent as he until they reached the gateway. Then she said, "Thank you for today. What a pity the officers aren't up to it! Luckily one doesn't have to bother about them, don't you agree?"

"You do not have to, *condesa.*"

He wheeled his horse, rode through the now darkened streets to the house where the major lived, and took up his position in the shadow of the wall. Eventually the major came down the street accompanied by two captains, all very drunk until they realized who was there.

"Señor Mendoza!" the major greeted him. "Is anything the matter?"

"Just now, when I was leaving you, in the company of Señora Bernadette and her companion, you laughed."

"Merciful heaven! Not at you!"

"At what, then?"

"Eh, what? I was telling the others a joke."

"Then tell it to me."

"It's not worth it. It's not very funny."

"Nevertheless."

So, miserably, in front of his embarrassed captains, the major fished up a joke and repeated it in the damp night air.

When at last he had finished, there was a pause. Then Mendoza asked, "Is that the joke?"

Sheepishly the major looked at his companions and muttered, "I must admit it sounded better the last time I told it." The two captains exchanged glances and then looked away down the quiet street.

"I am glad," said Mendoza, "you have told me this joke. It convinces me that army life is not for me. You see, I do not find it funny. I think you should take care, Major, not to repeat such jokes before civilians. Before the *condesa,* for example. Yes, I would be very, very careful, if I were you. Good night!"

The next time he met Carlotta, although they were in company he seized an opportunity to get her to himself, and made a grave avowal of his great regard. Then, before she could think of a fitting reply, he held up his hand.

"We belong to different orders; I know that. One day you will return to Madrid and make, perhaps, a fitting match there. I do not enquire when that will be. I prefer not to know. I am simply yours; you have only to ask what you want of me. It is enough for me to be by your side, like this." He gave her a pale smile.

Carlotta considered him and his inflexible bearing, and touched him with her whip: "This is very unwise, you know."

"The fault is mine. Where is the man who says that it is yours?"

"He will not say it to your face, but you cannot stop him saying it elsewhere. Nor can I stop you feeling as you choose."

Mendoza was always strictly correct in his deportment, and besides, she liked his rough talk and his hardness. As yet she did not realize that for her this grim man had opened a door in the fortress he had built around himself and, once she had passed through, closed the door behind her.

10

SHORTLY AFTER THAT exchange, a letter arrived from Philippo to say that he was coming home. Mendoza hurried around to tell Carlotta.

"I should like to meet this little brother of yours," she said.

"He is elegant, charming, and refined. Not a man whom you would take to be my brother."

"Yes? Take care, my friend, there is a difference between a charming letter and an upright man."

Mendoza listened, and went by himself to meet Philippo on the waterfront. When the barge appeared and drew into the shore, he saw a slim young man who raised one hand to greet him. Stiff-faced, Mendoza raised his own in reply. The barge drew closer, and shading his eyes he saw Philippo's eyes, the same detached, cool gray that they had been when he was three and Mendoza had fetched him his food beneath the high lighted window in Cadiz. His heart overflowed.

Philippo embraced him. "Thanks, big brother. You see, I am come home."

"You are welcome, little brother." And then they fell into each other's arms.

When they were both walking back to his house, Mendoza remarked, "You do not wear a sword."

"No gentleman wears a sword nowadays."

"Indeed! A man without a sword is like *cojones* among bulls—" He broke off.

"What is it?"

"I remember when I first heard that. Gaspachio said it."

"Have you met him again?"

"No."

"You don't still bear a grudge against him, surely?"

"Yes, I do."

"Big brother, you have not changed."

After supper, Mendoza, in his black waistcoat with a cheroot stuck between his lips, had several times started humming a tune and broken off, looked into the fire, stood up, and sat down again, when Philippo, touching his sleeve and looking curious, asked, "What is it, big brother?"

"Listen, I am in love."

"Madre mia! With whom?"

"The Condesa de Vilhasante."

"A *condesa!"*

"She knows how I earn my living."

"Can I see her?"

"Tomorrow."

"Pardon me, but what do you see as the end of the affair?"

"She will go back to Spain."

"And that contents you?"

"Nothing could content me more, little brother." He looked pensively into the fire. "We were born at the bottom; she was born at the top. If one can remember these things, one is content."

"Yes?" Philippo spoke in a tone of doubt, for he had never known his brother to be contented.

Mendoza took Philippo, in a brown suit, to meet the *condesa*. Philippo went, full of suspicion, and found his wariness reciprocated. Carlotta looked enquiringly into his eyes, and he peered frowningly back.

She was not, as Philippo had expected, his brother's age, but young and beautiful. Also, she was serious, and animated, and acute, deprived in Asunción of the things he, too, felt the lack of—philosophy and music and the search for truth. At times a troubled expression clouded her face as she looked up at him, giving her a grave, even a wise expression.

She had seen much, Philippo was sure of that; she spelled no threat to his brother's tranquillity. Seating himself on a chair beside her, he turned to her with that air he had picked up from accomplished talkers who would throw off a bon mot as if by accident and then apologize for being witty.

Carlotta saw that Philippo was handsome. Nay, to be fair,

when he talked of something that interested him, he was beautiful. Obviously he idolized his brother, yet not without a sensitive puckering of the brows for his anomalous status. Moreover, he was serious and cosmopolitan, with an up-to-the-minute knowledge of the most current French writers, and he talked to her about the English poet Alexander Pope, of whom she knew no more than the name.

Philippo was among the last remaining guests when Mendoza, crossing the candlelit room, said, "I think now we should go, Philippo," and led him out into the refreshing night air.

"Well, young brother, the cat has got your tongue," he observed complacently.

"The cat has got my tongue, and with it my heart."

And Mendoza said, in a hushed voice: "There, you see?"

As the days passed, many people scented scandal. Philippo and Carlotta were closely watched, and many were the witticisms that were made about the two brothers. Bernadette, however, was the only person who realized that the foundations of the relationship between Philippo and Mendoza, which both of them had regarded as unshakable, were now being undermined.

As Mendoza, Philippo, and Carlotta went about their affairs together, Bernadette kept her eye on them. When Mendoza was called away, she noticed, as did many others, how Carlotta and Philippo rode together, almost touching, and at a display of Italian fireworks, where they were seated far apart, how neither of them had a glance to spare for the pyrotechnics, but spent the evening gazing at each other.

Blasco said: "As long as they do nothing foolish—and you are there to prevent that—you need only watch."

Philippo said to Carlotta, "I am of the same stock as my brother."

"I, too."

"Yes. But I have picked up mannerisms that remind you of the Court."

"Oh, no. They are from the fashionable cafés. But what of that? They are good and they belong to you now."

"I have no money."

"Whereas I own a castle."

"I am aware of that."

She smiled. "Which produces the rent of three large farms."

"No more?"

"We could go back to Spain together and live off the rent."

"What about your relatives?"

"What about the hidalgos here? They are all negligible."

He kissed her hand: "You are the most amiable person I have ever met. I embrace you."

"Be careful," she said, looking around.

A buzz of innuendo followed Mendoza. He was the subject of prattle, behind the sedate walls of private houses, and of an obscene joke in the corners of cafés. He did not notice. In fact, he rejoiced. It was as if Carlotta and Philippo, walled up in his mind, could indulge in nothing more than a brotherly and sisterly relationship.

Some weeks later, Mendoza and Philippo attended a musketry competition organized by the messes of the garrison, where a number of marksmen shattered clay pans propelled on discs by Guarani. Philippo was just taking aim for his first shot when a door opened and Carlotta and Bernadette came in. He sent his first shot high over the clay pans, and missed with all his others. Mendoza and a lieutenant of the guard competed for first prize, a silver tankard, which Mendoza duly presented to Carlotta. To young Philippo, for it was a subject he took seriously, Mendoza said, "You must give your musket all your mind or it will let you down. You shouldn't let the *condesa* distract you."

There was a sudden quiet. It seemed that all Asunción was waiting for Philippo's reply. He looked at his brother sharply, but Mendoza's gaze was so guileless that he replied, "On the day the *condesa* can't distract me, I'll become a monk."

Carlotta, backing him up, said, "On that day, Philippo, half the ladies of Asunción will become nuns."

"Alas," said poor Philippo, keeping it up, "that is pure gossip. Rodrigo is the ladies' man."

Gazing at Carlotta, Mendoza repeated, "He is *this* lady's man."

He made his way out of the courtyard with a darkened face, amid general laughter. Philippo went outside at once to join his brother, who asked, "Did she say anything?"

"She blushed," Philippo replied.

"Blushed," repeated Mendoza, and they walked home together without exchanging a further word.

The next time Carlotta found herself alone with Philippo, she said, "I must tell him."

"Leave it to me," Philippo told her.

"He will not hurt me."

"Do you think he would hurt me?"

"I am not sure."

"Then I must face him," Philippo insisted.

"It would be like a boy facing a tiger."

"Indeed? Then decidedly I must face him." He strode off, she after him.

"If you do this thing, I shall not speak to you again."

"I go now!" Philippo said.

"Good-bye."

He stopped, and turned to face her.

"I mean it," Carlotta told him. "Swear to me that you won't speak to him. Give me your word. I will tell him myself."

"When?"

"Tomorrow."

The next day was the day of the Guarani Madonna, which was made the occasion of a fancy dress ball for those whose skin was white.

Coming from his study and putting on his sword, Mendoza said to his brother, "Wish me luck."

"Why, where are you going?"

He looked up at the sun, squinting, and then back at Philippo. "I shall tell you this evening."

He went to Blasco's house and asked to speak to Carlotta, but this time alone.

Blasco said, after a pause, "I see. Wait here." He led the way to a room where Carlotta softly joined him a few minutes later.

Mendoza said, "I have decided to put an end to this confusion. I have to ask whether you will marry me, yes or no? One word will make an answer."

Carlotta felt her blood draining away.

"The answer is no, I see. Forgive me." So saying, Mendoza made for the door.

She knew that now was the time. "Wait."

He stopped but did not turn around. She gathered her breath: "I am to marry Philippo."

The creak of a cart sounded from the street. He turned to face her. "Philippo?"

"Your brother."

Not understanding, he came back and sat on the couch, frowning a little: "But Philippo is a boy."

"He is the same age as I am."

Mendoza was struck by this. "Of course, he is a man."

"I love him, Rodrigo."

He stared at her. "Yes?"

"Oh, yes, indeed."

"Since when have you loved him?"

"Many months. I have been trying to tell you."

He recollected certain incidents. "So that is what you have been trying to tell me."

"Yes."

He looked at her sideways, snake-eyed: "Me you do not love?"

"Not as I love Philippo."

"And how is that?"

"Gently, sensibly . . . That is the love I need, Rodrigo."

He breathed. "Have I no need?"

She looked at him with fear and pity, wanting to comfort him but far more wanting him gone. "You need so much."

She raised her hand to stroke his cheek, but with a hawk-like speed he raised his own to cut it off. His face took on a masklike sadness. He rose and made for the door again.

She said quickly, looking after him, "Rodrigo—you will not hurt him?"

He stopped and turned a face like the half-hidden grotesques at Santa Anna, unforgiving, grinning like a wolf.

"Rodrigo!" she insisted.

He shook his head and left the house.

The city was thronged with Guarani, assembled for their Madonna. Carved out of a big piece of black marble many generations back by a Guarani hand, she was placed outside the Church of San Cristóbal, underneath a teakwood frame to protect her from rainstorms. Mendoza, unseeing, tramped out into the country, walking blindly through the clearings and the brushwood, his hand resting on his sword.

After a time dust clogged his pores, covering him with white powder. He took no notice. He felt dirtied inwardly. His brother had befouled him with the woman he loved. All at once he stopped, halted by the thought that all the inhabitants of Asunción had been rejoicing over this. He started off again, and a branch whipped his face. He brushed it aside, thankful for the smart, and went on walking. His hatred was turned equally on the guilty pair and on the world at large. They were all false.

The sun was going down now. His farm was over the next rise, he would go there and sleep.

When he reached the farmhouse, the glow of the fire lit up the surprised farmer who came to the door. Mendoza turned him out of his bed and threw himself down on his back, but could not sleep.

The farmer whispered to his wife, "Did you see how white his face is?"

"I think he is mad."

Mendoza came out again and asked for a horse. He spurred away from the farm in the moonlight, with his sword dangling by his side.

As he drew near, he saw the walls of Asunción lit by torchlight from within, and heard the confused uproar of guitars and laughter.

Entering, he found the tumbledown shacks of the Guarani servants on the outskirts of the town deserted, save for a few elderly natives dumped like heaps of old clothing. The rest were all assembled at the Church of San Cristóbal.

Mendoza rode through the bent little dwellings of tiled mud to the commercial quarter. Here, the outside walls of the houses were lit by candles, and mothers and children were standing in the doorways, looking up the street to a spot from which, out of sight beyond the turning, a chaotic din was sounding.

In Cabeza's house every room was illuminated. Inside it, and out in the street, people—bizarrely dressed as birds, jaguars, heroes of the ancient world, and satyrs—were uttering strange cries and mocking laughter. The air was loud with the beat of guitars and the blasts of a trumpet. Those outside carried long torches so that the farthest corners of the street were either glowing with light or suddenly plunged into blue-black shade. A dwarf, swathed in brilliant green feathers, came right up to Mendoza's bridle, grimacing obscenely, only to draw back at the sight of the rider's face.

Standing on a balcony overtopped by a huge tasseled standard of the arms of Spain, Cabeza was whooping and clapping at the riot below. Mendoza looked up at Bernadette, who was there on the balcony with Blasco and all the other dignitaries of the town. She knew, of course. They all knew. He made his way into a side street, for he did not want to go home.

The tiny square of San Angelus seemed to draw him. He found it crammed to the walls with Guarani, all kneeling or prostrate before the Guarani Madonna. All these worshipers were silent. Not a sound escaped them. They faced the black Madonna. She stood underneath a juniper tree, festooned with flowers. Huge pots of clay had been arranged with a mixture of reeds and cotton waste burning in them, casting an eerie light on the square. To the intoning of a Jesuit priest, they repeated a Hail Mary while a soft drum kept time. All hoped that their Madonna would come down and, by a miraculous and transcendent gesture, make them free.

Then the Guarani formed up behind the priest. They eased the statue out of its shelter and carried it away, four to each pole, still silently, out toward the first of the churches it was to visit before the night was through.

The square was empty now. The blast of a remote trumpet and the shout of a distant reveler were all that disturbed it.

There was an inn here that Mendoza had frequented in the days before he knew Carlotta. He sat down outside it. Nobody came, so he banged his sword on the table. A maidservant emerged, stopped, looked at him, and retreated indoors.

A moment later the innkeeper came out, wiping his hands on his apron and saying, "Welcome, Señor Mendoza, a thousand welcomes. It is quite a time since we last saw you here. This is an auspicious occasion—you don't join in the carousal up in town, then? No, why should you? It is idiotic, don't you agree? Thank God the slaves have gone at last—you have been in the country?"

"As you see."

"Does your farm fare well, *señor?*"

"Sufficiently."

"You look thirsty. You would like a glass of wine? I go now to get it—yes, in haste, *señor,* in haste." So saying, he hurried back inside, forsaking his usual dignity. But first he had cast a rapid glance up at the second-floor window.

Mendoza followed his glance. One window showed a chink of light.

Inside Carlotta and Philippo were clinging to each other, in the small walled space to which their world had shrunk, and she was crying. Philippo had earlier searched the city for his brother and, not finding him, he had become distracted. He would leave Asunción. After what had happened, how could Carlotta bear to be seen in his company? He smashed a mirror. Then he went off down a narrow passageway to the poorer quarters of the city, which Mendoza had shown him many years before, and proceeded to get drunk.

Carlotta, told of his wanderings by her maid, went out in the dusk, dressed as a nymph with veils, and found him near the inn. With the whole town in bedlam, they had taken this room on the second floor and made love. For a time that was all that mattered, but later he had to comfort her as she wept, rubbing her spine up and down with a strong hand and murmuring to her.

The innkeeper came out to Mendoza again with a bottle and two large stoneware mugs.

He called out, "Here we are, *se—*"

Mendoza snapped, "Who is up there in that room?"

The innkeeper placed the goblets and the bottle softly on

the table, and did not meet his eye. He shook his head.

"Pardon, *señor*, I have no idea." Then he went back inside and shut the door.

The square fell quiet. The shutters went up on the ground floor. The lights went out. Mendoza turned around, looked up at the one lit window, and began to tremble. Slowly he got to his feet and tramped up the outer staircase to the second-floor balcony. Philippo and Carlotta heard his heavy tread on the pinewood floors.

"Listen," she whispered.

The footsteps ceased. Outside the door, Mendoza went to the balustrade and scanned the moonlit roofs. His gaze passed on to where the outlying fields merged into the forest. Then he looked back over the roofs. The city was still brightly lit. What if it was not them behind that door? If so, what he was on the point of doing would add a new indignity to the one the hidalgos were already laughing at. The couple in the room heard his footsteps retreat and begin back down the stairs. But then they stopped. What if it *was* them? Mendoza asked himself? They heard his heavy tread come swiftly back to the door, and then it crashed open. The figure staring down at them looked gigantic.

He, for his part, took in two naked forms clasped loosely to each other. The two men's eyes met as if they had never met before. Then Mendoza spat full in his brother's upturned face, wheeled around, and went away.

Philippo, sitting up in the bed, said, "How did he know?"

"He thinks we have done this often."

"Oh, no! Rodrigo!" Pulling on his breeches, Philippo dashed out in pursuit of his brother.

Mendoza marched blindly along the camino real to the square in front of Cabeza's residence. A few late revelers in their outrageous costumes, with Cabeza bidding them a tipsy farewell, stood talking on the balcony, making a bizarre contrast with the red mud and carriages and clattering palms below them.

Here Philippo caught his brother and grasped his arm.

"Rodrigo, please!"

Mendoza stopped and said, "Take your hand away!"

Philippo was shocked motionless by the menace in that voice. Mendoza wrenched himself free and then made off across the roadway in the direction of his home.

But an elderly gentleman in the costume of an ornate bird gave a nervous titter. Mendoza stopped. Here was the mockery that had been dogging him for months. He was up to the offender in two swift strides.

"You laughed?"

"Not I, señor. I did not laugh." He appealed for corroboration. "Did I laugh?"

"Yes, you laughed. At whom?"

"Señor Mendoza, you are quite mistaken, I did not laugh." The gentleman licked his lips.

"That is a lie."

Philippo said, "Rodrigo," and his brother turned. "Quarrel with me."

Mendoza, though he looked as though this would entirely satisfy all his hatred for the world, said, "No," and turned back to his victim. Philippo tapped him on the shoulder and then struck him full in the face as he turned.

An officer of the guard thrust a rapier into Philippo's hand, but he had not time to find his guard before Mendoza ran him through with a thrust of his broadsword so accurate and violent that his brother was thrust backward, to be pinned against the ornate side of a carriage with two screaming ladies in it.

So Philippo died, looking into the face of his brother, who was forced to stand close against his victim, not daring to extract his sword lest the other should fall.

Then two officers of the guard came and took his sword from him and lowered the corpse to the ground. There was dead silence. Then the noise of the Guarani began to be heard. All Cabeza's hangers-on were witnesses, and Cabeza, too: It was Philippo who had struck the first blow. Mendoza could not be held accountable to the law. But the whole of Cabeza's party drew back from him.

11

IT WAS TWO weeks later that Gabriel received a letter from Father Ribiro, written in reply to one of his. Sebastian, who had found an easier way up the cliff, came to deliver it.

"A letter from the Father Provincial." Gabriel opened it carefully.

A group of Guarani were watching, as they did each day when he sat down to make an entry in his diary, shaking their heads. They still were awestruck at the art of writing. The sight of print they had now got used to, but the formation of the characters by a moving pen was magic.

"It is nothing," Tanretopra had said. "It is just a trick their people have learned."

And Gabriel replied, "You are right. Perhaps you could not learn to write, but your children could."

About a week later a child took hold of Gabriel and led him to where several lines of signs and symbols had been inscribed on the ground as if by someone who was learning to write. The Jesuits were excited, for they knew the Guarani were quick to learn. The musical instruments they had made since the priests' arrival were as good in ornamentation and tone as those made in Europe. For themselves, the Guarani had made canoes, longbows, spears, cooking pots, simple looms, and huts, and they were irresistibly attracted by new skills.

This was the Jesuits' opportunity. They had built a camp by a Guarani settlement, with a little lean-to church and a small hut. By then, five other Jesuits had joined Gabriel. They had constructed an elaborate loom and worked it painstakingly beneath the attentive gaze of the older women. One day a woman told Father Antonio to get up and change places with her. By the end of the day she had a six-inch-wide strip of cloth woven on the warp. The priests were jubilant.

The next day, however, they awoke to find the mission deserted. They stood discouraged among the abandoned huts and cooking places, and listened to the early morning noises of the forest.

"Why do you think they have run away?" asked Sebastian.

Gabriel said, looking up into the ululating trees: "It must have been Tanretopra's idea; he hates us and everything we bring. Perhaps he is right, save that we bring them the Blessed Word."

They waited for a month, but nothing happened. Gabriel said that evening, "I fear we have failed."

The next morning the Guarani were back. Unknown to the Jesuits, there had been a fierce confrontation, with much shouting across the campfires, between Tanretopra and his party on one side, and on the other Hacugh and the older men. Because of his skill with the bow and the hunting spear and the fishing lance, Hacugh had won.

When he led the tribe back, he saluted the Jesuits with "Here I am" and received the answer, "God be with you."

Gabriel told the other priests, "Just follow their lead. Behave as though last month had never happened." All the tribe came up and greeted them, save Tanretopra. Gabriel went up to him and said, "Here I am."

"I do not see you," Tanretopra said, ignoring his outstretched hand, and squatted down to watch.

Watched by the whole tribe, Sebastian and the five others began felling long scaffolding poles from the forest and dragging them painfully, inch by inch, toward the trampled earthenware foreshore by the river.

Breathless and exhausted, Antonio urged, "Why don't we ask them to lend us a hand?"

Sebastian replied, "We are the helpers; they are the helped."

"Right," said Gabriel, who was flat on his back.

When they had assembled twenty poles and started to lash them together, the Guarani laughed. One of the women stamped her feet and, going down to the riverbank, collected some fine yellow reeds, which were immensely strong. She

brought them back to the Jesuits and laid them out to dry, so
they thanked her, whereupon all the other women went down
to the river to collect the corded yellow reeds and lay them out
to dry. At the end of the day they were as tough as whipcord.

Hacugh inquired, "What do you want to do with that?"

Gabriel asked Sebastian to draw in the sand an accurate
picture of the uprights of a hut.

Hacugh and the others gathered around.

"Will it stand up?" someone asked.

"Oh, yes."

"In the rain and the storm?"

"Much bigger ones than this have stood up, down there,
for three generations."

The braves reported to the tribe, to be greeted by a shrieking diatribe from Tanretopra, which lasted far into the night.

Next day the shaman was gone, and Hacugh reported to
Gabriel, "We will help you at your work and see if your Christ
is pleased with us."

"Thanks be to God."

"I have not said that I will serve your God."

"He has plenty of time."

"Maybe, and maybe not. Tell him that. We collect how
many of the poles from the forest?"

Sebastian looked reflectively at the poles. "If only they
were thicker we could build an even bigger house.

Hacugh looked at him ironically. Sebastian flushed.

"You make a fool out of yourself by trying to treat me like
a fool," Hacugh said calmly. "How much bigger do you want
them?"

"About so big." He indicated a size six times as big.

"Like that?" Hacugh pointed to a tall juniper growing in a
clump nearby.

"That would do excellently."

By the end of the day the trunk was lying on its side by the
river, and the boys and old men had begun to trim its sides. In
two weeks they had twenty more. When they got bored they
went away, but always they came back. Then, directed by
Sebastian, they began to erect the framework of the church,
using the reeds to bind it. They seemed content to follow his

instructions initially and then, having carried them out, sought out a similar operation. Fearlessly, they ran about high up in the roof-girders of the growing church.

Watching all this, Gabriel gave thanks to God. Setting his eloquence aside, he told them the New Testament story in the simplest terms. He found their questions about it probed his beliefs, forcing him to go much deeper than he had expected. Then the women came, posing even more basic problems. He was compelled to elucidate fundamental principles to justify the simplest articles of faith, so that he was lost in deep thought and prayer for days. Then he realized that they were teaching him, and loved them for it.

Tanretopra came back and installed himself some distance away in a dark thatched shelter at the foot of a massive teak tree. He squatted there in feathered headdress, mixing the pigment of roots with blossoms and murmuring a harsh singsong. Many tribesmen went to hear him and listened to his heart-rending incantation, painful and sad.

In the middle of the night, Gabriel went to Tanretopra, coughing to give notice of his approach. He heard the shaman start awake, put on his feathered headdress, and recommence his melancholy song. Then he blew up the fire as his visitor came forward beneath the towering tree and asked, "May I sit down?"

Tanretopra went on singing, so Gabriel sat down without an invitation, facing him. He waited for two hours, but still the singsong did not stop. Then Gabriel drew out his breviary and began to read. Immediately, the high-pitched drone was broken off, and a skinny hand came swooping down on his book to send it fluttering into the fire. Gabriel glanced at it and snatched it out, dusting the ash off against his cassock. Tanretopra laughed softly.

"Well done, Gabriel."

"What can I do to make you heed my words, Tanretopra? They are good for your people."

"Good words, but false."

"No. I may be false, but the words are true."

For a few moments the shaman remained sunk in thought, and then, in a deep voice, he said, "You have won, Gabriel.

You have won today and tomorrow, but in the end you will have lost. Do you not know this?"

"No."

"Then you are a fool." Tanretopra resumed his harsh singing. Gabriel got up and returned to the camp, but still the painful singing followed him into the thick dark, until the night sounds of the jungle drowned it.

That was how things stood when he received the Father Provincial's reply to his report. With a long face he told Sebastian, "Father Ribiro calls me to Asunción."

It was a long-standing joke between them that Sebastian looked forward to these visits to the capital as much as Gabriel dreaded them. He responded, "I will come with you."

Gabriel gave a nod of his head and made a grunting sound, "Aye, if you like, then do."

The next morning they set off, leaving Antonio in charge.

When they got to the Mission of Santa Croce, they were met by Brother Itapua, who had been left in charge of the whole mission in Gabriel's absence. Gimlet-eyed, Gabriel sniffed into every crevice. He called for the accounts and asked many probing questions. Itapua had the answers at his fingertips. Finally, Gabriel closed the last account book with a sigh of satisfaction.

"All correct," he said. "Most orderly!"

Itapua, who, being Guarani, was a lovely olive brown, answered, "Did you think that I would cheat those of my own color?"

"Oh, no. I thought you would incline a little to their side. Instead, I see that you have kept the accounts strictly in accord with the rule."

"I see. You did not think that I and my people were capable of being faithful to the rule?"

"I ask your pardon. Bless me, Brother Itapua."

"I bless you." He looked proudly at Gabriel and swept out of the little chamber where Gabriel, left alone, jumped for joy. Then he caught sight of a frieze of little brown faces watching him from the veranda. He cleared his throat, put on a pedagogic air, and pushed his way out through them, for in fact he had no idea how to treat children. They followed him about, fascinated, clinging on to his cuffs, sensing that he was himself a child with a saint's bravado.

After a short stay at the Santa Croce Mission, the two priests set out on the long journey to Asunción. It was raining when they arrived. The low clouds scudding with the wind, emptied their contents all day and all night on the city, whose streets were thick with mud and whose walls ran with racing water. They tramped hurriedly along the deserted street to the entrance of the Father Provincial's residence, and Sebastian pulled on the bell. After a while, the door was opened by a brother who, immediately he saw who they were, came out into the rain and insisted on bearing their rolls up to the first-floor rooms that had been prepared for them. Then he brought two rough cassocks and two big jars, which he filled with water, one soapy and one clean, in front of the roaring fire.

After Gabriel had washed himself, he joined Father Ribiro, who greeted him with a smile. Gabriel bent to kiss his superior's ring and then, at the other's invitation, seated himself, with an inquisitive glance of his sharp blue eyes.

Ribiro returned his glance, thinking, How blue those eyes are! Is that sign of something? Or is it just a badge with which God has marked out that island race—well, no, not God—yes, God, God! Yet again, he smiled. "How are things at the new mission above the falls?"

Gabriel, who disliked these smiles, replied, "Insects and twigs, Reverend Father Provincial."

"And how many converts?"

"None."

"I see."

"But many who are almost ready."

"How do you know when they are quite ready?"

"They tell me themselves."

Ribiro frowned. He thought that Gabriel's regard for the Guarani as individuals was excessive. Mass conversion was good enough. "Tell me, are they as you expected to find them?"

"No. They are far more sophisticated."

"Sophisticated?"

"There is, for example, a shaman called Tanretopra. I have

to pit my wits against him continually."

"You don't think that it would have been better left as it was, with the Mission of Santa Croce as the last outpost on the river?"

"No, Reverend Father Provincial, do you?"

"I do think so. But you are the one in the forest. I have agreed that you should start another mission stretching from the head of the falls up to Portuguese territory, to be called the Mission of San Sebastian."

"Reverend Father Provincial, God's peace be upon you. As for us in the forest, we will do our best, guided by the rule of Saint Ignatius and under the superintendence of Christ." Gabriel got down on his knees and crossed himself, than sat down again.

Ribiro resumed: "I am anxious about Brother Itapua, your successor at Santa Croce, however."

Here it comes, Gabriel thought. "I am sorry," he replied. "Why is that?"

"What is his profession?"

"He is an agriculturalist."

"Not a soldier or a musician?"

"No, an agriculturalist," Gabriel repeated. But why beat about the bush? It was better to have it out in the open. "As an agriculturalist he is not handicapped by the color of his skin."

"Then let him remain."

Gabriel spread out his work-hardened hands with an expression of puzzlement. "But naturally. What else?"

"You know what I mean, Father Gabriel. Do you really consider this man qualified to take over your mission?"

"None more so."

"Has he any notion what the world outside the missions is like?"

"I do not know."

"Is he completely subject to the Order?"

"Reverend Father Provincial, he would perform whatever you commanded without question, and that is more, *mea culpa*, than I can say for myself."

Another ironic little smile from Ribiro. "I appoint him." The smile vanished. "May he follow in your footsteps and do as virtuously, Father Gabriel." He extended his hand, and Gabriel rose to kiss it.

Ribiro became the host. He went around to the glasses and bottles in the blaze of the crackling fireplace. "Wine? From the captain general's own stock. Excellent!"

He poured two glasses, held his own up to the leaping firelight to view its color. "Ah! How rich! You have heard of Condesa Carlotta de Vilhasante? She has been staying with Blasco de Bigorente these twelve months past."

"No. Why?"

"You know Rodrigo Mendoza?"

"Indeed."

"And his brother?"

"I know he has a brother."

Ribiro raised his eyebrows quizzically. "To be precise, he *had* one. Let me tell you what I know."

When he had finished, Gabriel said, "They sound like a well-assorted trio. Why are you telling me all this?"

"The *condesa* is here, in another room, waiting for you to see her."

"Me? Why me?"

"I suppose she will tell you that."

"I will not listen. This is merely a device to squeeze the last drop of excitement out of it."

"But I am asking you to see her."

"Because she is a de Vilhasante?" Gabriel asked.

"Perhaps. Remember, this day I have done you a favor."

"In that case, Reverened Father Provincial, take it back."

"I command you to see her."

"I can be very hard on the guilty."

Ribiro smiled. "Not always, perhaps!" Motioning his visitor to stay, Ribiro rose and left the room, still smiling.

For an angry minute, Gabriel sat there, waiting without curiosity or any other sort of interest. Fashionable suffering did not concern him. His duty called him to battle on a plainer field. Nevertheless, no sooner had Carlotta glided silently into the room than he was impressed. The features of the pale woman, who now composedly seated herself in front of him in the firelight, though youthful, had already settled themselves in a mask of resignation. He coughed irritably.

"Well, what do you want of me?"

"I want nothing, Father. It is Señor Mendoza who wants something."

Gabriel's expression was stony. "I know that he has killed his brother, and the law cannot touch him. Now he seeks absolution, too. Is that it? Well, I can't help him. God forgive me, I loathe him. Tell him so."

"I thought the Church could help anyone."

"There are better helpers in the Church than I am."

"He is lying in the hospice."

"Then let him be cast out so that another can take his place."

"You cast him out."

This made him raise his eyes to look at her. He gave her a faint, cryptic smile. "It seems that you love this man."

"Not love." She shook her head. "Fear," she said.

"Yet you are anxious about his spiritual welfare."

"Father, listen, if you please." She told him of Mendoza's love for her and also all that he had done for his brother out of love.

"I see." Gabriel frowned. "Has not one of the other priests already seen him?"

"He does not wish to see the others. He will only see you."

"He seized five people from the tribe above the falls, did you know that?"

"That may be why he wants to see you."

Gabriel yielded. He would see Mendoza once and only once.

Carlotta walked back, through the tippling rain, to Blasco's house. There was nothing left to detain her in Asunción. She would return without delay to Spain—but not to Madrid, not to Court. Her story would be common gossip there already. She would go back to her castle and perhaps—why not?—to marriage, if some tolerable hidalgo, who no longer expected very much, found her worth the risk.

Gabriel, too, went out into the rain, to the hospital. The lay brother took him to a cell, and the heavy door was shut behind him. He had to peer about, for there was no light. When he had got used to the dimness, he saw that the walls were running with damp. He seated himself on the only chair and looked at Mendoza, who was lying naked on the bed. Mendoza returned his gaze, but otherwise did not move a muscle. His eyes followed Gabriel's to where his sword was propped up in the corner among a heap of dirty clothes.

"You took five men from the forest," Gabriel said.

"Yes."

"Where are they?"

A pause, then: "Dead, I expect."

There was silence except for the crash of rain on the tiled roof and the plaintive howl of the wind outside. Then Gabriel got up and examined a cheap wooden image of the suffering Christ. This man is implacable, he thought, and the strain of his task weighed on him physically.

"To whom did you sell them?"

"I don't remember."

Gabriel resumed his seat, tilting it on its back legs this time, balancing himself against the damp wall with his hands stretched out behind him.

"And you feel no remorse over your treatment of the Guarani?"

"If I said I did, would you believe me?"

"No."

"Then it was a foolish question."

Gabriel gestured at the damp walls. "What's all this about, then?" he asked with hostility. "Remorse for your brother?"

Mendoza looked at him; his eyes were set deep in their sockets, but he answered, "Yes."

"Then why hasn't God forgiven you?"

"I don't know."

"Perhaps it is not remorse, only regret, that you feel."

The haunted eyes took on a wary look.

"Do you know the difference?" Gabriel asked.

"No."

Gabriel experienced a flood of exultation. He thought he saw his chance to make Mendoza recognize his need of grace.

"Regret is only for the consequences. A lecherous husband regrets that he married a plain girl. A usurious banker regrets that he didn't charge more for his loan. And you regret that the man you killed was your own brother. Of course you do. Who wouldn't? But to feel remorse you must renounce the deed itself. The very deed must revolt you. Does it?"

Mendoza, still looking at him, made no response.

"How did you do it? With this?" He went to the corner where the sword was leaning, and took it, glittering, like an instrument of justice, in his hand. "You enjoyed doing it."

Mendoza muttered, "I don't need your forgiveness."

"No man can be as good as you must be with a weapon like this, unless he enjoys using it."

Mendoza looked at the blade, his breath beginning to come short.

"Take it," Gabriel urged him, holding the sword out to Mendoza. "Are you frightened to take it?"

Mendoza grasped it and weighed it in his hand. At once his impassivity began to crack. Even as he opened his mouth to deny the charge, he was aware of a surge of irresistible power in his arm and shoulder, and knew that when he had driven that heavy blade into his brother, in and up, what he had felt was joy. He lowered it, replacing it gently in its scabbard, and went to look out of the tiny window into the night. He said nothing.

"Well?"

The mute figure did not appear to have heard. The silence remained unbroken. Gabriel waited for two minutes, during which his ardor was somewhat cooled. "Well?" he repeated. "What is your answer?"

"I am damned."

This sinner did not wait to be condemned! Gabriel thought. "And what are you going to do about it?"

"There is nothing I can do. I feel no remorse."

This was what resulted from attacking the sinner and not his sin. Gabriel realized he had contrived his own defeat. His own argument had been turned against him. He appealed to the sentimental image on the wall for assistance, but the figure of Christ only seemed to reply, Go on.

I have lost the way, the priest admitted silently.

Go on, the Christ told him.

Taking the baselard by the hilt, he said, in his thoughts This is a heavy burden, and Christ replied, Yes, he is relentless, that one.

Suddenly Gabriel asked Mendoza, "Are you prepared to carry this thing and your pistols, musket, powder, and shot above the falls?"

"Yes. What for?"

"The chief is there."

"He will kill me."

"You can turn back."

"I shall do it."

12

GABRIEL LEFT THE hospice without more ado, and next day took no particular notice when Mendoza presented himself at the place by the river where the Jesuits had moored their canoes. He was dressed simply in shirt, breeches, and boots, not like a soldier, and he carried his weapons like so much luggage, in a bundle slung over his back.

But all the other members of the party knew who he was and had heard the story. The Guarani paddlers slipped him dark glances out of the corners of their eyes and kept out of his way.

Sebastian was furious with Gabriel for imposing this incubus on them, but his protest received a short reply. Grimly, he offered the newcomer a paddle. It was his duty, as he saw it, to contribute his own strength to the voyage. But Sebastian's pride was also at work. Conscious of his own power, he counted on driving the canoe continuously around to starboard, but Mendoza kept sweeping it to port instead. Then, just when the furious Sebastian, red in the face, was about to ask Mendoza to slacken his stroke, the offender, frowning to himself, slowed down.

The shades of evening were already falling on the forest when they came to the first resting ground. Mendoza hoisted his bundle of weaponry out of the canoe and, after a moment's thought, tied it to his waist. It must have weighed a hundredweight of steel and lead, but he did his fair share of the work. The others looked significantly at one another and at Gabriel, but he was looking elsewhere.

Mendoza ate his food in silence and then, ignoring the conversation in which the brothers and the Guarani joined in common, turned on his side. He could not sleep, however, and his eyes were as wakeful as ever when the firelight faded and the rest were overtaken by oblivion.

When they awoke in the morning, he was already up fanning the fire, with his bundle still beside him. Gabriel looked him full in the face and said, "Good day. *Dominus vobiscum,*" but Mendoza uttered no word in reply. While they said morning prayers, he threw himself onto his back, sitting up to take breakfast only when they had finished. Once in the canoe, he guided it forward all day without a word.

Although he continued silent, however, after a week he sat up in the shade of the trees to listen when they said their prayers.

"Here," said Sebastian, offering him a book. "Take this."

"I cannot read," Mendoza answered, and rolled over onto his side.

For two days they stopped at the Mission of Santa Croce, where Brother Itapua gave an emotional greeting to Gabriel, who brought him the news that he was now the head of the mission. Some of the brothers were jealous of Itapua, in view of the color of his skin, saying that he was not fit to take command of whites, but others were agreeable, and all alike were swept up in the service when Gabriel, beneath the huge vault of the church, announced the appointment. All knew that they were eavesdropping on a communion between Gabriel and God. Standing at the back, with a large space cleared around him, Mendoza saw why Gabriel was revered.

When they went on upriver, they left the Guarani behind but took on two more Jesuits. When he could speak to them in private, Sebastian told them that Mendoza was a little mad, but made no mention of the man's spiritual condition.

Now, when they said their prayers, Mendoza for the first time stood up. In response to Gabriel's gratitude, however, he replied, "Your prayers mean nothing to me. It is just that I feel more comfortable this way."

It began to rain, and they came to the place where the peaceful flow of the river was impeded by huge blocks of basalt that extended upstream—nobody knew how far. The priests dragged the canoes far upshore, for fear of floods, and packed the lightest of their provisions into bundles.

Mendoza gazed over the rain-soaked landscape, stretching always uphill till it was lost in the seemingly immovable clouds that capped the mountains. Sebastian saw how he jerked the enormous load of weapons onto his back and brought up the rear. In an hour or two he had dropped out of sight behind. When they had started a blaze of twigs in a clearing high up in the hills, Mendoza was still not there.

With an air of preoccupation, Gabriel was reading. Nobody spoke. Then, silently, Mendoza appeared and lowered himself and his bundle to the ground. At once, all the Jesuits started chattering, only to stop suddenly when he got to his feet again to fetch armfuls of wood for the fire, still carrying his burden. When the meal was ready, he consumed his portion and then made as if to sleep.

The next day, Sebastian watched the rain-drenched bundle bumping, sliding, wrenching, and straining on Mendoza's back. When Mendoza stopped for a rest, he asked him, "How long can you go on carrying that bundle? It must weigh a hundredweight."

But Mendoza did not answer. He was scanning the next ascent.

That evening he appeared to fall asleep in the folded roots of a big ash tree. Gabriel said quietly, "Good; he sleeps."

Mendoza, without opening his lids, replied: "No, he does not."

When Gabriel and Sebastian went over to their sleeping places, Sebastian asked, "Father, how long must he carry that thing?"

"I want him to drop it; but he must decide himself when that will be."

A scarlet millipede, six inches long, was where Mendoza's hand came down to help him up among the trees. He cursed and threw the twisted, involuted shape to the ground.

Sebastian saw the blue-black of the sting on his wrist and quickly pulled his own knife from its sheath. "Here, let me do that!"

But Mendoza got a poignard out of his bundle and, holding his wrist against a tree, sliced into it this way and that. Then he wiped the blade and replaced the poignard in the load.

Sebastian said, "Better bandage that," but Mendoza was already off on the ascent of the cliff with his bundle clashing and banging against the rocks. The rain flowed down in rivers.

The next day the sky, a level sheet of dirty gray, disgorged itself. Within minutes, the wet ground was slippery. Mendoza's face was white and leaden with fatigue, but he slithered relentlessly along with his swaying burden, like a heedless automaton, up slopes and down. He had fallen behind. Only Sebastian was with him. All at once Mendoza was jerked off his feet. The bundle had got caught in a low forked branch, and he would not let go.

Sebastian, however, could bear no more of it. He drew his big knife and slashed the fastening. Thudding into the mud, the massive load began to slide downhill, the way they had come, impelled by its own weight. It started slowly but then, gathering speed, vanished over an edge into dead ground. Standing there in the crashing rain Sebastian stared at his companion, but Mendoza did not look at him. He turned back without a word.

"Let it be," shouted Sebastian. "Do you want to kill yourself?" There was no answer. Mendoza was already out of sight. "Do you think God wants you dead?" he called. No answer came from the pouring trees.

Retracing his steps, Gabriel came to the edge of a slope where, looking down, he saw Mendoza crouched in a puddle, surrounded by all his weapons. He had succeeded in collecting them, but was now staring at them as if he did not know what they were. At last, very deliberately, he spread the cover of his bundle out flat and began to collect everything onto it, methodically placing his pistol in the center, then arranging his armor, and then, in their exact positions, musket, poignard, and sword. Only when the four corners had been folded in and the rope tied did he look at Sebastian.

His face was a blank white circle of skin, with pits in which no light shone in place of eyes. For several seconds Sebastian stood without moving, receiving that deathly stare. Then he turned back to the track to rejoin the others.

That night he told Gabriel, "He'll never let the weapons go."

"What makes you say that?"

"I cut the bundle loose for him."

"That was foolish of you. Has he got it back?"

"He has. But he was going to kill me."

"Was he? That ought to please you, Father. He knows no other way of showing his affection."

The next evening they were back within sight of the river, now flat and calm beneath the setting sun. Sebastian checked the canoes. Then all the Jesuits waited until Mendoza had sunk, exhausted, into rigid unconsciousness.

Then, in one united body, the priests made their plea to Gabriel, through the senior among them.

"Father, we are all of one opinion. He has borne his burden long enough."

"I thank you for your opinion, but I do not share it," Gabriel informed them. "Christ laid that burden on him, and Christ will take it off. Happily we are not a republic but an Order. I am in charge. May the Divine Care watch over you all during this night." Then he unwrapped his oboe and wove a musical incantation over the dark water.

When they pushed off upstream in their canoes the next morning, Mendoza as usual took a paddle, but made no response to suggestions that he should abandon his load, so that in the end they left him to himself.

The thunderous falls came into view at last, and they reached the base of the cliffs the same day. The Jesuits gazed into the drifting vapor and then at Mendoza who, sitting apart, was staring at the cross that the priests had erected over the grave of Julien Lanzotti. Gabriel knew from his set, livid face that the man was locked in a grapple to the death with Christ, relishing the justice of it. He would never seek to palliate his guilt, nor would he weep or turn to the Church for mercy. Realizing this, Gabriel saw the error he had made in entering Mendoza in such a contest. He had underestimated the man's strength. He had overestimated the coercive power of hardship. Mendoza was ready to force himself to breaking point.

Death was what he sought. Frantically Gabriel prayed for guidance, but received none.

They camped for the night. At daybreak Gabriel sent the rest of the party ahead with Sebastian in charge, but himself remained behind with Mendoza, who stayed out of touch, bringing up the rear at a far distance. Gabriel kept ahead until they were halfway up the ascent, where he waited in the mist for Mendoza to labor up and join him. Then he made no move to carry on.

Without a word, Mendoza lay down on his belly, like an armadillo that had emerged from the forest, and drank muddy water from a hollow. Hair, body, and face, he was smeared with slime. When he had finished drinking he rolled over and stared at the waterfall.

Gabriel said, "You will kill yourself. You know that."

"Not if you order me to put this down."

"You yourself want to put it down."

"Not until Christ has shown mercy."

"Cannot you show mercy?" Gabriel asked.

"On whom?"

"On me, if you prefer it so."

Mendoza rolled onto his stomach again. "Did you not think of that earlier?" He stood up shakily, and resumed the climb, with his dripping burden hammering the back of his legs and catching in the thorns that grew out of the cliff face.

Toward the end of the day, Gabriel began to think about their destination. "What will happen when you meet the Guarani chief?" he asked. "What will you do? Have you thought of it?"

"Will he be there?"

"I think so."

"In that case, I shall submit myself."

"To be murdered?"

"Yes."

Mendoza stayed there in the gathering dusk while Gabriel went on ahead to where Sebastian and the others had already lit a great fire, and Hacugh, together with a company of warriors and children, had already joined them. When the greetings were over, however, Hacugh demanded, "What is the silence?"

Gabriel looked enquiringly at Sebastian, who shook his head. Nothing had been said yet. He took Hacugh to one side. "There is one who comes later."

"Why later?"

"He is called Mendoza."

Hacugh scanned the head of the falls. "He comes alone?"

"Yes."

"Why is he so far behind you?"

Gabriel explained about the bundle.

"Last year he took five of us," Hacugh said. "What has become of them?"

"Dead, probably. You will never see them again, that is certain."

"Then he must die. I shall kill him."

"If you murder him, then I and the other priests will have to leave you."

"I shall be sorry for that, but I shall kill him."

Then Hacugh went to get his spear and warn the other tribesmen. They talked in low voices. Hacugh put on his headdress of parrot feathers and went to stand in the shadow of the rocks.

Sebastian came and stood with Gabriel. "Tell me what to do."

"I have lost my way, Father Sebastian," said Gabriel. "Just stay with me."

"Gladly."

After they had all stood thus two hours, Hacugh suddenly stiffened. The ring of metal had sounded from the cliffs below. Priests and tribesmen together all froze.

Five minutes later they heard a louder clang. "That is the bundle I told you of," said Gabriel in a low voice.

Hacugh grunted, too intent for speech.

There was not much longer to wait. They could hear Mendoza approaching steadily now. The clinking of his load was continuous, and soon they could also hear his labored breathing. Then the group of Jesuits heard a stir in the undergrowth just down the slope and saw Hacugh moving stealthily forward with raised spear. Then he halted and stood poised to stab.

Sebastian glanced at Gabriel for a signal, but Gabriel gently raised his hand in a gesture forbidding interference.

Then, like an enormous reptile, Mendoza appeared. He was flat on the ground, hauling himself along, dragging his lurching, grinding bundle behind him like some trailed excrescence. With his face only a few inches above the mud and stones and roots over which he was dragging himself, he encountered a human foot. Then he saw its fellow. The feet were dark and bare. Rolling over onto his back he found himself staring up into a pair of coal-black eyes.

"Is this the one I met before?" asked Hacugh.

"Yes," Gabriel answered.

Frowning, the chief stooped to examine the mud-caked face out of which a pair of red-rimmed eyes stared back at him relentlessly. Then he straightened himself and surveyed the prone, mud-colored body in its entirety. He took a step to the bundle and picked it up and then, surprised by its weight, put it down again without opening it.

"He has brought this thing from his home?"

"Yes," Gabriel confirmed.

"He must be strong."

"Yes."

"Why has he brought these weapons here?"

"He has no more use for them," Gabriel explained. Then, turning to Mendoza he asked, "What happened to the slaves you took? Are they all dead?"

"Yes, they are dead."

"What does he say?" asked Hacugh.

"They are all dead, the people he took from you."

"It is a foolish thing to drag those weapons through the jungle. He could have left them, having no more use for them."

"He is still attached to them although he has no use for them."

"You joke. Do not think I have forgotten the debt he owes me. I have not forgotten." Hacugh's hand closed on the hilt of his knife. Sebastian darted forward, but Hacugh only cut the cord that joined Mendoza to his burden. Seizing the bundle, the chief carried it over to the riverbank and halted there. "Come here!" he called to his companions. "Feel that!"

"He is strong."

"Yes, potent and evil."

"I have not forgotten!" With a mighty heave, Hacugh slung the enormous weight away from him. There was a splash, and then the water closed over it. Nobody moved, and there was a moment's silence.

Then Gabriel started to laugh. Laughter shook the whole of his spare frame throughout its length. Sebastian joined in, and then the other Jesuits. Then the Guarani, too, began to laugh, delighted to have occasioned so much pleasure, although ignorant how this had been achieved.

Slowly Mendoza sat up and looked from one group to the other. Then his body, too, began to emit a sound that might have been sobbing but was indeed laughter. He gazed at the dark river into which his burden had just disappeared, then covered his face with blackened hands and laughed and cried.

13

WORN OUT, MENDOZA did not paddle when they pushed off upstream for the mission station. The Jesuits laid him in the bottom of one of the canoes. Passive and supine, watched over by a Guarani boy who was studying him closely, Mendoza, too, studied the moon riding with her stars beyond the festooned trees that leaned far out over the river. He saw enormous moths navigating through the dark, and heard the yells of monkeys and the snorting of wild pigs. It seemed to him that he had never noticed any of this before. His sleep was dreamless.

When he awoke he opened his eyes to a blinding blue sky and turned his head to find himself the target of the gaze of a frieze of children who had gathered along the riverbank. He had been left to sleep in the canoe. Seeing him now move, all the children fled except one boy who had been left in the canoe to keep a watch on him. Boy and slave trader stared at each other aimlessly.

Then Mendoza tried to sit up. His whole body shrieked for mercy. He did not groan, but he sank back. Then he tried again, and Gabriel, coming to the landing, saw the boy crouching down in the canoe behind Mendoza, who was gently easing himself up.

When he was on his feet, Gabriel led him away, and all the children followed to watch Mendoza bathe in the clear pool and rinse out his clothes. Then, squatting at a discreet distance, they watched him eat.

"What shall I do now, Father?" Mendoza asked.

"I cannot say."

"Should I go back to Asunción?"

"The river is always there."

"But what do you advise, Father?"

"You could stay here."

"I will stay here until I have made up my mind."

"You are wise. You need time. You must consider."

From a distance, Mendoza watched the Guarani. They were building a church and some big huts. The women were beating cotton they had gathered in the forest.

Realizing that it was impossible to prevent these new developments, Tanretopra had taken to joining the crowd of men, women, and children who gathered every day to watch the Jesuits say mass. When the ceremony was over, he sat and argued with Gabriel.

"Why did God make a devil?"

"The world God created is not without suffering. The devil prefers suffering to happiness. Suffering is the devil's choice."

"Why did God create a world with suffering in it?"

"He wanted to create a world in which we could worship him. Unless there was a devil, we could not turn from the devil to God. Men have to choose."

"Then let them know that God has given the devil power. It is the devil who commands prowess in battle."

"Yes, you are right. The devil has great power."

"And you also say that God takes women's graces for his share—tending and pity and self-sacrifice."

"And love."

"But I choose men's virtues. I choose bravery. I choose endurance."

"Those are Christ's virtues. What have you to say of cruelty and cowardice and deceit?"

"They are great virtues when the devil commands. Great virtues, great!" The shaman struck an authoritative posture. "The devil will win!"

"That depends on how many rally to his standard."

"Multitudes rally to him, and they are right to do so. Tell me why your towns and farms are built upon the backs of slaves."

"Alas, I do not know."

"I know."

"Then tell me."

"It is because you people are cunning. You worship the devil in secret and pretend that you worship this Christ."

"So we priests are liars?"

"No. You are the true believers. You serve the devil's worshipers. You form the screen they hide behind when they do the devil's will." Tanretopra suddenly pointed at Mendoza, who was standing at the edge of the group. "He knows what I say is true."

Suddenly Mendoza found they were all looking at him.

"Well, then," Gabriel invited, "speak up!"

"There are many servants of the devil in Asunción," Mendoza said. "But there are true servants of Christ as well. Back Father Gabriel with all your might. This shaman is false. He is telling you lies."

In the silence which ensued, Mendoza left, having nothing more to say, and went to the Jesuits' hut, where a bed had been allotted him. He stretched himself out on it. He had said nothing that he did not truly believe.

After that, as the days went by, Mendoza gravitated to the children and the women, away from the men. He watched the babies riding on their mothers' hips, asleep, or playing, or being bathed in the pool. His harsh features relaxed at the sight of them. At first, however, when their mothers spoke to him he did not reply, but turned away after a swift, curious glance. At first, too, he discouraged the children who followed him everywhere he went, trying to understand him. He answered their curious gaze with a threatening glare that drove them all away except Babuie, the boy who had watched over him in the canoe.

Babuie was not afraid of his opaque stare but looked straight back at him with puzzled eyes. Not that he stared at Mendoza perpetually. Sometimes he found Mendoza's doings boring, and on these occasions, to Mendoza's wonder, the boy simply fell asleep.

Babuie often poled a hollow log across the river. One day he challenged Mendoza, "You can't do that! Watch him," he told a circle of his friends who were also watching. "He thinks he can do it, but he can't."

Mendoza went down to the water's edge, took up the pole,

and, squatting in the hollow log, launched out onto the river with an easy shove. As soon as he stood up, however, to punt it, over it rolled, plunging him into the water. A score of times he tried in vain to re-embark. Then, rising to the surface after his last attempt, he saw the small watchers on the bank all rolling with laughter and joined in. Then they came rushing to help him and to show him what he had to do.

One day Mendoza was watching an old woman working a loom when she asked Babuie, "What is it he wants?"

"He wants to know how you do it," the boy answered.

"It is not man's work," the woman told Mendoza.

"I know, but I am not a man."

"Sit there," she invited. "I will show you."

He was astonished by the women's skill in communication, their patience and methodical ways. After he had received his first lesson in weaving, the old woman inquired, "Would you like to see how it's done really properly?"

"Yes."

She put him alongside five girls in a weaving team, showing him how to play his part, and then called the other women to come and see him at it. He found it a restful occupation. It employed that part of his mind which had been brooding endlessly on the death of Philippo.

Next, Babuie showed him how to stir the huge pots of food for the men when they returned from hunting or gathering honey.

"How long does it take?" Mendoza asked, breathing hard.

"You can keep on with it as long as you like," the boy told him, "but you must keep on without stopping. If you want to rest, you must hand over the task to a woman. But this is not man's work, after all."

"I am not a man," he declared again. Watched by a silent crowd of women, he kept on stirring the food for hours, because it employed that part of his mind which would otherwise have been in hell.

One morning he awoke in the early sunshine to find a young woman kneeling beside him. She pressed her hand to his lips, enjoining silence, and then led him by the hand through the silent village to a hut where many women had gathered. He was told to sit on a raffia mat.

"Mendoza, take off your clothes," said a very old woman. He looked at their faces. They were all grave, so he obeyed, pulling off the cassock to reveal his white skin, which was marred by many scars. These they examined closely, inquiring how he got them. Some came from fighting with Guarani, others from fights with his own people.

"This is a warrior," the old woman declared.

The space around him was cleared, and the old woman ordered a pot containing a sticky black fluid to be held beside her. Then she was handed a stick of bamboo with fanned-out bristles at one end. With this, very cautiously, she painted a wide stripe down the left side of his face. This she followed with three narrow stripes down the right side.

"That is good," the spectators said, and they crowded in closer to watch while more lines, serpentine but firm-edged, were painted over his rib cage and down into his groin, then around his arms and legs. The last lines were painted around his scars.

By way of benediction the women then offered him a young girl. He kissed her and said, "I am not a man." Then, after making a profound obeisance to the old woman of the tribe, he went out.

"What does this mean?" he asked Sebastian.

"It means that the tribe accepts you. Can you not now, through Christ, accept yourself?"

"It is not in my power."

The men took him hunting. Shouting, they steered a hog to where he stood drawn back like a bow with his spear at the ready. The animal was fizzing with rage. Mendoza made no move. The hog halted to stare at him with bloodshot eyes and then ambled off into the forest with tail high and rump thrust up.

"Why didn't you kill it?" Babuie demanded.

"I do not know. Forgive me," he said to the assembled hunters, but the eldest of them nodded and turned away.

"I have no faith in all this," Gabriel told Sebastian.

One day Mendoza went into the forest. He looked up and saw monkeys playing in the treetops, which met a hundred

feet above his head. He looked down, and there was Tanretopra, seated at the foot of a tree.

"You are not a Christian," the shaman said. "I have been
watching you."

"Yes, I am a Christian."

The shaman raised his hand to shake a finger at him. "Take
care. This Christ may be only a little god, but a god is what he
is."

"He is the one God. All other gods are devils."

Tanretopra grinned at him. "You do not believe in Christ at
all." He rose and disappeared into the forest, but his voice
declared, "The devil is your god."

"That may be so, but the only God is Christ," Mendoza
called after him.

Gabriel had taken good care to explain to the Guarani that
at their masses they consumed the blood and flesh of Christ
himself. As a result, they held the Jesuits in awe, watching in
strict silence when they administered the sacraments to one
another, but they could not be persuaded to take communion
themselves.

"Why will you not take communion?" he asked Hacugh.
"It is a joy. It is an honor."

"Why does not he?" Hacugh pointed to Mendoza.

"Because he has committed a crime against God and does
not believe he is forgiven. Is that not true?" He appealed to
Mendoza.

"Yes, that is true. And it is nobody's concern but mine."

Hacugh's expression became watchful. "I will take it when
I see you take it." He nodded and turned away. The other
Guarani men followed him.

Gabriel asked Mendoza, "Is your judgment higher than that
of the Society of Jesus?"

"It is in such a case. I learned that at my mother's knee. Is
it not so?"

Gabriel drove his fist into his palm and answered, "Yes, it
is. But still, you are mistaken. I, who have watched you say
Christ has forgiven you, I beg you to consider that."

Mendoza went away to think. There were only two who
could judge his conscience—himself and Christ. But what if

he were to be received into the Society of Jesus? As to whether he was fit for that, not he but Father Ribiro in Asunción was the appointed judge. And if he was judged fit, that could only mean Christ had forgiven him. In this way his problem could be solved for him by someone else. He had watched the happy priests joking together and realized that they were all united in obedience. It would be a good life here among the Guarani, with the Jesuits to keep spiritual watch over him. Perhaps he would be permitted to stay, not as an ordained priest but as a lay brother, having taken his vows. It would be good to die at the mission, without ever again running the risk of doing what was unacceptable to Christ.

In his tiny cell, where enormous insects veered into the candle flame to fall dead with shriveled wings, and where a ceaseless whispering of wind could be heard from the leaves outside, and the steady croak of frogs, he repeated a passage he had conned from Sebastian's Bible. "Though I have all faith, so that I could remove mountains, and have not love, I am nothing. And though I bestow all my goods to feed the poor, and though I give my body to be burned, and have not love, it profiteth me nothing."

If Christ accepted him as a lay brother, he would accept him as a being capable of love. "Love suffereth long, and is kind; love envieth not; love vaunteth not itself; love is not puffed up . . ." Love, say, for the Guarani. They told the truth.

A black beetle banked in through the window and droned on toward the flame. He blew out the candle, and listened to the beetle careering around the cell. Then came a steady drone that sank into silence. It was away, and his heart took flight with it.

"When I was a child, I spake as a child, I understood as a child, I thought as a child; but when I became a man, I put away childish things . . ."

Catherine, his mother, had told him that.

"And now abideth faith, hope, love, these three; but the greatest of these is love."

He went to Gabriel's cell, to present his request in the name of his love for the Guarani.

Gabriel was incensed. He lit his candle and asked, "Now

what in the name of Michael has put this into your head?"

"If Christ accepts me as a lay brother, I shall know that he accepts me at the mass."

Heavens above, but the fellow was no better than an idiot! "But it wouldn't be Christ who accepted you. It would be only Father Ribiro in Asunción."

"That I know."

"Then don't you know that if you made your application he would judge you as one man judges another?"

"But Christ would speak through Father Ribiro."

A man with the heart of a child! Gabriel asked Mendoza searching questions about Philippo and Carlotta and the souls he had sold into slavery and the helpless girls he had violated. Then he warned, "If Father Ribiro did permit you to take your vows, you would start right at the bottom and almost certainly remain there. Do you realize that?"

"It would not matter to me."

"I will write to the Father Provincial, seeking his opinion."

Mendoza went, leaving Gabriel to ponder the irony of the situation. When the Guarani saw Mendoza take the mass, they would all take it, too, and proclaim themselves Christians. Mendoza had been guilty of enormous crimes against them, but in their minds he had a special place. Gabriel dispatched a long and complicated letter to Ribiro.

It took four months to reach the Father Provincial, who roared with laughter at the array of saints and fathers whom Gabriel had mustered, first on one hand and then on the other. It was clear the writer longed for the request to be granted, and he obliged with an affirmative response, which cost him two hours' effort in the composition, as he knew it would be gone through with a mental tooth-comb. Like the other Jesuits who knew Gabriel, Ribiro regarded him as a nagging saint.

On receipt of the letter, Gabriel sent for Mendoza. "Are you still sure?"

"Yes, Father."

"Well, now the answer has come. Go away and spend to-night thinking it over. In the morning you will be received."

And so, the next morning in the presence of all the Jesuits and the assembled tribe, Mendoza was accepted as a lay brother and received the mass. Then Hacugh also took communion and many other Guarani after him, and Gabriel thanked God.

Mendoza lay down and slept. He dreamed of Philippo, who in the dream was dancing, and of his smiling mother washing the cane matting. Upon awaking, he knew that they approved of what he had done. His thoughts then turned to Carlotta, and he was thankful when the blaze of memories faded away.

Hacugh presented himself to the shaman. "I am a Christian." Tanretopra gave him a piercing look, nodded, and turned away. That day he moved a short distance out of the village and, with two others to help him, built himself a shelter with a matting roof, high in a tree. There he sat day after day. He was there when the sun came up and when it went down, sometimes alone, sometimes with his two companions staring at him.

Part
Three

14

SOLEMNLY, SEBASTIÃO JOSÉ de Carvalho e Mello, soon to be Marquês de Pombal, backed out of the bedchamber of His Majesty King Joseph Emmanuel of Portugal. Then, when the door was closed, he smiled up at the ornate ceiling. Carvalho returned the salute of the officer on guard outside the royal door, and proceeded with a firm tread beneath a row of lamps illuminating a series of paintings in which pompously benign generals, watched by angels, were depicted in the act of extending clemency to the kneeling or prostrate figures of alien wretches, ignorant of the True Faith, whom they had just defeated. Carvalho, who regarded the True Faith as an irrelevance and the Church as an obstruction, found these glorifications of the servants of the Crown old-fashioned. Here on the third floor of the Royal Palace in Lisbon, he wondered whether subsequent memorials to his own service would display the same provincial taste, for Carvalho—still only fifty-one years old and decidedly the most useful man to know at court—prided himself on his cosmopolitan sensibility.

His views on religion were particularly *au courant,* and he stopped to stare contemptuously at the portrayal of an event being celebrated by heavenly trumpeters while on earth below enraptured bishops were simultaneously thanking God for it—to wit, the nativity of King John of Portugal, which in Carvalho's view had been a national disaster. The bishops struck him as stupid-looking—stupid but also crafty, like all clerical advisers, he told himself, especially Jesuits. Carvalho was no deist. Provided people in authority did not take it seriously, religion in his opinion probably did more good than harm. What harm it could do in high places, however, he had witnessed to his cost during the reign of the credulous dotard the baby in the painting had grown to be.

In his last years, the fat, incompetent, devout old man had been invisible within a crowd of pale-faced clerics who had deliberately prevented him from even glimpsing the serviceable Carvalho, who was waiting in the wings. Well, wherever he might be now, bad fortune to him and all success to his chubby successor, the rosy-faced Joseph, whom Carvalho had just left snuggling down with his mistress in the royal bed. As heir apparent, Joseph had already chosen Carvalho to be his confidant, and devoted as he had always been to the less energetic of the deadly sins, he was not hard to humor now that he was on the throne.

So reflected Carvalho, recalling the scene in the royal bedchamber while at that same moment his royal master lay back with lips parted to admit the cherries fed to him, one by one, by a choice companion. If Louis of France could conduct his amours in public, so, too, Joseph had regally decided, could he. All that mattered was to make it absolutely clear who was in the saddle. He smiled domineeringly and congratulated himself on the lesson he had just taught Carvalho. Carvalho might be very clever, but he would rack those brains of his in vain to work out how his master had found out about the secret meeting he was off to have with the envoy from Brazil.

"Good night, Carvalho." The king had waited until the lamps had all been lowered and his minister was about to leave him to his pleasure before delivering his thrust. "By the way, as you're just going to meet him, remind the envoy from Brazil that he takes leave of me tomorrow in the morning, not in the afternoon as we arranged at first. Which brings me to another point, Carvalho. I'd like to be informed officially when you arrange meetings like this in future, instead of having to rely on my other sources to find out what you are getting up to."

The astonished minister could not conceal his consternation. His response, the king recalled with pleasure, had been gratifyingly confused. Well, it would do him good to realize a monarch had more ears than other people. As the woman (whom he had decided to make a *duquesa*) pressed herself against him, King Joseph decided to reward Carvalho's secretary, his source on this occasion, with a little cash. He rolled over and said, "No, sweetheart, we'll have some wine," finding that statecraft made him thirsty. In point of fact it was Carvalho, now passing down the corridor to his suite of rooms, who had himself instructed his secretary to tell the king about his private meeting with the Brazilian envoy. Evidently the fellow had been convincing. He must remember to congratulate him; congratulations spoke louder than coin, and the king would be bound to pay the rascal something, in any case. It would be overdoing it to reward him twice over for one trick. Another thought followed. Suppose his secretary decided to change sides in earnest? There was nothing to hinder him. But the fellow knew what was good for him. He, of all people, knew where the real power lay.

When he got to his rooms, the minister found the envoy waiting. He bustled in, offering wine, and then settled down to listen to familiar arguments. The envoy was a member of the Council of Brazil, and these Brazilian councillors all said the same thing. This one came fresh to the customary performance but had no new notes to sound. He opened by lamenting the diminishing supply of silver and gold to the Royal Treasury. The mines were down to a mere trickle now. Heaven knew where it had all come from in the first place! But the problems of the Royal Treasury, he declared angrily, were of no interest to the grandees of Brazil—if one could call them grandees when one could not imagine them in a European court. Descendants of mere traders or civil servants, they put on what they absurdly imagined to be aristocratic airs. Of course, half of them passed their entire lives without paying civilization a single visit.

But their rusticity was only a source of amusement. What caused concern to the loyal subjects of the king of Portugal was the grandees' attitude to the colony. They seemed to think it belonged as much to them as it did to the Crown, and, as they were on the spot, no project, however beneficial to the Treasury, had the least chance of succeeding if they did not like it. Unless their selfish interests were involved, no problem caused them any concern.

Take the slave trade, for example. As long as slaves were available, the grandees cared nothing about where the slaves were coming from. The scandal was that in a Portuguese territory nearly all the suppliers were foreigners. Take Colonia del Sacramento. The slaves docking there flew the flags of every seagoing nation except Portugal—England, France, the Low Countries. As a result, the profits of the trade all went abroad. Thank God at last for the Treaty of Madrid! Things would start to get better once all those thousands of Guarani, whom the Jesuits kept secluded on their missions in Spanish territory, were brought onto the market.

Courteously, impassively, Carvalho inclined his ear. This information was relatively new, but he had heard it before as well. He was learning nothing, but then he had not expected to. What mattered was to send the speaker away with the belief that he had a friend at Court who understood him. This he proceeded to do by thanking his visitor for clarifying his ideas with illuminating arguments and unrivaled information, and then rising, as a mark of favor, personally conducting him all the way to the farthest door and remaining there to give him a farewell wave as he disappeared into the gloom of the corridor.

Carvalho quietly closed the door and consulted his pocket watch—made in Augsburg. It was half past twelve. In another half-hour a visitor the king knew nothing about was due—the last of the day and the most important. The minister had arranged a meeting with the Jesuit Father Altamirano, who stood as high in the inner councils of the Pope as in those of the General of his order. This was going to be an encounter with a foeman worthy of his steel. The meaning of this priest's words was not to be discovered in a dictionary but by looking behind them. Well, Carvalho was ready. He had taken the first important step in his career in diplomacy.

He returned to his salon and sat down comfortably to wait, folding across his chest the muscled arms of one who had been a keen swordsman in his early manhood. With his confident bearing and his autocratic stare, standing six feet in his stockinged feet, he made a formidable figure—a fact he frequently confirmed before a looking glass. It was not, however, his physical presence that created the strongest impression. From his youth, everybody had been struck by the sense of some unquenchable fire in him. Impatience and resentment had left their mark on him since then, but the flame within had not gone out. Age was powerless against it. It was still burning on the altar of ambition.

His first attempt to make his mark was as a hanger-on of aristocratic rowdies. When he arrived in the capital, to the neglect of his small estate, he found the Duque de Cadaval had earned a reputation by rioting in the streets at night with a gang of regimental officers, so the young Carvalho attached himself to them and did his best to behave no less disgracefully than his models. Nobody was more feared by shopkeepers. The Duque de Cadaval took note of him accordingly. Nevertheless, despite his convincing impersonation of a lounging bully, he loathed the role and vowed that when his day came as he was sure it would, he would stamp out privileged delinquency.

What sharpened his hatred of his lordly accomplices was their refusal fully to accept his claim to be one of them. As a Carvalho he was a member of the nobility of the sword, but they regarded him as nothing better than a farmer. He loathed them all, realizing they did nothing with all their privileges. Yet how he envied them for not having to earn their power! What bliss to be a member of one of the dozen ruling families of Portugal! To enjoy unchallengeable authority from the moment of his birth, even if he was born a halfwit, as so many of them were. (Intermarrying down the centuries, what else could be expected?)

It was not only envy that he felt for them. There was disgust, too, at the spectacle they presented, eating with their fingers, which they then wiped on damask napkins worth one year's income of an honest tradesman, or a year's rent for a fine town house. Many of them could not even read and write. They mismanaged their estates. They could not even drink without incapacitating themselves. They knew little of Brazil and nothing of the world outside it. They had to ask the king's permission if they wished to go abroad, but hardly any did, in any case: Outside Portugal they knew of no families blue-blooded enough to consort with. And yet these squalid no-bodies were repositories of unquestioned power—together with the ecclesiastical hierachy!

The ecclesiastics were even more dangerous, however. They were more cunning, and the superstitions they fostered enabled them to maintain a steady stranglehold on the privi-leged. This was particularly true of the favorite confessors of kings, princes, and dukes, namely the Jesuits. When death was approaching some royal sinner, sweating in abject fear, a Jesuit could make him do exactly what he wanted. Those schemers knew what they were doing when they took such pains over education. It was madness to entrust responsibility to anybody who believed in hell.

Ironically it was by means of the only ecclesiastical con-nection in his family that Carvalho contrived to break into the outer circle of power. The only use the Duque de Cadaval could find for him was to toss him to the constables when the needs of justice called for the infliction of punishment on an aristocratic scapegoat, and thus Carvalho abandoned his first patron. At that point, he bethought him that his uncle, on his mother's side, was a priest, and he started to pay strict ob-servance to evening attendance at his church, allowing himself just the hint of a smile at his own behavior. His approving relative rewarded his hypocrisy by bringing him to the atten-tion of no less a person than the late king's confessor, a Jesuit who saw through Carvalho immediately. Continuously prom-ising that something would be done for the young careerist, this devious cleric kept him idly dangling for three years. Nevertheless he was dangling where he wished to be. He seized this chance to study the ways of great ministers and eccelesiastics, and the spectacle of power stoked the blaze of his ambition higher. In the end, tired of being trifled with, he went back to his modest estate in a rage.

But life in retirement was impossible for him now. The passion to succeed was only intensified by the boredom, which outdoor pursuits and solitary reading in his library failed to relieve. Fragments of Court gossip, trickling into the depths of the countryside, served to remind him of what he was missing. Inevitably he was driven back to Lisbon, where he looked about him with an eye that was now as coldly calculating as success demanded. It alighted on Teresa Norhona, straitlaced and grave-faced, in no way pleasant to the officers but, as he realized, ready to fall in love with whoever might make a plausible show of being in love with her. Another fact he registered was that she was a niece of the Conde de Arcoa.

It took Carvalho just two months to reduce Teresa to readiness to elope. He carefully weighed up the odds and decided to risk it. Then he married her and retired with her to her small country estate, from which she wrote pleading letters on his behalf to her uncle. For months Carvalho waited to see which way the dice he had cast would fall. The marriage might have meant lifelong banishment from Lisbon, but in the end Arcoa summoned Carvalho to a family meeting where, after a thorough dressing-down, he was offered the post of minister plenipotentiary to the Court of St. James's.

Carvalho knew he had his wife to thank for the appointment. Nevertheless, he did not take her with him to the embassy in London. She had served his turn, and at last his foot was on the ladder. After all, he had never loved her.

Those who had sent him had not the least idea what use he could be to Portugal in England, a far-off corner of Europe, not to be compared with Spain, for example, or France, let alone Portugal herself, mistress of half the globe. The English monarchs were not even Catholic, but members of some petty ruling house of a minor Protestant state in Germany. Their aristocrats for the most part were a crowd of *nouveaux riches*. A man might rise by his own efforts to become one of their viscounts, or even a duke like the soldier Marlborough. It was a thoroughly upstart kingdom. Carvalho ought to find it to his taste.

England burst upon him like a revelation. Unlike his masters, he was not reluctant to draw comparisons between the Empire of Portugal, crippled by conventions he regarded as preposterous and rituals he found superstitious, on the one hand, and on the other the bustling, noisy, energetic and above all prospering Kingdom of England and Scotland. What if the blood of the royal house of Hanover was not to be compared

with that of Hapsburgs and Bourbons? In this particular kingdom, the salient point about the royal house was that it was of
no account. The business of government was in the hands of
people who saw the direction their country had to move in to
achieve prosperity. Even the English equivalent of great aristocrats devoted their energies to their estates, enlarging their
fortunes by improving yields and livestock. Some of them
even employed machinery in their fields. And there was no
shortage of money. Instead, ingenious ways and means had
been devised to make it available—not for the poor, of
course, but for enterprising people who knew how to set
money to work, for this was a commercial kingdom. You
found no antique regulations here, of the kind that were regarded as so sacred in hide-bound Portugal. The merchants
might not be in charge of ministries—they were too busy
making fortunes—but the whole kingdom was run in their
interest.

Nevertheless, his ceremonious manners stood him in good
stead. Apparently the English thought of his country as a relic
of the days of chivalry. He contrived to turn this condescen-
sion to his own advantage. Alas, he had no English, but luckily French was acceptable in enlightened circles and he spoke
it fluently. He learned to speak the name of Newton rever-
ently, and came to understand that his old instinctive distrust
of the Church did him great credit. One English expression he
did learn, and made it his watch-word: *self-interest*. It meant
the same as selfishness, but was commendable, as he had
always secretly believed, even in Portugal.

He was not so interested in philosophy however as in the
competence of bankers, the acumen of brokers, and the inge-
nuity of new manufacturers. Fascinated he observed a novel
world springing up, of turnpike roads, canals, shipyards and
mills, glass-houses, kilns, and breweries. He vowed that this
would be the future of Portugal as well, if he had anything to
do with it. Self-interest was the key, and that was something
he understood thoroughly.

On his journey back to Lisbon, at the end of five stimulating years, Carvalho was filled with admiration and envy at the
spectacle of the Thames Estuary, thronged with every descrip-

tion of ship, from great Indiamen to colliers, flying many different flags and sailing to and from all quarters of the world.

In the course of his residence in London he had repeatedly received intimations, occasionally laughing, sometimes contemptuous, but to him always humiliating, that his own country was no longer a power of any account, but merely the decrepit ruin of a bygone kingdom with an empire hanging on to it, waiting to be taken by a more efficient state. He dug his nails into his palms and vowed that Portugal would regain her proper place in Europe, thanks to the firm hand of a master at the helm—which would have to be his own.

Back in Lisbon he found nothing had changed in his absence. Ignorant of the way things were in the rest of the world, and oblivious of the cleansing breeze of self-interest that was blowing away the cobwebs of superstition in the rest of Europe, ecclesiastics joined complaisantly with aristocrats in a petty display of useless pomp, effecting nothing, ignorantly devoted to antiquated rites that spelled their doom. Particularly offensive was the display of ecclesiastical power at Court, where John V had become the willing puppet of creeping priests. The ministers had no policies worth the name. They were capable only of repeating maneuvers that were already ceasing to be relevant in the previous century.

But woe to any man who questioned them! Woe in particular to the ambassador freshly returned from a den of thieves and moneylenders, even if he had impudently contrived to connect himself by marriage to that pillar of the establishment, the Conde de Arcoa. Carvalho spent a few unhappy months at home in the company of his wife Teresa and then went to Court to find himself an outcast. He made the only move open to him: He began, as stealthily as possible, to devote his attention to Prince Joseph. Perhaps in ignorance of this development or, more probably, to thwart it, he was sent on an obscure mission to Vienna. Once again he left his wife behind, though not without a scene this time.

On arriving in Vienna, he was chagrined to discover that his mission did not entitle him to the ambassadorial status he had enjoyed in London. His chagrin was due not only to loss of dignity but to practical disadvantages as well: He was no longer immune from proceedings for debt. As a result, nagging anxieties were added to the agonies of a thwarted ambition, which he began seriously to consider abandoning for country retirement in the style of an English squire. It was at this stage, as he liked to say later when people hung on his words, that fortune did him the one solitary favor that she ever granted him: The wife he had left behind in Portugal conveniently died.

The convenience was romantic. He had fallen in love, and his love was passionately returned. The young woman who found this mature and somber lover irresistible was not endowed to restore his financial fortunes. She was poor, but that did not prevent him from loving her. She was also a Hapsburg, which was a more serious obstacle. It meant his suit could not succeed without the approval of the Empress Maria Teresa herself. Inquiries to the Queen of Portugal, however, elicited the information that Carvalho's blood just marginally qualified him for the honor he sought, and he returned to Portugal with a partner he could share his inmost thoughts with. No longer as tempestuous as before, he soberly set about securing his position with the heir apparent, Prince Joseph.

Suddenly King John was stricken with a flux. His death, however, took time. It was over a year later that he was gathered to his forebears. Meanwhile, month by month, to Carvalho's secret fury, the king's Jesuit advisers prayed night and day for the fat old man's benighted soul, and all the Court made a great show of joining them in their petition. Prince Joseph held himself most meek, and Carvalho walked warily. Nevertheless, remorselessly, a new faction was forming around them and growing so that when, at the very end, the dying king gave signs of recovery there was widespread concealed alarm. The improvement in the monarch's health was fleeting, however, and at the age of fifty-one Carvalho at last found himself in possession of the power he had so long been conscious of deserving.

The late king had done little to merit the tolling and chanting that now filled the air, and, knowing how little affection he had inspired, Carvalho sneered at the mourning that overspread the entire Court. There was no time to waste on hypocrisy. Those whom the new king had called to power must bestir themselves to drag the kingdom into the light of day. The first task was to destroy the influence of the Church.

Carvalho was appointed minister for foreign affairs, the empire, and war. The new prime minister was a very happy choice, being an innocuous dotard whose antique presence would serve as a cloak for innovations. The only other minister who ranked above Carvalho was a courtier of the old school, whose interest in society was confined to pedigrees.

The field was clear for Carvalho, and he had his program ready. At home he started by tackling the immediate debts the old king had incurred as a consequence of his munificence to the Church. The time-honored way of dealing with such a burden was to perpetuate it; Carvalho's was to clear it. Then, faithful to his early memories, he clamped down on gentlemanly street rowdyism in a series of harsh edicts, which he then made sure were strictly enforced.

Pope Benedict XIV, whom Carvalho suspected to be an atheist, had rewarded John V with the title Most Faithful King. Carvalho's first adventure in the field of foreign affairs was to claim that Joseph Emanuel now inherited this honorific and, accordingly, to refuse to accept missives from His Holiness that were not properly addressed. This was, however, no more than a mild foretaste of the treatment he was to hand out to abbeys and religious orders at home.

A more serious diplomatic problem was posed him by the Treaty of Madrid. As he had inherited this agreement with Spain from his predecessors, he had initially been tempted to abrogate it. The treaty sought to end the long-established friction between the two empires in South America. Carvalho at first could see no harm in permitting that friction to continue. On closer examination of the terms and circumstances, however, he perceived that the treaty was all to Portugal's advantage at the expense of Spain. Centuries ago, a Pope had used a pair of calipers to divide a map of the world into two halves, one for each of the two Catholic kingdoms, drawing an imaginary line between Brazil, which went to Portugal, and the Río de la Plata, which fell to Spain. The recently concluded Treaty of Madrid shifted this boundary. Portugal was to lose the haven of Colonia del Sacramento to Spain. In return, Spain was to transfer to Portugal certain territories, which included the areas occupied by the Jesuit missions.

With the eye for profit and loss he had acquired in the city of London, Carvalho calculated that Portugal benefited by both halves of the exchange. Even the loss of Colonia del Sacramento must be accounted a gain. In the first place, although it was a port, it contributed nothing to the Treasury, and it was of no commercial benefit to Portugal. The only people to make commercial use of it were the English, French, and Dutch slave traders about whom the envoy had just been enviously complaining. Moreover, as Carvalho also learned from three naval captains whom he took trouble to consult, the place was a nest of pirates whom an up-to-date administration would have to eliminate.

That would be a difficult and expensive business, however, calling for a full-scale naval expedition. Far from being a source of revenue, therefore, Colonia del Sacramento constituted a heavy liability to whichever monarchy was responsible for it and that was not what colonial possessions were for. Fortunately, if the liability was passed on to the Spaniards they could be counted on to meet it because the Spanish trade suffered the greatest losses to the pirates.

The surrender of territory by the Portuguese therefore landed the Spaniards with a liability. The surrender of territory by Spain, on the other hand, endowed the Portuguese with an enormous asset. Carvalho found it hard to believe the Spaniards would execute the treaty in good faith. To make sure, he cautiously sounded out the opinion of Spaniards on the spot by establishing contact with the Spanish captain general at Asunción. He found this dignitary, whose name was Cabeza, eager to become a subject of the Crown of Portugal, for reasons of self-interest which were after Carvalho's own heart. A further point of sympathy was Cabeza's hostility to the Society of Jesus.

The Jesuits, as he now learned, had caused an artificial shortage of slaves in the colony by sheltering thousands of Guarani tribesmen in their missions, thus keeping them off the open slave market. The existing Spanish law forbidding slavery was bad enough, and the settlers were counting on the Crown of Portugal to abolish it. Nevertheless, it was possible to escape the prohibition in practice while observing it in the letter. What could not be infringed, however, were the peculiar rights granted to the Jesuits by the Crown of Spain, because the Jesuits were there to protect those rights. As a result thousands of Guarani idled their lives away under Jesuit protection instead of making a contribution to the prosperity of the colony by working for the industrious settlers. As long as the colony remained a Spanish possession, the captain general could do nothing to rectify this deplorable state of affairs. For this reason the colonists all hailed the Treaty of Madrid as their salvation.

Carvalho discovered that Cabeza was a curious fellow. A fouth-generation colonial, apparently he did not feel the slightest desire to visit Europe. Nevertheless, he was clearly going to be useful. He had an eye for essentials. For instance, he had already estimated and reported that taxes on the land now belonging to the Jesuit missions could be raised to ten times their present sum as soon as the Jesuits were deprived of their control over them. He was a good Catholic—quite devout, apparently—and yet commendably possessed by a banked-down fire against Saint Ignatius Loyola and his mischievous Order. Carvalho reflected with satisfaction that the Jesuits' enemies were increasing every day. Madrid itself—Carvalho was sure of it—would be secretly relieved to see the last of those missions. They were a bulwark of the old paternalistic order and had no place in the settlers' more up-to-date view of what colonies were for.

The Jesuits, however, still remained to be dealt with. There ought to be a special section of the law dealing with sanctimonious meddlers who thought they were a law unto themselves —a legal means of placing them where they deserved to be, out of harm's way. Jail was the proper place for people who tried to create a state of their own within every nation that was prepared to tolerate their presence. The priests even collected their own revenue! Well, Carvalho would be happy to knock one more nail into their coffin.

South America was really the only place where they still counted as a force to be reckoned with. Everywhere else they were adroitly giving way without appearing to do so. They knew their days were numbered, just as their priestly claptrap had at last gone out of fashion. (Of course, if truth were told, they had never believed a word of it themselves. Carvalho had a deep respect for them as politicians.) In private nowadays, if their tastes inclined that way—or even publicly, when it suited their purposes—they were not above revealing an acquaintance with the new philosophy.

In these circumstances Carvalho held a good hand. The Pope knew very well what was brewing in the courts of Europe and did not want to provoke a crisis over the issue of the Society of Jesus. The General of the order also wished to avoid a confrontation. His response to the Treaty of Madrid, therefore, had been to depute a special representative to visit South America and ascertain the treaty's consequences for the Jesuit missions. In view of the gneral situation, it was not hard to guess what the answer to this local question had to be. Naturally the removal of the Jesuits would have to be a lengthy process. No doubt significant local interests were inclined to the *status quo*. That was why the veteran negotiator, Father Altamirano, had been selected for the operation.

Carvalho had not yet met Altamirano, but he had collected information, including the detail that the preferred indulgence of this priest, despite his almost venerable years, was dalliance. Also, according to reliable informants, he was not above taking a bribe. Nevertheless this corrupt priest was not only the trusted agent of his general but was also privy to the inner councils of the Holy Father. He therefore undoubtedly knew which way the wind was blowing and could be relied upon to reach the conclusion he was being sent cross the ocean to arrive at. In any case, if he chose not to cooperate . . . ! Seated now in his salon, awaiting the arrival of this very special dignitary, Carvalho struck the globe beside his chair a smack in the region of Asunción, setting it spinning.

15

Altamirano, approaching at that moment down the gloomy corridor, treading softly in the wake of a tiptoeing undersecretary, did not affect the dark habit that might have been expected of him. Indeed, the figure he cut was suited to more vivacious, brilliant surroundings. Due allowance, he was thinking, should of course be made for official mourning for the defunct king—a deplorable creature! Nevertheless, the total lack of social activity in Lisbon as early as midnight did compel certain comparisons—for instance, with Versailles. He allowed himself a smile of reminiscence, which he prudently converted into one of gratification as he followed the undersecretary into Carvalho's anteroom.

His guide departed to announce their arrival, carefully closing the door behind him, leaving the alert Jesuit to look about him. It was a businesslike chamber, with a row of chairs to accommodate a considerable number of people who might be compelled to wait hours for the privilege of seeing the minister. At the long desk he pictured an overworked secretary, delighted by his position, sitting all day. A painting hung on one wall, but, moving to examine it, he found it dull, even though the artist, as he noted with approval, was a Frenchman. The subject, a group of councillors, was admittedly unpromising, but a perceptive brush would have made something more amusing of it.

Suddenly Carvalho stood bidding him good morning in French from the door of his salon and then advancing into the anteroom to take his hand. The undersecretary stood inconspicuously waiting at the inner door to close it quietly behind their backs as they entered the salon.

Carvalho indicated an upright chair and stood waiting, a

masterful figure, for his visitor to be seated. "Forgive me, Father, for detaining you one moment. I must deal with this while it is still in my mind." He picked up a document from a table. Altamirano, outwardly respectful, inwardly entertained, watched his performance of wrinkling his brows at it. Meanwhile the minister was assessing the papal representative. He had often sneered at Jesuit Order's military pretensions, but there was something in the settled expression on this one's face that reminded him of an experienced commander. He signed the document carefully and put it on a pile. Then, seating himself and casually crossing his legs, he asked, "Have they made you comfortable here in Lisbon?"

Altamirano realized that the man who had made this polite enquiry knew about the girl awaiting him at his lodging. "Thank you. My Order has arranged everything as it saw fit. It is most considerate of you to think of my comfort, with so many other things to keep in mind."

"Ah, yes!" Sighing, Carvalho riffled the pile of papers on his desk. "Alas, I have to get through all this before I see the king tomorrow morning." Ruefully he shook his head and shrugged.

Courting scrutiny, Altamirano looked about the room and nodded in the direction of a picture behind the desk. "That looks interesting. May I?"

"Of course."

The Jesuit rose and, with a natural gesture, picked up a candelabrum from a side table on his way to examine the painting.

"It's by Martin Scaffner," his host informed him.

"Really!" Altamirano exclaimed with studied surprise. "Was it, perhaps, your personal choice?"

"None of the paintings was my personal choice."

So there was nothing to be learned from them, the Jesuit reflected. Carvalho knew how to secure himself from observation. He sat down with an air of frankness to meet another polite inquiry.

"I trust your passage to Asunción has been taken care of?"

"By your Admiralty. Yes, many thanks."

"I have been corresponding with Señor Cabeza."

"Señor Cabeza?"

"The captain general in Asunción."

"Thank you for reminding me."

"He is in favor of the transfer."

"So I should hope, Senhor Carvalho."

"I mean, as it affects the territories at present administered by your missions."

"I see. Thank you for explaining."

"So you see, you should have no difficulty in reaching a decision."

"If only the question had been settled in the treaty. Then there really would be no difficulty."

"Are you of the view that the will of Ferdinand of Spain still presents a difficulty?"

Changing his position, Altamirano seemed caught by the painting on the far end of the room. "That really is a masterpiece. By Tiepolo, isn't it? Superb!"

"Indeed." Carvalho gave no sign of impatience at the Jesuit's crafty change of subject.

"Superb! Yes, your splendid Admiralty has seen to everything. Do you suppose the voyage will prove as onerous as they make out?"

"I would say the burden the Holy Father has entrusted to you is not a light one."

Altamirano fluttered his hands deprecatingly, with a rueful smile.

"But Ferdinand of Spain was always an obedient son of the Church." Carvalho went on, easing the conversation back on course.

"Of a certainty, yes."

"Then do you think we have to be governed by his will?"

"Is there a provision in the will that you wish to ignore?"

"Perhaps you will ask Cabeza."

"Assuredly," Altamirano answered in his frankest style. "I am going to Asunción to ask questions."

"Then you will hear from Cabeza that the missions should be included in the colony."

"Indeed? And that would involve several hundred thousand natives, I am told."

"You are told? You surely know."

"My dear sir," the Jesuit said, "I know nothing without being told."

"There are about three hundred thousand natives on the missions."

"If you say it, then it must indeed be so." Altamirano smiled thinly. "No wonder the hidalgos are so ready to change kings."

"As the treaty, may I remind you, requires them to. And you must understand that, as matters stand, these mission natives make no contributions to the Treasury."

"Yes, I believe I have heard that. And what *do* all these natives on the missions do?"

"Grow maté and make musical instruments, apparently, in the mission workshops."

"Well, it sounds as if it should all be very interesting to see."

"But what is your opinion? Should the mission lands be part of the colony or should the mission natives be allowed these special privileges for no good reason?"

"I shall listen to every opinion on that subject at an open hearing when I get there." So saying, Altamirano closed his mouth in another smile, an innocent-looking one, seemingly unconscious that the question he had just avoided was the only one which interested either of them.

Carvalho tried a new tack. "There is another side of the bargain, as you must know. On our side, we are giving Colonia del Sacramento to the Spaniards."

"Yes. Tell me. What sort of place is this Sacramento?"

"A nest of pirates."

The Jesuit nodded. "So I have been told." A thought appeared to strike him. "I shall beg the captain to keep a sharp lookout when we approach those shores."

"The pirates will give you a wide berth. Don't worry."

"Thanks to your naval escort. I am most grateful for all your help, and also for this instructive meeting. One thing I have heard already," Altamirano continued smoothly, "is that this part of South America produces a steady stream of gold. Can this be true?"

One of Carvalho's qualities as a statesman was an ability to distinguish the possible from the absurd in rumor. "No," he said flatly. "You only hear that because whenever the word 'gold' is uttered, His Majesty's advisers prick up their ears."

"Very naturally, too," commented Altamirano, shooting a glance at Carvalho out of the corner of his eye. "Not all your royal master's advisers are as disinterested as you."

"I am not a man to dismiss the thought of gold lightly," the minister assured him. "Gold is always a welcome addition to the Treasury, but where could this gold they all talk about be coming from? Not from the earlier inhabitants. The Río de la Plata isn't Peru. You'll find no ancient ruins there that used to be ablaze with bullion, and there aren't any mines in the jungle either. Even if the gold were lying there, waiting to be extracted, the natives wouldn't know what to do about it." He shot a sharp glance at his questioner. "Unless it was on the mission lands and the holy Jesuits showed them how to get at it. There is a story going to that effect, you know."

"I assure you, there is no question of that happening."

As if you would tell me, if there were, Carvalho thought. He knew there was no gold there on the authority of the unfailing laws of nature. Aloud he agreed. "I believe you, although it does need something like a gold mine to explain the high returns you get on those missions of yours. They all seem to make half as much again as comparable plantations. If they aren't running secret gold mines, how do they do it?"

"Until I have been there and seen for myself, I can have no idea. Why don't you tell me what Cabeza has to say about it?"

"The explanation is simple, according to him. The missions have taken all the best land."

"And do you believe him?"

"I have no means of knowing. No servant of the Crown is permitted to enter a mission, not even Cabeza himself, the captain general!"

"In accordance with an enactment of King Ferdinand, that is so."

"As you say, by an enactment of a bygone king. It is by a similar enactment that slavery was made illegal in those territories," Carvalho pointed out, "but surely you would not contend that slavery will continue to be illegal after the Treaty of Madrid comes into effect." He smiled his most superficial smile.

"Slavery will of course become legal," Altamirano agreed, returning his smile, "in the territory transferred to Portuguese administration. The question that still remains for me to settle, alas, is whether the mission lands should be included in that territory." He sighed.

Carvalho felt the time had come for him to show displeasure. He frowned. "In your honest opinion, is there really a serious possibility of a decision against inclusion?"

"Senhor Carvalho," Altamirano answered, mockingly wagging his finger, "you can hardly suppose I am traveling halfway across the world in my declining years to come to a foregone conclusion."

"But nevertheless, just on the face of it, you must find yourself inclining one way or the other."

Altamirano tugged his waistcoat. He was beginning to enjoy himself. "Unfortunately," he confessed, "I find I have two turns of mind."

"Indeed!" Carvalho responded dryly. "Which turn inclines you to exempt the missions from our administration, may I ask?"

"My theological turn."

"And will you take that turn of mind with you to the public hearing in Asunción?"

"Undoubtedly," the Jesuit said, again tugging his waistcoat. "I am never without it. But then again, my other turn of mind is always with me, too."

"And what do you call that one?"

"My other turn of mind is distinctly practical," Altamirano gravely informed him.

"And what would that one incline you to?"

Altamirano again wagged his finger. "Oh, as to that I must wait and see. It will depend on the advice of practical-minded people on the spot. I'm sure the colony is full of them, and they will all attend my meeting and tell me what to do."

"I promise you, they will tell you to abolish the missions so that the whole area can be opened up to enterprise."

"Thank you, thank you. I shall store that promise away. But of course I must also listen to what any theologically minded people have to say to me. I expect to meet some of them as well."

Carvalho sat back in his chair and looked at his visitor with alarmed respect. He had hoped to catch an inkling of the directive Altamirano had been given by the Pope, but found himself no wiser than he had been at the start of the interview. Indeed he was now less sure about it. And no doubt he had also received additional instructions from his General.

"A glass of wine?" Carvalho offered.

"With pleasure. From a Portuguese vineyard?"

"Spanish." The minister rose to pour the wine. "If it does so fall out that you have occasion to withdraw your missionaries from the colony, whereabouts in Europe will you put them?" He approached his opponent with the glass.

Instead of answering, Altamirano held his wine up to the candelabrum and asked what region it was from.

"Granada."

"Your health!" Altamirano took a sip. "Oh, excellent! I remember being particularly appreciative of a wine from Granada in the days of my youth, at the Escorial."

"Would you perhaps take them to Rome?" Carvalho persisted.

"The missionaries, you mean, if they have to leave America? I fear that Rome as it is nowadays might give some of them a shock." He shook his head as if amused.

"Please believe we could arrange something very acceptable for them here in Portugal. You may count upon it."

"Thank you. Oh, thank you. That is most kind. I shall certainly remember that—if the need should arise, of course."

"We could offer them a generous endowment, and their labors would be clerical, not physical. They will be assigned to study."

"And teaching?"

"Preparing men for the business of life is no work for priests. My own opinion, I must tell you frankly, is that your order is too much involved in secular pursuits—even in state affairs sometimes."

Altamirano made an exaggerated show of thinking this opinion over before responding. "Ah, well," he said after a moment, "you and some others may be right to say so. I must confess, however, it is a view I do not share."

He leaned forward in the manner of one who is prepared to learn, provoking his host to a prolonged harangue the memory of which subsequently caused him some dissatisfaction with himself, in which he dwelt particularly on the Jesuits' predilection for the spiritual guidance of the great.

Altamirano bowed his head appreciatively. "I have heard it said," he admitted, "that in France things sometimes are indeed as you describe, but until I heard this from you, I had no idea that it was going on in Portugal, too."

"In Portugal," Carvalho continued tartly, "certain men of a rational frame of mind say that the Curia should curb the activities of your Order, lest calamity befall the entire Church as a result of the presumption of a small but dangerous section."

Altamirano, who was aware of the precarious situation of his Order, recognized this as a serious warning. Stretching back in his seat, he rested his wineglass on his stomach, and said, "As it has been left to me to judge for the Church in this particular matter, you can rely on me to judge ecclesiastically, not jesuitically." His smile this time was sweet.

A clock over the fireplace struck two.

"I must leave you to your bed," the Jesuit said, "unless you have more advice to offer me."

"We have said all that can be said at this point, don't you think?" replied Carvalho. "Later, perhaps, when you have reached your decision, we may have more to say to each other. My bed, however, is another matter. Before I can give it my consideration, I must address more matters in behalf of His Majesty." He indicated the pile of papers on his desk.

"I am more fortunately placed," Altamirano confessed, thinking of the attractive young creature waiting for him at his lodging. "I will leave Your Excellency to your endless labors." He rose and went over to examine the Tiepolo again, then turned around to face his host. "Impressive," he said, thus summing up his personal impression of the minister who, he hoped, was not immune to flattery.

Carvalho rang a little bell to recall the undersecretary from the anteroom to usher out his visitor with several God-be-with-you's for his coming voyage.

Outside in a coach, rumbling over the flagged court and rattling under a threatening arch, where he was halted while the young officer of the guard poked his nose into the carriage, Altamirano sat thoughtful. Carvalho had not attempted to conceal his hostility and he had delivered a threat he might well be able to execute. He would engineer a concerted move against the Order of Jesuits throughout Europe if he did not get his way in South America. Altamirano knew that if the conflict did reach that point, Carvalho would probably succeed. On the other hand, he had also indicated—for what such hints were worth—that if the missions were subjected fully to the terms of the Treaty of Madrid, his catastrophe would be at least postponed. He decided to write a categorical report on the conversation to his General, and a less frank but no less forceful letter to His Holiness the Pope. Portugal must now be numbered among the enemies of the Faith, whatever claims might be made on behalf of its king to an honorific papal title.

Considered simply as a man, Carvalho—bureaucrat as he so boringly was—had all the telltale characteristics of the parvenu. Witness his pretense of ignoring admiration of his paintings while so obviously enjoying it. As a bureaucrat, however, he was also dangerous—one more sign, Altamirano reflected, of the enormous change that had come over Europe since he had chosen his career. In those days the director of a royal or ducal conscience had been a force to be reckoned with. Defending the Order had not been a grim battle in those days but just an agreeable intellectual amusement.

Nowadays, however, though monarchs still occupied their thrones, kingdoms were ruled by men like this one, and a religious order was too antiquated a mechanism to be incorporated into the new machinery of government. If he instituted a concerted move against the Society of Jesus throughout the courts of Europe, Carvalho was very likely to succeed.

Of course the Order itself had made things easy for him. Concentrating all its efforts on making itself indispensable to the old order, it had rendered itself suspect to the new one. Altamirano struck the window jamb of his carriage with his gloved fist, attracting the footman's attention, so that he had to change his gesture of impatience into a thoughtful stroking of the window through which he now peered into the night. Somewhere out there in the murk was the fleet that would carry him to Buenos Aires across the storm-tossed and, later, sultry South Atlantic. This was the first inordinate journey Altamirano had undertaken for the Order and the Church. He was getting old, as he would not forget to mention in his letter to the Pope.

Altamirano had no faith in the simple cures of the spirit. Some twenty years earlier he had tried treating the sins of the flesh—sins that he had no trouble in acknowledging—with prayer. It had been in Rome, and he remembered the unresponsive silence in the vault above him when his experiment had ended. Then all at once everything was shattered by a clamor of bells. Well, if critics of the Order wanted suitable targets, his case would suit their book. He smiled at the thought and, removing his wig, pressed his cheek against the embroidered linen lining of the carriage. A moderate meal of figs, white wine, and duck awaited him in his room. It would be followed by temporary solace in the arms of a woman who doubtless deserved a less venerable companion—more supple, less subtle—but who would find the aging man who had engaged her for the evening could still enjoy himself.

In the palace, the man Altamirano had just left was now the only person still awake save for the night guard and the undersecretary, who was staring, yawning but still apprehensive, at the anteroom door.

Carvalho, drinking deeply now, had shifted the candelabrum onto a side table so that he could examine his Tiepolo in comfort. He was sure now that it was a masterpiece. Not that he was a connoisseur of painting, but he was a judge of men, and he knew his recent visitor's admiration had been genuine. The fact that the Jesuit had also been using it to create a conversational diversion was incidental. Tiepolo was a master! Strange, nowadays, how good Italians were at everything except the one thing needful—power! He decided to have

some more Tiepolos brought into the larger suite of rooms into
which he intended to move before the year was through. It
was situated at the end of the opposite corridor and contained
eight rooms, twice as many as Pedro de Morta's suite, and
what was more it had a balcony.

He foresaw the day—indeed it was almost come—when
the proudest aristocrat would leap to his feet at the announce-
ment of Minister Carvalho's arrival, whoever else might be
present. His was the hand on the tiller of the ship of state, and
soon the time would come when everyone would realize the
vessel had changed course and that, thanks to Carvalho, Portugal was again one of the foremost nations, strong as Prussia,
prosperous as England. He would be rewarded with a duke-
dom at least, perhaps a princedom.

After all, King Joseph was already planning to make a
duchess of his whore. One way or another, certainly, Carvalho
must be raised above mere dukes, for unlike them he would
have earned his title. He bared his teeth in a grimace which
even his wife had never seen and, listening to prolonged applause, accompanied by drums and trumpets, remembered
how the ancient Romans had expelled their kings. Kings were
not necessary. In ancient Rome, men like Carvalho had been
declared dictators.

This was not the first time these lunatic aspirations had
invaded his mind, usually so cool and practical. The smothered fires of ambition threatened to scorch his brain. He had
been forced to wait too long for his day to dawn. To relieve
the blind force that agitated him, he got up and strode up and
down the room, recovering a touch of ceremony with each
turn, backwards and forwards. Then he stood still, drew himself up to his full, splendid height, and condemned all his
opponents, clerical and aristocratic, to death by hanging or at
the stake. Suddenly he directed a guilty, cunning look in the
direction of the door, reached it with long, swift strides, and
flung it open. The undersecretary at his table in the anteroom
contrived to look genuinely busy before looking up startled.
Resuming his normal air, Carvalho recovered his equilibrium,
too, and shut the door, reminding himself to be more careful.

Back in his office, his mind a blank, he sat at his desk and picked up a paper. Altamirano, of course! A typical Jesuit! There could be no knowing what was hidden in a mind like that. People talked of church mice; why didn't they talk of church chameleons? He chuckled. What a labyrinth of sophistry that lecherous, avaricious old sinner's conscience must be! (For Carvalho all ethical questions were simple. He solved them on the spot by rule of thumb.) What he had in his hand was the last letter his agent had forwarded. It was Cabeza's fulsome welcome to the Treaty of Madrid.

The worthy captain general's thinking was obvious, of course, but sound. He was counting on the Treaty of Madrid to increase his colony's prosperity by releasing restricted land and labor onto the open market. It was wonderful how self-interest could teach an unthinking man to see things for himself —things to which the deepest thinkers of the Church were blind. Dispensing with the aid of hypocritical claptrap, Cabeza was ready with one bold stroke to cut the knot that priests, entangled in theology, could never rise to. It must have called for enormous effort, Carvalho realized, for this obscure Spanish settler to jettison the prejudices bred of ancient enmities and old traditions and voluntarily transfer his allegiance to Portugal. Indeed, it was one more proof that the real law of peace was the law of the market. It was absurd that the decision about the missions did not lie in the hands of the captain general on the spot. If it had been a question of an English colony, Carvalho was sure Altamirano would not have been permitted as much as to set foot in it. That the final decision of a practical question should finally be left to a priest was intolerable, and now, after their interview, Carvalho was no longer even sure which way that decision would go! Well, whichever way that jesuitical cat happened to jump, Carvalho could prevent him from doing any damage. Drawing a sheet of paper toward him, the minister began writing additional instructions to the representative he had sent to Asunción to keep an eye on the implementation of the Treaty of Madrid.

Part
Four

16

THREE MONTHS LATER in Asunción, Carvalho's letter was opened by its addressee—Hontar by name—in the captain general's residence, where he was a guest. Senhor Hontar—thin and elegant, homosexual, with a long, humorous, sad-eyed faced—sighed in anticipation of disagreeable reading and gazed out upon the exotic garden with distaste. The heat was stifling, and he wished he were back in Portugal where—a failed diplomat with a pedigree receding into the fourteenth century, ministered to by a valet who understood his tastes—he could live comfortably enough on an income which, though slender, permitted an elegant if unostentatious way of life. The confidence Carvalho had displayed in him by dispatching him to this barbarous region, although flattering in its way, had been unwelcome. Failing a posting to Vienna or some almost equally attractive capital, his preferred residence was his villa in the foothills, not too far from Lisbon. Here, on the edge of the jungle, he dabbed his skeptical, sweating face and guessed what Carvalho could be up to this time. As the newly appointed minister of foreign affairs was fifty-one, he was in a hurry. Worse still, he was eager to wield a new broom, and consequently Hontar would put nothing past him. Carvalho's views might well be sound, for all he knew or cared. No doubt the upstart worked hard and well, in the new efficient style. To Hontar, however, modernity was no recommendation. Long ago he had decided he was born at the wrong time. In his own pondered opinion, he should have lived in fourteenth-century Venice, a gray-bearded savant living in a cool apartment by the sea, flocked to by muscular sailors straight off the wharves from Middle Eastern voyages, and strapping soldiers fresh from frightful wars.

But here he was instead, in Asunción of all places, involved in a dirty business that contributed almost as much to his discomfort as did the heat. The contents of the letter in his hand proved worse than he had feared. He was dismayed to learn what lengths Carvalho was prepared to go to in a final reckoning. What could it be, he wondered, that enabled a man to contemplate drastic decisions? Surely honor—if you called it that—was not worth it nor was wealth. Could it be the fellow actually believed he was called upon to be some sort of instrument? There was no denying a new spirit was abroad. It was no longer just a case of being greedy. There was something actively destructive in the air, and Carvalho had caught it. What made it worse was that he was bound to win. Even if the Jesuits tried to make a stand, they would find they had no backing. Hontar decided they must have realized that already.

All of which meant it would be interesting to watch Father Altamirano, who would soon arrive in Asunción, playing his difficult hand, because now his real opponents were his own people, the Jesuit fathers from the missions, whom Hontar had watched assembling at their house here in Asunción over the past weeks, in readiness for the public hearing that had been arranged. Grim-faced, resolute men he found them, men who would defend their position inch by inch. The new spirit received no welcome from priests like that.

Carefully assessing the actors who were to take part in the coming drama, Hontar had already taken note of the Irishman, Father Gabriel. It was extraordinary to find such childlike eyes in an old face ravaged by suffering. Even more extraordinary, though, was the one who silently dogged his footsteps—the lay brother with the dark, scarred face, who, despite his habit, looked downright dangerous.

The summons to Asunción to assist in the presentation of the mission's case had reached Gabriel two months earlier at the new mission he had established above the falls.

"What question can there possibly be?" he asked Father Ribiro as soon as he arrived. "There is no argument on the other side."

"His Holiness has dispatched Father Altamirano, who has

his complete confidence, to listen to both sides of the debate, with an even mind" was the warning answer.

Gabriel peered at the carved face of his superior for a sign. "Do you think it possible he might actually decide to close the missions?"

"I think you need to make your arguments convincing."

"I see. And may I tell this to the other priests, Father?"

"That was the purpose of this conversation."

So Gabriel told the others, including Sebastian and Mendoza.

Two years had passed since Mendoza had taken his vows. Since then he had been at peace, working quietly, devoting his attention to the work of building, and learning to read, piecemeal, at night. From his arrival he had been adored by the Guarani children and accepted by the braves for the man he so recognizably was. The women also trusted him. He exchanged his inmost thoughts with all of them and listened to their replies, in a way that even Gabriel could not do. He frankly discussed with them whatever question happened to be uppermost in his mind.

It was not without some envy that the other brothers saw how easily he conversed with the Guarani, on the shadowy forest tracks by day and by the fire at night, and how the Guarani always stopped talking if a priest or another brother came near. Father Antonio, in particular, took it badly; he had always wanted to be close to the precious hearts of the converted. At last he complained to Father Gabriel about it.

"Building is what you put him in charge of," he pointed out, "not the care of souls."

"That is so. But it is Christ himself who, in the end, appoints the pathway."

"This," Antonio said firmly, "is not of Our Lord's devising, no, certainly not. There is no denying Mendoza is a murderer, and now he holds new converts in the hollow of his hand. It is not right."

"Then you should tell him so."

Antonio went and, finding Mendoza at work in the forest, sat down and explained to him all afternoon what was so objectionable about his intimacy with the Guarani converts.

Meanwhile Mendoza worked away silently at several felled trees, and listened to Antonio's words with concentration. The sun was low before Antonio finished with the declaration: "A brother must do the work that he is set, not invent his own duties."

"I am not helping them with their difficulties," Mendoza explained, "any more than they are helping me with mine."

"If you have difficulties, you should seek help from Father Gabriel or some other brother."

Mendoza laughed and said, "Father Antonio, some of my difficulties are very minor. It is those that the Guarani help me with."

"And what about *their* minor difficulties? Should you be helping them, or should it not be Father Gabriel?"

"Father Gabriel, of course. But they talk to me to prepare themselves to go to him, because they would rather start by talking to an equal."

Antonio, astonished, protested, "An equal?"

"I hope I am their equal."

Father Antonio fell silent. Then, in a pious voice, he consented. "Of course. We are all their equals in the eyes of the Lord."

"But also in the eyes of men I am their equal. That is why they can talk to me of the sort of thing that happens to ordinary men."

"What things are those?"

"I suggest you work next to me tomorrow. Perhaps they will chat with you as well."

But when Antonio did work next to him, the Guarani did not come at all. When he slipped off, however, they came back immediately.

"You have told them to stay away from me," Antonio accused him.

"They keep away from you because you scare them."

"Me, scare them?" Antonio, frail and tiny, was indignant and amazed.

"Yes."

"How?"

"They say you are severe."

"But how?"

"They think that you are a misery, a moper."

"Nay, truly—do they say that of me?"

"They all do."

"Perhaps they are right." He puffed his cheeks in his unhappiness. "A moper. How would you describe a moper?"

"A moper cannot help a man decide how to treat his extra wives when he becomes a Christian."

"I see. And what do you tell him he should do?"

"I do not know; they just discuss it with me."

"What do they say Gabriel is?"

"A man who has Christ inside him but does not realize it."

"Well," said Antonio, "that at least is true. And what do they say you are?"

"I only know they say that I build well. Now I have told you all I know. Shall we get back to work?"

"Yes, let us. You have shown me a great sin that I was unaware of, and I thank you."

"I thank you, too. I will remember what you said." Antonio was excited when he repeated all this to Gabriel. "I think," he declared, "I really and truly think we have some sort of saint among us."

Gabriel flung both his hands up in the air in irritation. "One minute you tell me he's a murderer, not fit to be a member of our Order, and the next thing I know, here you are telling me he's a saint. Well, I tell you he's neither, but there's no denying he's fit to be one of us, for all his faults—and his virtues, too, if it comes to that."

Gabriel realized that Mendoza's virtues were those of a soldier, not a priest, but after all, Saint Ignatius Loyola, the Founder, was once a soldier, too, and thought of the Order as Christ's army. In his eyes the missions were Christ's forts, outposts in a holy war. As for Mendoza, Gabriel was ready to accept him, like the Guarani, for what he was.

Mendoza himself, however, struggled with his weaknesses —in particular with illiteracy. He would stay awake at night with pen and paper to sweat over a primer by firelight. It was a long, hard struggle for him to learn his alphabet, and when he had done it, he found it no less difficult to join letters into words. The ease with which the Guarani children accomplished this task filled him with admiration.

When he received Father Ribiro's summons to Asunción, to assist at the assembly Father Altamirano wished to hold to enable him to ascertain the truth about the missions, Gabriel knitted his brows. Everybody knew the truth already. Enemies spread calumnies about the Guarani—well, not all of them calumnies, perhaps, but the obvious intention of such stories was deception, and everybody who knew about the missions spread their fame abroad as bastions of Christ's kingdom. Altamirano must surely know this. What was his purpose, then, in calling this meeting?

The summons instructed Gabriel to bring with him any companions he thought likely to prove useful. He decided on Sebastian and Mendoza. Altamirano would be able to see at once that Sebastian was incapable of lying; he was a straightforward, stalwart, horny-handed ex-commissioned officer of a foot regiment. Mendoza, in his flesh and blood, supplied live testimony to the existence of the slave trade and in his own words, should he speak at all, could bear awesome witness to Christ's readiness to employ the missions in his service.

It was night when Gabriel announced his decision, and the brothers were all seated around a fire. Sebastian blushed scarlet when Gabriel laughed out loud at his schoolboy attempt to conceal his gratification by pulling a long face. Mendoza, however, was deadly serious when, shaking his head firmly, he said, "Father, let me stay as I am."

"You must not stay as you are. It is time for you to spread your wings a little."

"I do not know how to speak. Take one of the others." He gestured toward the others.

"You will not have to speak, except perhaps in ordinary conversation, and I shall be there."

"I do not wish to set foot in Asunción."

Gabriel looked at him, understanding, and said nothing immediately in reply, but taking an opportunity to move apart with him a little later, he murmured, "You don't believe the death of Philippo has been forgiven you?"

Mendoza did not reply at first. His face was expression-

less, but Gabriel held his gaze. The crackle of the fire sounded
very loud. "As long as I am here, I feel forgiven. That is why
I do not wish to leave," he said at last.

"You fear that in Asunción certain feelings might return."

"Yes."

"God's mercy is everywhere."

"Father, let me be."

"You cannot pick and choose the form God's mercy takes.
I will speak to you again about this, in the morning after I
have meditated on it."

Lying in bed that night he realized how deep had been
Mendoza's wound and how shallow his own sympathy had
been, not to realize that before. If Mendoza did not come to
Asunción, his wound would eventually cripple him.

Gabriel prayed to Christ that he might be shown how to
proceed, and in the darkness he could tell how much Christ
cared. His prayer, however, was not answered. He was still at
a loss the following morning when he urged Mendoza, saying,
"I beg you. I beg you to come."

"No, Father Gabriel."

"It is most important. I need to have you with me at this
gathering."

"I regret it very much, Father, but I must say no."

Gabriel shuffled his feet. "Very well, then, I command
you."

"Then I obey." Mendoza scowled. "That could as well
have been said last night."

"That means you know it to be right," Gabriel insisted,
pleased.

Mendoza, however, only said, "Perhaps."

"Tell Hacugh I need him, too, and a pair of his braves. And
we shall also need Babuie."

This was the boy who had adopted Mendoza from the day
of his arrival. Gabriel wanted him to sing the Canticles he had
taught him, for his voice was very pure.

"I will tell them all," answered Mendoza and walked off,
leaving Gabriel thanking Christ, who foresaw all, for making
Obedience the first vow of the Jesuit Order. Obedience came
unhesitatingly to Mendoza, who saw a chain of command

passing from God through Gabriel to himself—a chain that
was a lifeline—although it was through the Guarani that the
peace of God had come to him.

But when they arrived in Asunción after the long and arduous voyage down the river, Mendoza followed at Gabriel's
heels, with his face sunk far into his collar and his eyes unseeing. The soldiers sought him out, swaggering, and one
called out, "Hey, there, Mendoza," but he gave no answering
sign.

The hidalgos and their ladies nudged one another at the
sight of him, remembering the scandal, and Cabeza took the
opportunity to remark that if it had been left to him to decide,
the fratricide would not have got away with his atrocious
crime. "As things are at present," he reminded them, "I am
still hamstrung by the antiquated enactments of bygone kings
of Spain, but I can promise you, ladies, things will soon be
very different."

When Mendoza visited the spot where he had slain Philippo, he found a load of melons had just been dumped there.

Ribiro, the Father Provincial, took the assembled Jesuits
through four rehearsals of the public meeting to make sure
they would present the best possible case and to anticipate any
attacks on the missions. Discussion on these occasions was
keen, but Mendoza sat through them like a stone, simply
shaking his head when Ribiro at last asked him directly for a
comment. By the day of Altamirano's arrival, they were fully
prepared.

17

ACCOMPANIED BY A flotilla of small boats, decked with the flags of Spain, Portugal, and the Vatican, Altamirano arrived, seated imposingly in a state barge, to the accompaniment of trumpets and drums, and made a sweeping gesture of greeting to the crowds watching from the waterfront and from moored lighters. People of all sorts and conditions had gathered for the occasion—hidalgos and their ladies, tradesfolk, clerics including the visiting Jesuits, and last of all yet outnumbering the others, a host of half-naked Guarani.

The hidalgos removed their hats as, supported by his secretary, Altamirano got unsteadily to his feet to dispense a universal blessing. He had already raised his hand when the mob of natives shifted in a mass before his eyes and he paused, impressed and startled, while they knelt. This spectacle left him uneasy. He told himself how explicable it was: They were converts; they were pious; naturally they thought of him as their savior come from Rome, associating him, as a Jesuit dignitary, with the missions. Nevertheless, what perturbed him as he gazed for the first time, fascinated by those platelike faces with their gem-hard eyes, was a sense of quite impossible proximity, as if he wished to flee from them but could not leave them.

The priests from the missions were led aboard the barge and presented to him one by one, and as they bent before him in turn to receive his blessing, he took note of their eyes. One blue pair in particular reminded him of another man's eyes, which had been equally clear and youthful in a worn face, although the owner of the remembered eyes had been elderly, unshaven, and white-haired. These were the eyes of Altamirano's first teacher, eyes so transparent that they continually revealed the old man's feelings, whatever they were, to the perceptive boy. He remembered the face, too, now—gentle, usually melancholy, but occasionally smiling, and the long neck, shrinking into the vestment below it, and the slap of the water of this American river against the boat carried Altamirano back to his Italian boyhood in a villa by a narrower stream beneath a more opalescent sky. For a moment he could even hear the frogs. Undoubtedly, he told himself, he was fatigued. This was a very long voyage he had been sent on.

It was in that village that the feet of Altamirano had been guided to the path that had brought him where he was now. He had become a consummate negotiator, thanks to the example of a pious but simple man. Each year when the family was in the country, his father used to call the village priest in to teach him the elements of the doctrine of the Church—"because," he used to say, "this priest can do no harm." This priest was the old man with the expressive eyes. In the village, the hale and hearty accounted him a fool. A shepherd, they would say, should not allow his flock to fleece him if he values their respect. Altamirano, who always enjoyed being with him, regarded him as a kind of clown. When, for example, he tackled the old man on the way the villagers used to rob him, he received in reply a passionate explanation of how much they needed the money. A story from the Bible then followed, as usual and, also as usual, was listened to attentively.

It seemed that telling Bible stories, which he did irresistibly, was the only form of discourse the old man had mastered. When two self-styled philosophers who had heard of his simplicity—an upholsterer and a goldsmith's clerk—came from the local market town to bait him, they had no difficulty in completely baffling him. To the great delight of the villagers, whenever he tried to answer one of his inquisitor's questions, the questioner seemed always able to answer him back, and even the priest himself seemed to expect it. His view was that his real business was plodding the roads on visits to the sick or sad or dying, who prized his company.

So did Altamirano, and when the priest died, he had gone to his house and wept, burying his face in the old man's vestment, comforted by the familiar smell. It was then, after a week of silence in the villa, that he had informed his father he was going to be a priest when he grew up. His father, surprised, understood the reason, and took care not to forbid him or to ridicule him. There would be time enough for him to get over it, he had told himself. Later he had realized that his son's ambition might have to be taken seriously. He had paid a visit to a relative who was a bishop and returned favorably impressed.

"There may be something in this idea of yours," he said when he returned. "I shall make enquiries." He did so, and the eventual verdict, Altamirano recalled, had been: "You're a clever boy. If you are still inclined the same way at the end of the year, a priest you shall be, and if anybody laughs at you, then he's a fool." Altamirano recalled how, at those words, he had nearly changed his mind.

It was his mother's delight that had held him to his choice. She took this decision as a blessing conferred on her constricted soul by the Virgin Mother.

Altamirano's own admiration for artless love had not survived the education he received at a Jesuit college. His original resolve was lost there, but his personal resolution grew. Here in Asunción, however, in an unsteady boat, at last he felt his resolution weakening.

Ceremoniously he was handed ashore to be accosted rather than welcomed by a rude fellow, gorgeously dressed, who planted himself in front of him with an exaggerated bow and the words, "Good day, Visitor General. I am Cabeza, the captain general. Allow me to present to you Senhor Hontar."

Altamirano was then led to the residence of the captain general, where he was to hold a preliminary discussion with Cabeza and Hontar in preparation for the public hearing. After the Visitor General had been given time for a brief rest, he was joined by Cabeza, who busied himself by making a show of his importance.

At that moment, Hontar, having completed his rereading of Carvalho's instructions, folded up the minister's letter and buttoned it inside his linen coat. Quite unnecessarily, a majordomo was waiting to conduct him across the upper floor on

which he was accommodated, down the marble stairway, and
across the flagged ground floor to the room occupied by his
fellow guest, the Reverenced Visitor General. Descending the
stairway he saw two Guarani in livery planted on either side of
it in the hall below. In honor of the European visitors they
were wearing throttling cravats, but their feet were bare and
their impassive faces betrayed no flicker of recognition of the
significance of the event they were witnessing.

Altamirano, in his room on the ground floor, was watching
Guarani servants and laborers preparing the courtyard outside
for the public meeting to be held the next day. Cabeza, who
had already presented himself, had opened the door between
the courtyard and Altamirano's room and was shouting at
them. Descending the stairway, Hontar flinched at the sound
of the captain general's raucous voice and pitied himself for
being tied to such an ally. He would have preferred to be
associated with his opponent, he reflected, admiring the distinguished Jesuit's style as he entered his room.

Altamirano had casually relieved himself of an elegant buff
coat and laid it on a table to reveal an admirable waistcoat and
fine cambric shirt. Now, with studied informality, at a cough
from the majordomo he turned toward the doorway where
Hontar was standing, to greet the man whom he thought of as
Carvalho's watchdog.

"I wonder how long it will be before I tire of watching
these natives," Altamirano said. "There's something very
strange about the way they never look at you."

"At you, Father, surely they must gaze."

"Not at all. They may have the utmost veneration for my
office—"

"Of course they have!" barked Cabeza, coming in from the
courtyard to join them.

"—yet I have not caught as much as a passing glance from
one of them. Last night they unpacked my books." He picked
up an elegantly bound volume, which, Hontar noted, was by
Voltaire. "I told them to unwrap them carefully, and so they
did, but they also kissed them."

"Naturally," explained Cabeza. "Because the books are
holy."

Altamirano showed the book to them. Embossed on the cover was a nymph surrounded by admiring animals.

Cabeza, squinting at it, said, "You read such books?"

"A priest must be able to recognize evil," Altamirano informed him, with a sober face.

"I do not allow any book into the province if it attacks Mother Church."

"Would there were more of you!" Altamirano commended him. Clearly this ruffian was not aware of being a hypocrite; he supposed himself to be devout. "Can we have privacy?" he asked, nodding at the door Cabeza had left open to the courtyard. The captain general obediently went and closed it. While he was doing so, the Visitor General seated himself unhurriedly in the highest chair. Then, with a gesture more of authority than hospitality, he motioned his two visitors to seat themselves, too.

To Hontar's irritation, Cabeza spoke first. "Will you be sailing back on the same vessel?"

"That depends on how long it takes me to reach a conclusion."

"No more than two days, I'd say. The hidalgos certainly can't afford to stay more than a week away from their farms, you know. In any case, there aren't any problems I know of for you to settle, and there's nothing of consequence in these parts that I don't know all about. If there's anything you don't understand, you may as well tell me now. I'll clear it up for you before you start."

"Why, look!" Hontar intervened hastily, "a monkey!" He rose from his chair and stole softly to where the tiny creature, wearing a bright red turban, was clinging to the curtains, peering at him inquisitively. "Does he bite?"

"It's a she," Cabeza told him. "It belongs to my wife. It's quite harmless."

Hontar stretched out his hand. The creature hesitated. Then, with a flick of its tail, it climbed up his arm, nestled in the crook of his neck, and began examining his ear. Hontar, pleased, delicately resumed his place, making a soothing noise.

So, Altamirano told himself, this one's a sentimentalist.

"Do monkeys travel well, Don Cabeza?" Hontar inquired, stroking the pet.

"No. They usually die on the voyage."

"I'm sorry to hear it." He turned once again to the monkey. "You'd be worth a gold coin in Lisbon, my little friend."

"Presumably," remarked Altamirano with a stare, "that is why they do not travel. They prefer to stay in a place where they have no market value."

This was the Jesuit's first reference to the issue of slavery. The time had come to make them realize he was not just a papal underling.

"But she never tries to escape from here, does she?" Hontar asked Cabeza.

"Never!" came the answer, delivered with a hostile glare. "Now, can we get back to business? Visitor General"—he turned back to Altamirano—"as I just said, if there's anything you want ironed out, best tell me now before the hearing starts."

"Surely," chimed in Hontar, "the Visitor General already knows he can count on your assistance in every way, is that not so, Father?"

The response caught Altamirano off balance. "About this letter you have just received from Senhor Carvalho."

Hontar stiffened and thought, How did he get his information? Or is he just guessing? He uncrossed his legs in an effort to relax and answered, "Thank you. It was delivered safely."

"May I be told about such of its contents as pertain to my business tomorrow?"

"The answer to that is simple. Nothing, nothing at all. The letter was about my next appointment, not this one."

"Ah, so? And what is that to be?"

"Unfortunately he doesn't say," Hontar managed to answer with an easy laugh.

Altamirano thought, He dares not tell me. My worst fears are confirmed: There is no point in any of this. And he sighed at the prospect of the next day's charade. "These natives," he asked, "the Guarani, what are they like as a people?"

"Ignorant," Cabeza answered briefly.

"And yet," Altamirano pursued his question, "when I was

watching them working outside just now, they were far more anxious to preserve your splendid furniture from damage than your Spanish overseer appeared to be."

"Of course," Hontar confirmed, with a warning glance at Cabeza. "They are the craftsmen."

"Indeed?" The visitor ran his finger over the elaborate carving on the arm of his chair. "You mean to say that this was not shipped from Spain?"

Again Hontar glanced at Cabeza, but the captain general was not a total fool. "No, Reverenced Visitor General," Cabeza said smoothly. "It is mission work. So is all the rest of the furniture. These people can make anything, just as long as they've been given something to copy. Without a model, though, they're helpless. As I often tell visitors like you, they didn't even know what a wheel was until we arrived on the scene to show them one."

"In the forests where they live I suppose they had no need of wheels."

Cabeza reflected that this was typical jesuitical talk. "All the same," he sneered, "the wheels have started turning now!"

Hontar, who had identified one quotation from the captain general in Carvalho's letter, reflected that the minister might even adopt this gem to be his motto. Aloud he observed, "Naturally, the local population are attracted by the amenities of a superior civilization. Naturally, too, Captain General, you cannot imagine the fascination your strange country and its people hold for visitors from Europe, like the Reverenced Visitor General and my humble self. I blush to confess it, but before the Treaty of Madrid was negotiated, I did not even know that such a place as Colonia del Sacramento existed, let alone that it was a haunt of pirates. Have you heard about Sacramento, Father?"

"Yes," said Altamirano, "from Senhor Carvalho in Lisbon." He began to stroke his leg. Hontar watched him curiously. What was coming now? "The minister also spoke of gold. Is there much gold these days at Sacramento?" Altamirano's eyes flashed as he asked the question. Hontar, who was not avaricious, was amazed.

Cabeza's manner, too, changed at the introduction of this

new subject. Suddenly he had become hesitant. "I do not know."

"You mean, then, it is not impossible there is some?"

"No, it is certainly not impossible."

"Where could they get the gold in Sacramento?"

Cabeza looked unpleasantly sly. "There are those who say there are mines on the missions." He shrugged.

"What do the Jesuits themselves say?"

"They deny it, of course. But I have to tell Your Reverence that there are those who do not believe them."

"Do you?"

"I am bound to," Cabeza leered. "Am I not?"

"Any gold mines on the missions," said Altamirano, "would have been accounted for." He looked out of the window and reminded himself that somewhere out there, before the end of that distant forest was reached, lay the city of El Dorado.

Amazing! thought Hontar, watching him. He's too clever to believe the rumors, but he believes in the dream.

When his visitors had left the room, Altamirano, discouraged, said to himself, I shall be leaving on the next sailing, just as that animal said. The word "animal" reminded him of the monkey. It was still there in the room, but it refused to come to him as it had gone to Hontar.

Hontar is no fit servant for Carvalho, he thought. Cabeza is his man. The captain general wouldn't sully his lips with the name of Newton—supposing he had ever heard of him, which is not likely—but all the same he is in tune with the new philosophy, there can be no doubt of that. Just as there can be no doubt the Order will survive it. The Order must. But survival, he reminded himself, will call for the sacrifice of much that would be worth keeping if the world were a different place. My life, as I see now, has involved much sacrifice of this kind, and those Jesuits I met when I landed must sacrifice the simple, skillful people they have brought to Christ. They must do it for the sake of the Order to which they belong and to which they have sworn obedience, but how am I to tell them?

In his mind he felt a pair of eyes upon him. That will be my sacrifice, he told himself. In order to obtain their obedience I must sacrifice their fellowship.

He felt calm but tired, and above all else, he wished to be alone, but that night the Guarani were presenting a pageant in the main square. It was an annual affair, Cabeza had told him, arranged by the nearest mission, but this year, in view of the coming assembly and the arrival of so many visitors in the city of Asunción it should be worth attending. Cabeza himself was going!

Altamirano had already explained to Ribiro that he could not go to the Jesuits' house in Asunción to celebrate mass there, much as he longed to do so, because he had come on behalf of the Pope and must on no account appear to identify himself with one of the parties in a case in which he was the appointed judge. To refuse to grace this occasion as well would be to promote distrust—premature distrust—so he joined the captain general's party.

Darkness had fallen hours before they arrived, and the square was crowded as far as the side streets—hidalgos and officers and their families in the front, tradesfolk at the sides, and a solid mass of Guarani at the back. Even before they left the residence, the captain general's party could hear the din, which rose to a roar as they joined other, less distinguished figures on a temporary gallery. Every tree and wall was decorated with flowers. Their arrival was the signal for the pageant to begin.

Altamirano soon gave up trying to understand what the pageant was all about. There was enough to engage his attention without attempting that. He could have listened to the orchestra all evening. It astonished him with its precision. A massed choir sang. There was also a moment when a clear space beneath him was invaded by horsemen in fantastic costumes—not savage but strangely sacerdotal.

A Jesuit appeared at the top of a tower, where he set two torches ablaze, turning all eyes in his direction. The music died down, and there was silence. In a resonant voice, the Jesuit spoke a prayer in Guarani. Altamirano could sense the devotion in the listeners below him. Then it was over and a noise like the sea sounded across the square. Suddenly Altamirano realized that thousands of faces had turned in his direction and knew what they expected. He bowed his head and blessed them.

18

EARLY THE NEXT morning a small crowd of watchers had already gathered in front of the captain general's residence from which the three flags—Spanish, Vatican, and Portuguese—were hanging listlessly against a dull gray sky suffused with cloud. The crowd saw the Jesuits arrive two by two, led by Father Ribiro. Then by back streets came the upcountry Guarani led by two Jesuits who disappeared into a side door. Came the hidalgos and their ladies on horseback—even a few in coaches—leaving their mounts under the trees outside, heads drooping, in the care of grooms. Confident that the decision would go their way, they called out cheerily to one another. For them, this public meeting was something of a festivity.

Altamirano came, flanked by a choir, not of Jesuit origin but from a local church, singing a Psalm. When the Visitor General entered the courtyard to take his seat facing them, the entire assembly rose. The choir completed the Psalm and then the prior of the Franciscans said a prayer. Altamirano stood and, with an expressionless face, looked across to where Ribiro sat in the midst of ranks of Jesuits on benches ranged to the same side as that on which, crowded into a corner, a group of upcountry Guarani, all but naked, had been placed.

The Visitor General then turned his head to direct a smile at Cabeza and make a friendly gesture to Hontar, both of which were acknowledged. The three men were seated in the front row among the hidalgos and their wives and daughters. The arrangements had been good. Satisfied that everything was perfectly in order, Altamirano was about to make his opening statement, inviting each interested party to state its case fully, because justice would be possible only after everything had been taken into consideration, when Ribiro asked permission for a choir of recent converts to make an opening contribution. He was confident the captain general would agree that sacred music would help on this occasion.

Cabeza, with a shrug, signaled agreement, but then, instead of introducing a full choir, Ribiro summoned a small boy from the group of upcountry Guarani. There was a slight delay while the child sought permission from a Jesuit who was standing apart from the others, in whose care he appeared to be.

Then the child came forward, the introduction of a Palestrina solo was heard from a harpsichord, and the boy, lifting his flat expressionless face, began to sing. It was as if he were a natural spring and the notes were water, even softening Cabeza's surly look. Altamirano, however, knew well such skill was not spontaneous, and marveled that the training necessary to produce such a voice should be available in such a place. Even now the singer's eyes were fixed on somebody who was unobtrusively directing him. Following the boy's glance, with a shock of interest and recognition, Altamirano found himself staring at the worn face and limpid blue eyes that had transported him back to his childhood on his arrival. Gabriel was discreetly conducting from his sleeve.

When the boy had brought his piece to an end in a trill of quiet notes, Altamirano told Ribiro it would give him particular delight to hear the singer render the same composer's "Plenum." Ribiro bowed his head and consulted Gabriel in an undertone. Then both turned to the boy.

"*Si,*" said Babuie, in answer to a question in Guarani and, without accompaniment, proceeded to sing the ecclesiastical music. Altamirano, astonished, watched peace descend over the crowded courtyard—on all but Cabeza. Pulling angrily at his collar, the captain general scented some sort of trap. Altamirano saw Hontar frowning a warning at Cabeza to be patient. He knew he had only to wait.

In sudden hostility to the pair of them and what they stood for, Altamirano clapped loudly when the child had finished, and the ranks of Jesuits enthusiastically joined him. The hidalgos and their womenfolk did not. Hontar, however, deprecating any whiff of demonstration, clapped, too. The Visitor General watched the boy return to his place among the up-country Guarani next to the one Jesuit who sat among them. The Jesuit handed him a little monkey, like the one that had so captivated Hontar. The pet clung immediately to Babuie's arm.

After nodding toward the boy, who was now seated, Alta-mirano turned and attacked Cabeza with a question: "Señor Captain General, was that the cry of an animal we just heard?"

"Reverenced Father, a parrot can be taught to talk." The retort earned a volley of shrill laughter from the hidalgos' wives. Altamirano looked at them and in their faces saw scars resulting from years of wresting from a hostile environment the goods and services they could never enjoy at home in Spain.

"Are parrots here so melodious?" the Visitor General asked.

A man's voice called out, "Yes, Father. A brute beast can be taught anything, with a whip."

At the word "whip" there was a murmur of rejection from the Jesuits and of approval from the hidalgos and their wom-enfolk. Father Ribiro suppressed the Jesuit clamor. Good, thought Altamirano, this priest has authority. I shall need him later.

Cabeza rose truculently to his feet and stood with legs apart. He thought of himself as a settler. He had never cared twopence for the Crown of Spain and no longer had to pretend to.

"Reverenced Visitor General," he began unctuously, "we have just heard a child of the Guarani sing, and it appears Your Reverence was much taken with it. Very well, but before Your Reverence goes on to make a mistake, I'll just describe the barbarity that produced that little angel. I am able to tell you this because, as anyone who lives here can see at a glance, the boy is one of the untamed ones from above the falls, and in that part of the world things still go on the way they did everywhere in the Río de la Plata, before we arrived and brought the twin blessings of religion and trade here. Up there the Guarani live like beasts."

A burst of applause sounded from the hidalgos, at hearing

their spokesman tell what they perceived to be the truth. Encouraged, Cabeza went on. "I'll tell you this. If what we heard just now was not an animal with a human voice, then it was something lower. It was a human with animal vices!" He paused to hear his wit applauded. "No, worse than that even, for it has vices any beast would flee from. Reverenced Father, let me tell you just one thing about these people. Even here in your very presence they've got practically nothing on, as you must have noticed. When they get back into the forest up there, they'll go around stark naked. You ought to see the state they get into, all smeared with earth and scratched with branches! In other words, as I said, they live like animals!"

The women behind him had often discussed the Guaranis' gross indecency, but that did not prevent them from displaying outrage anew. Some shook their heads with pursed mouths, while others broke into exclamations.

Cabeza continued, "What's more, they don't live in human homes. In fact they don't live in any particular place at all. They turn up in some corner of the jungle, kill everything that moves, and eat it, and then wander off to some other part. While they are there, they just pile up a few branches and huddle underneath them."

He turned to appeal to the hidalgos behind him, and there was a rumble of agreement. He was enjoying himself hugely. "Do the Guarani have arts? Well, I must admit they can chip stones and they can squeeze clay. They also weave a kind of crude cloth from wild cotton. I'll grant them that. And then there is their painting: They paint their naked flesh all over with dots and stripes, let's not forget that! But that's the sum total of the arts of the Guarani, which reminds me, talking about sums, they can also count. Yes, like this!" He held up one hand and displayed his fingers. "One, two, three, four, and plenty! Anything over four, is plenty! Plenty! Can you believe it?" His supporters joined him in a fit of cackling laughter.

"Can they cultivate the soil?" Cabeza continued. "Some of them scratch around with digging-sticks on patches of land they have cleared by slashing and burning. Then, when they've emptied all the goodness out of the soil, they wander off somewhere else and start again. This, Reverenced Father, is the condition from which we have rescued them, and I defy anybody to deny it." Jutting out his lower lip, he stared across at the Jesuit ranks while his supporters cheered. However, his prime audience, Altamirano, while continuing to make a show of inclining an attentive ear, showed no sign of shock or outrage.

"Reverenced Father and Visitor General," Cabeza went on, "I do not wish to weary you, but before ending this pitiful list I must inform you of one or two more details that tell the Guaranis' story. For instance, one thing they do go in for is lethal weapons. They have clubs and swords and bows and arrows, and what is more they take a lot of trouble over them. Some of their bows are eight feet long. Their swords have basket handguards. Their arrows have barbed heads, and if they are war arrows, I am sorry to tell you they are tipped with human bones. Savage? They want to be savage! When they paint themselves, they add jaguar ashes to the colors, on purpose to become like beasts of prey."

Gabriel, the Jesuits' chosen spokesman, turned his lean, sunburned face to Ribiro, but the Father Provincial shook his head, and whispered, "Wait."

"The two things they devote their lives to are drunken orgies and cannibal feasts." Even Altamirano seemed shocked at this. Gratified, for he was prepared for this moment, Cabeza produced something from his pocket. It was a piece of hard meat wrapped in cloth. He held it up. "A chop from a tribal hero," he said, and paused to let them all look at it, before concluding, "That's all I have to say for the present. Such, Reverenced Visitor General, are the converts the Jesuits would have you believe are equal with us in the eyes of God!"

He sat down to a storm of applause. The hidalgos drummed their handsticks on the pavement.

Ribiro got to his feet and said, "As the world well knows, we Jesuits who cleansed the Church of Jansen's heresy, accept—nay, we maintain—there can be no salvation where there are no good works. Nevertheless, we are confident that Guarani will be numbered among the redeemed, which is to say that they have souls as acceptable to Christ as our own.

This does not mean that we deny they are sinners. But such we also freely confess ourselves to be."

The entire gathering nodded. Ribiro was known to be the cleverest theologian in the Río de la Plata. But what had this pious truth to do with what Cabeza had just said?

"Father Gabriel," announced Ribiro, "is best qualified to comment on the remarks we have just heard because he directs our mission above the falls."

Gabriel came quietly forward. Again Altamirano felt the presence of his old teacher. This man's conscience, he thought, was as clear as day. The work of God was all he could contemplate doing. "As Father Ribiro has told you, Reverenced Father, my mission is upcountry, above the falls. Here where we are now, below the falls, this province belongs to Spain and is under the protection of the captain general, but the land above the falls belongs to the Guarani under God and the Crown of Spain."

I see what you are trying to say, thought Altamirano. Aloud he said, "I understand that Portugal, too, was awarded territory in the mountains."

"Reverenced Visitor General, indeed that is so, but although none can say with authority where the division runs, there is no doubt that it leaves the land beyond the falls to Spain. The falls were placed there by God to be a barrier. Standing above them and looking down, a man can have no doubt of that. Reverenced Father, I have to tell you that up there the Guarani behave very much in the way the captain general has just described, but as to the existence of their precious souls, the evidence is in their music."

"Their music?" interrupted Cabeza, guffawing at the hidalgos. *"Theirs?"* he repeated to Gabriel. "The savages above the falls? When you arrived up there, what instruments did they have?"

"The gourd rattle and the stamping tube."

"So!" said Cabeza, turning around again to share the joke with his followers. "The gourd rattle and the stamping tube. From these we see their wonderful gift for music, do we?"

"No, indeed," Gabriel conceded. "When first the Jesuits came among the Guarani," he explained to Altamirano, "they found they would not stay to listen to the Holy Word of God, but they were drawn by the evening canticles—though all they had known before our arrival was, as I said, the sounds of the gourd rattle and the stamping tube. Hearing the strains of rarest music—Purcell, Scarlatti, Lully—they laid down their weapons and came out of hiding. The first Jesuit fathers traveled up the river with their instruments to play to them, and the Guarani came and stood knee-deep in the water to get close to them and listen. Then, later, the fathers would speak words to them and tell them the holy story. I can show the Reverenced Father various old texts from which this can be verified."

Cabeza said, "There is no need to see the texts. Everybody knows that those old Jesuits used music to impress the natives. What does that prove?"

"I must admit, Father Gabriel," said Altamirano, "much as I relish these stories of our ancient forebears, I cannot accept them as evidence to be assessed by this assembly."

"Of course not. They are only old wives' tales," commented a hidalgo.

"But I also have living evidence," said Gabriel. He then related how, when he first ventured above the falls, he established contact with the Guarani with his oboe, and how they came out of their hiding places to listen first to his music and then to the Word of God.

Sneered Cabeza, "Obviously they had already heard some. They must have sneaked down below the falls to one of your missions and heard one of your choirs."

"No, on the contrary. Far from going down to where we were, they wanted nothing to do with us. There was bad blood between us, in fact."

"How so?" queried Altamirano. "What bad blood?"

Gabriel looked at Father Ribiro, who nodded, so he told them of the martyrdom of Julien, the first to carry the Word above the falls.

"And are these the same people who killed Father Julien?" asked Altamirano. He pointed to the group of Guarani.

"Yes, Father. And yet they are not the same, thanks be to God, and the power of music in God's work!"

"And it was you yourself who went beyond the falls after Julien's martyrdom?" asked Altamirano admiringly.

"Yes," said Gabriel. "That is how I know for myself that they are spiritual beings."

"Spiritual!" exclaimed a hard-faced woman, as if somebody had insulted her. "As you have just heard from a man who knows them like the back of his hand, Reverenced Father, the natives are perpetually drunk."

"Sometimes," Gabriel said swiftly, "it is true that they are drunk. I have also heard that the captain general goes to the trouble of sending all the way to Europe to stock his excellent cellar with wine, which must surely have the same effect on those who drink it as the liquor that the Guarani brew has on them." He cocked an Irish eyebrow at the captain general, who was forced to look away, and many of the hidalgos laughed, for Cabeza's drinking was renowned.

Hontar decided to come in. It was the first time he had opened his mouth that morning, but the time had come to return Altamirano to a sense of realities. He had become too interested in this dangerous witness. "Father, have you established a permanent mission up there?" The question was addressed to Gabriel, but it was aimed at Altamirano. Clearly he needed to be reminded who had the whip hand.

Gabriel looked at him, puzzled, and asked, "How does that concern you?"

"Why, Father, I am a representative of the Crown of Portugal at this assembly, and so the question is of legitimate interest to me. If you have established a mission there, you have in effect annexed the territory above the falls for Portugal."

"We do have a mission there," Gabriel stated. "I am, however, surprised to learn that Your Excellency knows in advance what conclusion the Reverenced Visitor General will have reached at the conclusion of this assembly."

"Ah, no!" Hontar protested. "No, no, no. I am distressed if I have conveyed such a wrong impression to anyone present, Reverenced Father."

Altamirano, who had understood this intervention very well, was fuming at it inwardly, but with a forgiving wave of his hand he answered mildly, "Pray do not distress yourself."

Angry as he was with Hontar, however, he knew that if he was to save appearances he must not allow the formidable Father Gabriel to make his case so well. "So you deal with the untouched Guarani, Father Gabriel," he said, apparently encouragingly. "Tell me, do they indeed employ the system of counting that Don Cabeza explained to us just now?"

"All Guarani count that way."

"Then how are they able to make a splendid chair like this, or this magnificent table?"

"Let us take that table as an example. There would be no difficulty about the length and breadth. They could measure those all right. The problem would come with the curves on the legs. They would have to trace around them to make a pattern they could transfer onto a piece of timber. Then they could reproduce it in the finished article. And so on, with the other curves. There is really· no limit to what they can do, using methods like that. In the mission of Santa Croce they have constructed an organ, complete with stops and listening pipes."

"What you mean is they can copy someone else's model," Hontar pointed out. "You see how it is, Reverenced Father, as scriveners are to poets, so they are to us Europeans. It seems the Muse disdains them. They can do nothing without a master copy."

To Altamirano's annoyance, Hontar's contribution was received with applause and more thudding of sticks. In the belief that the cool voice of reason sounded better than the hot tones of prejudice, even when they were saying the same thing, he had deliberately forestalled Cabeza from making the very point he had made the previous day. Much to his chagrin, however, the hidalgos were completely satisfied.

"Nothing!" they echoed him. "They can do nothing!"

The combative father, who, Hontar thought, had already dealt neatly with Cabeza over the matter of intemperance, now paid the diplomat the compliment of picking up his reference to poetry. "If any Muse has visited you, Excellency," he began, "and inspired you with a practical idea that I could pass on to my Guarani for them to copy—I mean something that would be as useful in the forest as accountancy is useful in the town—I beg you to impart it to me now."

"Alas," Hontar said dryly, "the Muses have always shunned me for some reason. But to return, with your permission, to the question we are supposed to be considering, you cannot deny the reason why your Guarani have turned to you for guidance is that they recognize the superiority of what you have to teach them—be it music, be it joinery—over what they have achieved themselves, even in the very forests they and their ancestors were born in. In other words, they acknowledge Europe's natural superiority—even in using their own local materials, for example, to erect buildings they could never dream of for themselves."

Impressed by this philosopher, the hidalgos started whispering among themselves. Disgusted, Cabeza pulled at his lower lip and looked sulky, feeling eclipsed.

"I suppose," Gabriel reflected aloud, "if what you say is true, that would make the Guarani my bond-slaves, wouldn't it?"

"If that is the word for it," said Hontar.

"It is a word whose meaning is well known to your countrymen," answered Gabriel, seizing his chance. He would explain the origin of the Jesuit missions. Without that knowledge Altamirano would not understand the need for the missions' special privileges and immunities. "Your countrymen were very quick to decide that *slave* was the proper word. I am speaking of the Paulista *bandeirantes*, as we call them, Reverenced Father, men from São Paulo in Brazil. They used to raid Spanish territory here, looking for slaves for their plantations; they headed bands collected from the wild Chaco Indians, half-trained *mamelucos*, who are men of mixed race, and also Negroes—all violent, desperate men for whom there was no honest, settled way to live. They raided the Guarani villages, killing many and carrying off the others into slavery. There was terror everywhere, and there was good reason for terror, but its effects were horrible. Fleeing their villages, the Guarani had to kill their old people and the feeble and infirm, because they would not be able to keep up with the speed of flight. I am telling you the truth completely. And these Portuguese called themselves Christians, Reverenced Father. Small wonder the Guarani flee from us, when they hear that we are Christians!"

"This is ancient history," Cabeza objected. "You have embarrassed Señor Hontar. We have a treaty with them now. That is why we are here."

"Is this information relevant to our inquiry, Father Gabriel?" Altamirano inquired.

"It bears directly on the Treaty. It explains why the kings of Spain saw fit to give our Order special rights and privileges," Gabriel answered. "At the time I speak of, the Jesuits were the only Europeans who attempted to protect the Guarani. They sent letters to the courts of Spain and Portugal, complaining about what was happening. Nothing was done, however, by governments to stop the Paulista *bandeirantes* before it was too late. By the time order had been restored and the Province was safe, the Guarani were no longer to be found in their villages. Many of those who had not been killed or captured had taken to wandering in the forest where they would be safe.

"There was another thing the Jesuits did besides writing letters. They did not help the Guarani resist by force, but they took many thousands of them to safety. They established mission settlements for them in the fertile regions of the Paraná and Uruguay rivers, where they could live in peace away from the Portuguese, and prosper. As Senhor Hontar has explained to us so clearly, by coming to these missions the Guarani have unmistakably acknowledged the superiority of Europeans—as in their situation who would not? And it is true they have acquired many skills on the missions: animal husbandry, poultry-breeding, agriculture, weaving, carpentry and joinery, pottery, tailoring, boat building, architecture..."

A suspicious-looking hidalgo interposed: "Mining and metal refinery." His tone was deeply significant. Altamirano pricked up his ears and waited.

Gabriel paused. "Do you mean gold?"

"I did not mention any particular metal."

"Whatever metal you had in mind," Gabriel informed him, "you will find none of it on any of the missions. I have heard talk of gold arriving in Sacramento. Some gold may do so. I do not know. What I do know is that any gold there may be in Sacramento has nothing to do with any Jesuit mission. Quite simply, we run no mines."

Many there resented him, some even hated him, but nobody disbelieved him.

"I thank you for explaining the history of these missions," Altamirano said. "That was most helpful. Tell me one thing more about them. To whom do the mission lands belong?"

"To the converts."

"Don Cabeza, is this true?"

The captain general shrugged. "Perhaps."

"Perhaps?"

"I cannot say. How can I when I am not allowed into a single mission? If I wanted to enter one for any reason, I should have to apply to its Father Superior for special permission. So what is going on inside them is something I can only guess at."

Altamirano turned to Father Ribiro for an explanation.

"King Fernando decided that the Guarani should be administered completely separately from the Spanish settlers, in their own interests, which he thought were best entrusted to the Society of Jesus. And that is why, in my opinion, both the spirit and also the letter of his legacy require that the missions be excluded from the terms of the recent Treaty, whose application to this question we have gathered to discuss."

"In this connection," Gabriel added firmly, "it must be remembered that, although they may no longer call themselves *bandeirantes,* slave-traders are still operating legally in the territories belonging to the Crown of Portugal."

They had reached the nub of the problem more rapidly than Altamirano had expected or desired. But at that same moment Cabeza, who had been listening with growing impatience to a discussion from which he felt excluded, rose to his feet and, striding up to the table behind which Altamirano sat separated from the body of the meeting, burst out, "Reverenced Father, this could go on endlessly. I don't see any point in it. I therefore beseech you—"

"There is no point in beseeching me," Altamirano told

him. "I am not here to please you in particular or anybody else. My duty—"

"Nevertheless," Cabeza impatiently insisted, "I implore you to stop this talk and give us your decision now, at once!" Then, having delivered himself of this request, he remained standing there, as if he expected his wish to be granted immediately.

Altamirano stared at him, biting back the crushing reply that rose temptingly to his lips, but which would later make it harder to do what he had to do. As a result he found he had nothing to say at all and avoided looking at Cabeza. The mere sight of the man robbed him of his normal self-control.

The captain general's sudden prominence caused Mendoza, sitting with the Guarani in their corner, to raise his head and stare at him, remembering. His visit to Asunción had affected him deeply as he had feared. He was haunted by the murder of Philippo as if he had committed it repeatedly, and not only by that act but also by the long succession of other horrors which had preceded it and which he now realized he would never forget either. He would have done better to disobey Gabriel. There was nothing for him to do here but suffer. What could a man like him contribute to the conversation over there at the Reverenced Visitor General's table? If Cabeza had looked back, he would have trembled at the sight of Mendoza's dark shadowed eyes contemplating him so steadily from his scarred face, but his own glare was aimed at the indifferent profile of the most distinguished person present. A moment later Mendoza lowered his eyes lest Gabriel, who had taught him the first Christian message, which was forgiveness, should see them. Only Babuie saw.

Hontar, who already respected Gabriel, again cursed the luck that had given him Cabeza as an ally. It was easier said than done to ignore Cabeza, he reflected, but well worth attempting. He addressed Altamirano.

"Reverenced Father, earlier this morning we heard a charge of cannibalism which, in view of what Father Gabriel has just told us, I find hard to understand. Can he explain it?"

This had the effect of taking Cabeza's eyes off Altamirano.

"It's true," declared Cabeza, pulling his wrapped meat out of his pocket again and showing it. "If you want details, they eat their enemies' muscles and testicles."

Gabriel said quietly, "Reverenced Father, the truth of the matter is that they are guilty of a childish identification of a man's muscles with his strength, just as some of the faithful at church here in Asunción confuse the virtue of the Blessed Virgin with her image."

"Nobody is to be blamed for an honest confusion," Hontar agreed. "But it is not permissible to eat human flesh. Is the truth that they do eat it?"

"I will put the question to them," was Gabriel's reply. So saying, he went across to where his Guarani, with Hacugh in their midst, were deep in amicable conversation which he had to interrupt. He spoke briefly to them and they all joined in a common reply, adding to one another's words and amending them. Gabriel then put another question to them, apparently a summing up in which all concurred. "They are very clear about this," he reported, turning toward the others. "What they say is that they did once eat the flesh of enemies but no longer do, being now persuaded that the spirit is something separate from the flesh. Moreover, they no longer wish to do it, as it is against the wishes of Christ, who they hope will act as their protector from the Spaniards."

"The Spaniards?" Altamirano exclaimed.

But before he could pursue that question, a hidalgo had risen to his feet and asked accusingly, "Why doesn't he ask them why they kill their own children?"

Altamirano glanced confidently at Gabriel. "I suppose this is just another story," he suggested, "like the gold?"

Gabriel's eyes sank to the flagstones. "No," he admitted. "This is not just a story. This is true."

There was total silence.

"Then what need is there to hear more?" demanded Hontar.

Gabriel replied, "There is need to hear the explanation. The Guarani who do this thing are those who live in the woods, the ones you call untamed. Because of the danger they are constantly in, their women can never have more than two children—one for each hand. If they have more, they cannot run away. Of course, with bigger children it is different. They can run on their own. I will tell you from whom they are running. They are running from us."

Sitting among the hidalgos was an old lady. Gabriel's attention had been largely concentrated on Altamirano, but she had caught his eye because he liked her face, although it was clear from her expression that she disagreed with him. She had shaken her head suspiciously when he had dismissed the idea that there were secret gold mines on the missions. When he had compared devotion to the image of the Blessed Virgin with cannibalism, her face had stiffened with contempt. At this point, however, she surprised him by rising to her feet, supporting herself by gripping the back of the chair in front of her, and declaring in a high voice, "In case that sounds like evil calumny, I would like to say, as an old woman, that I know it's partly true, I have heard my father speak of it. They had to kill some of their own children in that way when *mamelucos* were after them." She sat down carefully, having done her duty.

"Who knows what truth there is in the stories of those days? Both empires were still settling down and nobody knew what was what. Both sides believed lies about each other, if you ask me. What matters now is that everything is going to be quite different, thanks to the Treaty we are here to serve." Cabeza turned and bowed ceremoniously in the direction of Hontar, who rose to his feet to return the courtesy.

"Nonsense," Gabriel responded coldly. "It makes no difference to them who drags them into slavery. Listen to the word of the Guarani." He turned back to them to question them, but the courtyard broke into an uproar as the hidalgos tried to stop the Guarani from answering by shouting them down. The Jesuits, too, had erupted. Half a dozen fathers had risen to their feet in support of Gabriel's allegation and were trying to make themselves heard. Watching the scene with detachment, Altamirano saw how at first even Ribiro hissed and signaled a return to discipline in vain. There was, he noticed, just one saturnine, scar-faced brother who, alone among the others, remained impassive, staring at Cabeza.

Following his glance, Altamirano saw that Cabeza was re-

ceiving some sort of swift advice from Hontar. A few seconds
later the captain general waved his arms and bellowed for
quiet. The hidalgos fell silent. The Jesuits had already done
so, and in the resulting calm Cabeza was addressing Altamirano again.

"Reverenced Visitor General," he said, "in the territory
which His Catholic Majesty has entrusted to my hands, there
is of course no slavery, nor has there ever been since the days
of Ferdinand the Fourth. The institution of slavery has been
permitted, however, in the territories of our Portuguese neighbors"—he broke off to bow to Hontar—"a fact, to my mind,
much misunderstood. But here in Spanish territory, plantation
labor is employed on the system of encomienda."

"Exactly," confirmed a settler. "Encomienda."

"In strict accordance with the laws of Spain and the pre-
cepts of the Church." Cabeza was well pleased with his own
style and felt flattered by Hontar's murmur of assent.

Just then, however, the scar-faced Jesuit sitting next to Gabriel raised his head, looked across at Cabeza and Hontar, and
quietly said, "That is a lie."

A sign ran through the courtyard, followed by perfect silence as Cabeza, in instant fury at this unlooked-for insult,
glared into the steady eyes of the man who had uttered it. He
remembered that many a man had looked into them as he was
doing now, just before he died. Drawing himself up with the-
atrical hauteur he blustered, "In the name of the monarch
whose majesty I embody I demand an apology. A gentleman
ignores challenges from priests. Their cloth protects them."

"Don Cabeza, this assembly can judge for itself whom my
cloth protects," the Jesuit replied.

Revealing the bull-like set of his head, Cabeza snatched off
his powdered wig and flung it to the ground. "By God!" he
raged, "I will not suffer this," and under cover of this declaration, escaped by striding off into the shelter of his residence.

Hontar rose slowly. "Reverenced Father," he said quietly to
Altamirano, "I feel compelled, most unwillingly, to observe
that the worst enemy of your Order could not have hoped to
witness such damning proof of its contempt for temporal authority. Your priests here seem to consider themselves a law

unto themselves, citizens of a state within a state." So saying he made his own more stately exit in the wake of Cabeza, whom he joined in the hall.

Cabeza was heavy with outrage. Hontar was laughing silently to himself. "Perfect," he whispered. "That could not have been better."

"What did you say? Are you mad?"

"You don't understand, Captain General. Come here. Just listen."

Even through the closed doors, the angry voice of Altamirano could be clearly heard, calling on Father Ribiro, Gabriel, and Mendoza—whom he addressed, like a schoolboy, as *you*—to accompany him to his private chamber.

"That little flash of temper," Hontar confided, "was exactly what the reverenced father has been working for all morning."

"So? Why is that good? Altamirano is against us. He's a Jesuit."

"And therefore we can count on him to be obedient."

"To his Order, not to the King of Portugal."

"To his Order, yes, but above all to the Pope."

"Perhaps. But the most important thing to remember when you're dealing with a Jesuit is that you can't count on him for anything. Nobody really knows the sum total of the orders he's been given."

Meanwhile Altamirano had passed straight out of the courtyard into his ground-floor apartment, taking Ribiro, Gabriel, and Mendoza along with him. Without more ado be began questioning the lay brother sharply.

"What is your name?"

"Mendoza, Reverence."

"And how long have you been a brother?"

"Two years, Reverence."

Altamirano scrutinized the bone-hard face with its narrow eyes, clamped mouth, and scars. "And what were you before that?"

"A slave trader, Reverence."

"So, Father Gabriel, you admit slave traders to our ranks?"

"Yes, Reverenced Father," Gabriel replied, "as in the Old World, the Order recruits former soldiers."

"There is no comparison. And why bring him to the assembly?"

"To tell about the slave trade, Reverenced Father."

Altamirano seated himself and considered the figure before him. Mendoza stood meekly, with eyes cast down, each arm thrust into its fellow's sleeve. "Brother Mendoza," he ordered, "you will apologize to His Excellency Don Cabeza, and you will do it in the open courtyard for all to hear."

"Yes, Reverence."

"Now go."

Mendoza went out, and closed the door behind him. He did not resume his old position out in the courtyard, but moved across to a flight of steps leading to a balcony, along which he withdrew. Babuie had seen him and made to join him, but Mendoza shook his head.

Turning to Ribiro and Gabriel, Altamirano asked, "Will he obey?"

"Like any other brother," Gabriel told him.

Then Gabriel spoke of the old Mendoza and his gang, and their eruption into the placid world above the falls. He went on to tell the story of the two brothers' love for the same woman, with its tragic outcome. Last of all he explained Mendoza's bitter struggle to atone for his sin, a struggle that had made him the most docile member of the mission.

Listening to Gabriel, and watching his compassionate expression, Altamirano again recalled his old teacher, who—to him, at least—had always seemed noble in the threadbare clothes that contrasted so starkly with the splendor of his father's villa. But then he remembered Hontar and Cabeza, who were waiting for the next move, and returned his attention with a sigh to the present.

To the missionary Altamirano said, "Whatever your reason may have been for bringing this Mendoza with you today, Father Gabriel, he is no longer in a position to help your cause. I trust you understand that."

"I acknowledge it, Reverenced Father, which makes me wonder why I brought him," said Gabriel.

"You could not have foreseen his fit of spleen."

"But Christ must have foreseen it."

"You are talking like a zealot, Father Gabriel."

"I may not speak of this with Your Reverence?"

"No. I wish to see no further sign of this enthusiasm."

Father Gabriel looked at him and then slowly nodded.

After an inner imprecation, Altamirano asked, "Is it true the Spanish here own slaves?"

"Yes. They term them "Encomiendaros," but that means exactly the same thing. The encomiendaros get no wages and are taught the truths of Mother Church."

"By whom?"

"Such priests as work for Don Cabeza."

Ribiro added, "As for the Portuguese, the last time they made a raid, carrying off four thousand into slavery, the raiding party included two justices from São Paulo and two aldermen. We Jesuits have been expelled from all Portuguese settlements. These facts appear to us as reasons against inclusion of our missions in the Treaty of Madrid. I draw them to your attention, Reverenced Father, in case you, too, judge them relevant."

"And Don Cabeza connives at all this?"

"And profits by it, too."

"I understand. And is it also true," asked Altamirano, closely watching their faces, "that there are gold mines in some of your missions?"

For answer Ribiro turned to Gabriel, who smiled grimly. "No, Reverenced Father," he said, "nor have there ever been. These gold mines are a myth, based on the ancient history of Mexico and Peru."

"The settlers appeared convinced, nevertheless."

"Reverenced Father, come to our missions and see for yourself," Gabriel invited.

Altamirano's immediate response was to flinch at the prospect of a further trip up the interminable river. "No, no. That is impossible." He saw Gabriel look at him again and lower his eyes. Then Ribiro nodded again, as if the old Jesuit's reaction was only to be expected. Altamirano demanded irritably, "What is at stake here, as you see it?"

"The work of Christ," said Gabriel.

Altamirano decided that the man must be a simpleton unless he was some sort of saint. "Where were you born?" he demanded.

"In Ireland, Reverenced Father."

"Ah, yes." He looked thoughtful, recalling that one Father Hildebrand, distinguished by a flyaway headpiece and an infinite knowledge of papal edicts, had come from Ireland, too. "Now I will explain to you what is actually at stake—nothing less than the sheer survival of our Order, do you understand? Not only here but throughout Christendom. Furthermore, by comparison with the courts of Europe, your jungles here in South America are well-kept gardens."

Ribiro lowered his brows to protect his eyes from his superior's stare and murmured, "Ah, yes indeed," but Gabriel asked quietly, "Father, are we not the soldiers of God?"

Altamirano stared at him, bereft of a reply, pushed back his chair, and strode to the window. He looked out just as Hontar and Cabeza chanced to pass below him. Cabeza, with his waddling gait and vehemently working face was speaking. Altamirano heard him say, "Christian amity between two empires is more important than the work of a mission. That is what I maintain, with or without the approval of a reverenced father."

Altamirano's face betrayed no sign that he had heard Cabeza's comment, but he was listening with interest for the answer.

"Don Cabeza," Hontar said at last, "be assured the reverenced father has been sent here by His Holiness the Pope to do a certain thing, and he will do it, never fear, only provided we can exercise a little patience. Patience is all I ask of you. And try to be more modest."

"I will wait a little longer," was the reply as the speakers passed out of hearing.

Conscious that Ribiro and Gabriel might also have overheard that compromising interchange, Altamirano turned to show a troubled face to his two companions, then fell to pacing noisily up and down the resounding floor until his features had recovered their customary composure. "Father Gabriel, make sure Mendoza understands what is required of him. See to it at once."

Gabriel went up to the gallery and seated himself beside Mendoza while Ribiro and Altamirano resumed their places in the courtyard. "Now, listen," he said quietly to Mendoza, "you have undertaken to do a deed. Perform it now, before the whole assembly, on your knees."

"It was a lie he spoke. Why should I apologize?"

"It is an order."

"Altamirano's order?"

Gabriel gave him an ominous look. "It matters not to you. It is my order now."

"I will do it, Father." But then, as Gabriel was moving off to rejoin the others he added, "But it will still be a lie."

Down in the courtyard, where Gabriel rejoined the Jesuit ranks, the murmur of conversation suddenly died into silence as Mendoza went over to Cabeza, sank to his knees, and with arms outstretched, said, "Humbly and without reservation, I ask you to pardon my presumption and my insolence."

Cabeza turned to the hidalgos. "Very well; why not? As I said, a man of honor cannot quarrel with a priest."

"Which makes my insolence doubly impertinent and your pardon doubly courteous," came the response, at which Hontar half smiled. Then, addressing himself to Altamirano, Mendoza continued, "Reverenced Visitor General, I ask your pardon, too." Turning to the Guarani, he said in their language, "I ask your pardon, also."

"For what?" asked Hacugh.

"For insulting His Excellency."

Hacugh looked at Cabeza and weighed him up and down. "That needs no pardon."

A ripple of amusement stirred the Jesuits and the one or two others present who understood Guarani.

Gabriel said hurriedly, "Reverenced Father, may he resume his place?"

Dismissing a pang of envy at the glimpse he had caught of a different world, Altamirano brusquely signified his assent, and the meeting was resumed.

As he often did when he was about to make a crucial move in a conference, Hontar crossed his elegant legs. Then he said, "And now, Reverenced Father, may we be honored by acquaintance with your attitude to the transfer of the mission territories from Spain to Portugal? Because"—turning, he faced Cabeza—"unless we know the reverenced father's sentiments, we shall find ourselves, a year from now, still parleying here."

Cabeza grunted, "Very true," and looked expectantly in the visiting Jesuit's direction.

Altamirano nodded sagely and declared, "From the moment I departed from the Holy City, the question that has brought us together here today has been continuously in my mind, although, as many of you will know, it is a hard business crossing the Atlantic Ocean, and, as you all know, the journey up the river to Asunción is far from pleasant. I am also aware how difficult it has been for many of you to get here from your homes." He paused, noting with satisfaction the expectant look on Cabeza's face, before continuing: "Nevertheless, I have to inform you, Senhors Hontar and Señor Cabeza, I am less decided now than I was before I started out. Accordingly I have resolved to visit at least one of the missions in question before making up my mind. I am sure that from his vast experience Senhor Hontar will agree with me," he concluded, turning to his adversary with the gravest possible face, "that in dealing with a matter that involves such major issues, the sine qua non is modest patience."

Impatiently Cabeza said, "If it please Your Reverenced Father, there is a little mission not above forty miles from here that we could easily visit if it pleases you. What good such a visit might do I can't imagine, but this mission will surely do as well as any."

"No," Altamirano answered blandly. "It pleases me to visit the Mission of Santa Croce."

Hubbub swelled in the hall. "But Reverenced Visitor General," Cabeza protested in consternation, "you do not understand what that involves. That mission is more than two hundred miles upstream, and all the other members of this conference will have to accompany you, to see what you see. The number of boats required will be enormous. Besides, it will be a very arduous journey for Your Reverence."

Altamirano's eyes were fixed on Father Gabriel as he said,

"Nevertheless, that is where I have decided I shall go. Is my proposal agreeable to you, Father Gabriel?"

"Emphatically," agreed Gabriel, "but, it will take a long time to collect the boats."

"The Christian amity between two Catholic empires," Altamirano said, with his face turned solemnly to Don Cabeza, "surely deserves our highest endeavors."

"It is also an issue too important to be postponed until the crack of doom," Cabeza replied.

The considerations that had forced Altamirano to decide to visit a mission were political. Hontar's public confidence in his cooperation required him now to make a gesture to suggest that the missions' fate was not yet sealed. In choosing the Santa Croce Mission, however, Altamirano was yielding to a personal inclination—above all, as Hontar acknowledged to himself, yielding to a simple desire to please the disconcerting Gabriel. He had learned from Gabriel's story that Santa Croce was the mission that the Jesuits had founded below the Falls of Iguaçú.

So it came about that one month later, toward evening, a fleet of boats approached the Mission Santa Croce. The first three vessels were full of soldiers, a guard of honor for the dignitaries following. The next boat contained Hontar and Cabeza, their relationship considerably strained by two weeks of voyaging together. Behind them came some half a dozen settlers who had trailed them up the river in a worsening temper and without their wives. The boats of the Jesuits followed, in the middle of the fleet, and last of all came barge-loads of Guarani, servants, tents, and baggage.

The farther they proceeded up the river the narrower had grown the gap of light above their heads, while on either bank black trees were densely tangled in a confusion where dusk reigned even at midday, save where a random shaft of light shot down through a gap in the foliage. An eerie silence invaded the river from its overgrown banks, broken only by occasional forlorn howls, repeated a second later in the distance, only to be followed by silence again.

But now, in the falling dusk, a very different note was heard as from the leading boat—three trumpets sounded in unison to announce their arrival. A few moments later, around the next bend in the river, a massive timber jetty swung into sight with a group of Jesuits gathered on it in readiness to receive them while, from the tower of a great church nearby, bells began to peal.

Once ashore they were welcomed by the waiting superior of Santa Croce Mission. His formal greetings completed, he immediately added, without the slightest shift of tone: "And finally, Reverenced Father, I apologize for the color of my skin." He was a Guarani.

Altamirano found it impossible to tell whether this was a joke, for the speaker's face was expressionless. He replied: "In case you are serious, let me assure you no apology is called for. We are all one color in the sight of God."

"Reverenced Visitor General, it was to you alone I was apologizing."

Again Altamirano could not tell whether this was a joke. "Are there many fathers in the missions such as you?" he asked.

"No, Reverenced Father. But then, neither are there many such as Gabriel." So saying, Itapua seized his old superior in a fierce embrace.

Cabeza watched gimlet-eyed. Hontar, after a pause, came up and formally greeted his host. This time it was Itapua who looked taken aback. Hontar smiled.

Mendoza kept to the rear as, behind the dignitaries, the long line of visitors formed up in procession. His own face, when he raised his head, was expressionless, too. At his right hand walked Babuie with the monkey and, at his left, Hacugh.

In the failing light, the procession crossed the square to the enormous church. Altamirano, keenly observing everything, took note of the neatly ordered stone huts on either side, each raised up on a plinth, with a wooden roof and five doorways. The occupants, however, were not to be seen. They were all in the vast church, awaiting him. Save for hens and goats, the only sign of life in the vicinity was a couple of old women. They were lying in hammocks and gave no sign of noticing the grand procession. Gabriel, however, went over and greeted them.

Meanwhile the clamorous summons of the bells, cast in Italy, became more urgent. Rearing itself high above them, the shadowy tower looked menacing to Altamirano, crowded as it was with unrecognizable winged creatures, half angels, half demons, executed long ago by sculptors from the jungle. Once through the wide doorway, however, and into the dim coolness of the lofty candlelit interior, he was greeted by a reverential hush. A second later the "Te Deum" sounded from four thousand throats in unison, thundering down from the distant roof. At the front of the choir an orchestra of viols, clarinets, and trumpets sounded a strong accompaniment. Outside, the music pouring forth from the church inundated the entire settlement and spread out and away through the darkening trees.

As he knelt at the altar rail and let his eyes adjust to the dimness, Altamirano was amazed by the spectacle of that vast Guarani congregation, all wide-mouthed in praise, packing the full space, nave and transept. Hontar, for his part, found the presence of so many Guarani made him cough with unaccustomed awkwardness.

Next day, mounted on a white mule, Altamirano was led by Itapua, together with Ribiro, Cabeza, and Hontar, through miles of farmland. Gabriel walked beside him, and the rest of the Jesuits followed thirty paces in the rear.

To left and right, the Guarani laborers went silently on with their work unless he halted and faced them, whereupon they all knelt as one man. So it came about that eventually he found himself seated on a rise, where he had stopped to rest in an orange grove, surrounded by kneeling Guarani.

Looking Hontar directly in the eye, he said, "I find this place impressive, don't you?"

"Yes, very impressive," the diplomat agreed.

Cabeza, however, was resentful at having been called at six in the morning to trail around on an ambling nag in the retinue of a treacherous cleric. Moreover, he had a headache. "I may be blind," he commented, "but to tell the truth I don't see any difference between this lot and the ones who tend my own orange trees, back in Asunción."

"There is this difference," Itapua said softly. "Here at Santa Croce the trees are theirs."

"Theirs?" Altamirano exclaimed. "In what way theirs?"

Mendoza came a few paces forward from the procession and replied, "Nine-tenths of the produce goes to them; we receive only one-tenth." He turned to a laborer who was kneeling close by and asked him a question in Guarani.

A score of other laborers took up the answer this one gave, and then more, until the grove resounded with it. "Yes, they all say yes, the grove is theirs," reported Itapua.

Altamirano, watching Cabeza wipe his forehead, went on: "They certainly seem contented."

"Indeed, Reverenced Father, I would say they seem no less contented than my own Guarani do."

"Reverenced Father, there is another difference, by your leave," declared Mendoza, returning to the group of visitors, leading a laborer by the hand. He stripped the Guarani's thin clothing off his back, revealing a welter of old scars. "As you can see, this man has been living here at the mission long enough for the wounds he received from his owner's whip to heal. Before he escaped, however, they rarely stopped bleeding. He tells me he used to belong to a Spaniard, who bought him from a Portuguese."

At first nobody spoke. Then Ribiro broke the silence. "There is a very fine plantation along this way, Reverenced Father. Would you care to see it?"

Mendoza raised his eyes to Altamirano's face. The latter hesitated, then turned on Cabeza. "Captain General, tell me, is such a thing lawful?"

Cabeza's face was dark with rage. "What meets a public demand is surely lawful!" Then he did what he had been longing to do all day. He drove his spurs into his startled mount and left the whole lot of them at a gallop.

Altamirano followed him with his eyes until he was out of sight. Then he looked at Mendoza. "Father Ribiro," he said a moment later, "which way is it to the plantation you were speaking of?" and he urged his mule forward.

There were even more plantations to be visited—orchards of pears and apples, groves of apricots and lemons—and Altamirano was taken to each in turn. Devout laborers crowded around his mule and knelt to receive his blessing. Accustomed to mass piety, at first he suffered these demonstrations with a fixed expression of indifference, but at last they began to irritate him. These alien flat faces with their burning eyes seemed to make him irritable. When they reached the lemon grove, reining in his mule he said, "I have seen enough fields. Show me something else."

Itapua said, "But you haven't seen the clearing yet. That's where we keep the cattle. I beg you to inspect our cattle, Reverenced Father. The people have been cleaning up the steers since yesterday."

"I have seen sufficient," Altamirano repeated, and it was he who led their departure.

Hontar looked after him thoughtfully, and gently turned his mount to follow at the head of the accompanying notables. The crowd of Guarani trailed faithfully along behind. Last of all came Mendoza, walking with Babuie, apart from the rest.

They took Altamirano next to the carpenter shop. Here Itapua took the two halves of a flute and fitted them together. A hairline ran the length of the flute. "Like the blowpipe," he explained.

"Yes, indeed," Altamirano agreed, admiring the workmanship. "I see." He looked around the commodious shop at the viols, violoncellos, and other instruments being fashioned there, and at the dignified carpenters standing by. He stroked the strings of a guitar and was surprised by the murmur of sound that came from it. After a careful inspection, he made his way out of the shop.

Still accompanied by the crowd he was then taken to a vast open shed, with some forty women in it who stood up at his arrival. It was a carpet factory, and he was conducted around it, invited to finger, one after the other, the half-completed works still strung up to be woven. He turned, and there was a whirr of wings. He glimpsed a bird flying through the place and out into the bush beyond, where it emitted cries of warning.

He saw the schoolroom, deserted now. Drawn on a slate were the fingers of a mother and father with three strong children; it could have been the work of any child anywhere.

Altamirano next visited the living quarters. In a Guarani dwelling containing rolled-up bedding whose gaudy pattern was reflected on the white-washed walls, he found a mandolin leaning against a wall on which a picture of the Virgin hung. When they visited the cells of the Jesuit fathers, an elderly priest showed them a case of Guarani bows and arrows. Each item was neatly labeled, and the collection was displayed on the wall. To Altamirano he seemed proud of these primitive weapons, though Itapua looked away. "There, you see?" the priest said. "Beautiful . . . how beautiful!"

"But surely they don't make them still?" Altamirano asked.

"Oh, no, not nowadays." The Jesuit replaced the bow he had been handling and swung around to face his visitor. "I hope they never regret that, Reverenced Father."

Altamirano noted all this, but kept his thoughts to himself. So did Mendoza. Like all the other brothers, he could only wait.

Later, when evening was beginning to fall, the Jesuits sat outside the mission storehouse. The eaves of the pantiled roof served them as a veranda. The Guarani sat quietly outside their own dwellings. All eyes were on the refectory, whose interior was already illuminated by a lamp, where Altamirano was interviewing Itapua, the mission superior. Ribiro, too, was there.

Inside the storehouse, Altamirano shut the account book he had been examining. He looked at Ribiro, but the look he received in return said nothing. Outside he could hear the breeze in the trees, the croak of frogs, the soft, indecipherable utterances of the distant forest. He rubbed his face and, for the first time, felt cornered by his responsibilities.

"Brother Itapua," he asked, "are all the other missions much like this one?"

"Yes, Reverenced Father."

"There is no gold, then?"

"None."

He said to Ribiro, "How many Guarani are you responsible for?"

"All told, three hundred thousand."

"These figures are good, Brother Itapua."

"I know, Father."

"One-tenth of the earnings you take on behalf of the Order?"

"Neither more nor less, Reverenced Father."

"And how is the rest distributed?"

"By families, in equal shares. By this arrangement we avoid the sin of envy."

"That is the doctrine of some modern French thinkers. Did you know?"

"No, Reverenced Father, but I do know it is the doctrine of

the founding fathers of Holy Church."

"And are all who live here brought up in the practice of true worship?"

"As you have seen them, Reverenced Father."

Then Altamirano said to Itapua, "I am inexpressibly impressed by your work, Brother." He said it dutifully but formally.

"Father, will the good impression you have formed suffice to save us?"

Altamirano turned away. "Request His Excellency to attend me here."

Itapua went out without a word. He passed by the Jesuit fathers sitting beneath the eaves of the storehouse and through the Guarani lines to the guest house on the far side, where Cabeza and Hontar sat waiting—and Cabeza drinking—while their guards lolled outside, yawning or playing cards.

Cabeza's drinking showed. When he heard Altamirano's request, he slapped the table with his hand and replied, "Present my compliments to the Reverenced Father and tell him I await him here." Itapua looked at him, but, receiving no addition to this message, went out without a word to deliver it.

"Softly," said Hontar. "Don Cabeza, softly now!"

"No. Not softly."

Watching from the storehouse, Gabriel and Mendoza saw all that was happening, and in common with the rest, rose to their feet as, guided by Itapua, the Visitor General passed by them on his way to what they all expected would be the conclusive consultation.

On arrival, without waiting to be invited, he seated himself and said at once, "Don Cabeza, I address you as a true son of Mother Church. The royal house of Portugal, which for all its seeming confidence and greatness, is lost and desperate because it is faithless and godless, whereas you, my son, are a joyous believer in life everlasting in the company of Christ and all his saints, to which, as a member of our Holy Church—"

Hontar, appearing deeply shocked, held up a protesting

hand. "His Catholic Majesty, the King of Portugal whom I serve—" he started.

Altamirano turned to him and said flatly, "The man you serve is Señor Sebastião José de Carvalho e Mello, the sworn enemy of Holy Church, and most unhappily he rules your king as well as you."

The surprise on Hontar's face was genuine. As an experienced negotiator he had patiently thought out his opponent's possible moves, but this direct onslaught had not been one of them. What devil had got into him?

The Jesuit was leaning forward in his chair, which was crowned with an evil, or a seraphic, pair of wings, carved by the Guarani. "Which being so," Altamirano went on, "I cannot advise the transfer of mission territories to Portuguese administration. At the same time," he concluded, forestalling protest, "the treaty clearly does cover those territories, so Portugal is not to be deprived of them."

"What other way is there?" Cabeza demanded.

"You can advise your king, and I shall inform His Holiness, that Portugal should guarantee survival of the missions, pending which guarantee any operation of the treaty in respect to mission territories will be postponed. This I call upon you to do together with me, as you have hope of heaven through the intercession of our merciful Redeemer."

Hontar was thoroughly alarmed now, but the heavy features of Cabeza, thus appealed to, swelled into those of a bullying hooligan. "In my opinion," he said with hatred, "and most truthfully as I have hope of heaven—which I do—in my opinion, which is that of one whose family has been here for generations, the work of the missions is the devil's work!"

Cabeza's sincerity, too, astonished Hontar. What astonished Altamirano now was his own naiveté. Because Cabeza obviously accepted whatever he had been told in the name of religion during childhood, Altamirano had expected him to be equally obedient now. He opened his mouth to protest, but Cabeza rose to his feet to deliver a further thrust.

"Let me tell you something: Even I, the captain general, have to ask Father Ribiro for permission—*permission,* do you hear?—to enter a mission in my own territory."

"Not yours. Only your king—"

"His Majesty's and mine. He's made it all the same now."

"Not at all—"

"The same, the same." Cabeza loomed threateningly over the table. "And where are the gold mines?"

"In the imaginations of the settlers."

"Yes?" The word hung heavy; it was the first time Cabeza had questioned the Jesuit's integrity. Altamirano raised his eyebrows.

There was an awkward silence for the time it took Cabeza to realize how far he had gone, and he added, "Well, maybe, maybe you're right. Who knows?" He walked to the window and looked at his soldiers resting outside beneath the overhanging roof. Beyond them, in the darkness, he sensed hundreds of Guarani faces turned to watch.

Altamirano smoothed his brow and began again. "What I find true is that they teach these people—"

Cabeza flung himself around to interrupt. "What they teach them is that they are equal to us. They also teach contempt for property and lawful profit—"

"And slave owning?" Altamirano asked in a level voice.

"I have explained that. I'm tired of explaining it. The point is that they teach contempt for lawful trade. They scorn civil authority and those who have been appointed to rule over them."

"Not so. The paramount vow of the Jesuit Order is the vow of obedience."

"Then let Jesuits obey!" Cabeza struck the table. "Tell them to obey. Or your own head be it, Reverenced Father!"

Altamirano said, "Consequences will be on your own head, too, from your doings, Don Cabeza." He pushed back his chair and added, "For my part, I will obey my conscience." Then, turning away, he walked out of the guest house.

As he made his stormy way across the square, he thought, So, I am to consult my conscience! Conscience, are you there? My pride is there, certainly, and it has a lot to— He pulled up, finding himself face to face with Gabriel and

Mendoza; without a word, he veered off toward the river.

When they were alone in the guest house, Hontar gave Cabeza a profound sigh. "I fear you have been foolish, Captain General."

Cabeza glowered, shifted his heavy buttocks, and sat down. "It's time he heard the official view in these parts."

"Ah, so that is what he heard, is it?"

"Shall I go after him?" Cabeza offered.

But Hontar said quite sharply, "No. Not you." In the soft shoes he persisted in wearing despite the climate and the sand, he went out of the guest house and, watched by hundreds of Guarani eyes, strode through the gathering dusk across the square in pursuit of his opponent.

Altamirano walked out onto the jetty. The river looked leaden, and the trees, from which night noises now emerged, were darkening fast. A short distance downstream, half a dozen empty barges had lost their reflections, but children were still scampering over them. An older girl, posted to watch them, gazed dreamily at the water. Altamirano took no notice of the children's shrill cries, and when Hontar came up behind him he did not stir.

"I fear that I bear bad tidings from Senhor Carvalho," Hontar said.

"Give it to me." Altamirano held out a hand.

"What?"

"The letter in which Carvalho threatens to expel the Jesuit Order from Portugal if I decide in favor of keeping the missions here."

Hontar took the letter from his inside pocket and held it out. "He will also have you driven out of Spain and France."

"And throughout the world," said Altamirano. He took the letter and read it attentively.

"He will do it."

"Of course." The Jesuit returned the letter to its owner. His gaze went back to the half-dozen children now straggling home. It would be completely dark soon.

"I should like to express my personal regret," Hontar said. "I did not expect to see what we have seen. I had expected to find the Jesuits ready to compromise."

"So had I." Altamirano turned to face Hontar. "But you see what they are like."

"I did not expect to find such rigorous application of the saying 'Love thy neighbor.' It is quite refreshing to see people being nice to one another."

"That, too."

"Anyway, you can still have a noble failure. You see, your Christian community has its uses. Settle for a noble failure; there is something moving about that."

Altamirano stared at him, for Hontar was using the exact words he would have used himself before coming out here. Then, without answering, he strode off the jetty and back to the mission.

"Well, what is your decision?" Hontar called after him, but Altamirano ignored the question.

No less resolutely Father Gabriel intercepted him. Their eyes met, and for the first time since he had been involved in this affair, something like fear appeared in the Visitor General's eyes. Without disguising his evasion he changed direction. The cross on the church seemed to beckon to him, and he went toward it.

Gabriel rejoined Mendoza and the others. He stood there in silence for fifteen minutes. Then he went after Altamirano into the church. The sound of the door he closed behind him reverberated through the gloom. Only a few candles had been lit. Watched by a few Guarani worshipers, Altamirano was kneeling at the altar rail. Seating himself at a distance, Gabriel waited until the kneeling figure rose with a sigh and, peering through the shadows, asked, "Is that you, Father Gabriel?"

"Yes, Reverenced Father."

Altamirano came and sat down next to him. "I cannot. Cannot pray."

Then Gabriel said, "Come with me beyond the falls to see the mission of San Sebastian."

Another prolonged pause and then, "Why should I do that?"

"It's very much easier to see there; here it's all so visible."

"And you invite me?"

"Yes, Reverenced Father."

"How long would it take?"

"A month, and it would be a hard journey."

"I'll come."

Two days later the visiting notables, with Cabeza and Hontar at their head, stood on the jetty watching a few dugout canoes paddle away upstream. When they were out of earshot Cabeza observed, *"Puerco de Dios,* there goes a traitor," and stamped his foot on the sounding timber.

"A traitor?" queried Hontar.

"A traitor. The Jesuits make their own false church within the true one."

"Don Cabeza, your motives do you credit."

"Confound your impudence," said Cabeza. "I speak in all sincerity. I am the Catholic son of the Catholic Church."

"Then you alarm me."

"Why? I am saying that I am a good Catholic. Why is that alarming?"

"If you regard yourself as a good Catholic, perhaps the Jesuit regards the Catholic Church as Christian; in which event," he said, waving after the dugout canoes, "there's no guessing what he'll do."

Altamirano, in a pair of sturdy boots and a wide straw hat, despite his fine black cassock, sat trailing his hands in the water beside the canoe, and found that he could not guess either.

Ahead, in the leading canoe, he could see the back of the stern paddler, Mendoza. It seemed militarily hard even under the cassock. Mendoza's face, however, when from time to time he turned to stare back over his shoulder, looked more and more relieved as the Mission of Santa Croce, with its garrison, was left behind. He began to crack jokes with Sebastian, Hacugh, and the boy, who were in the boat with him. The words must have been Guarani; Altamirano could not catch them, although he heard the laughter. His own companion sat hunched and silent as though beneath a burden it took all his strength to bear. This was Gabriel.

On both sides Altamirano saw the jungle closing in—sometimes with high, dark, tangled branches; sometimes a wilderness of flowering bushes stretching away over acres blazing in the sun. Once he suddenly found himself staring into a predatory eye. It belonged to a monstrous creature with the hard, unnatural skin of a fiend or dragon in a medieval painting—an alligator.

Day followed day, and he began to forget why he was there. No longer mindful of responsibilities to the Holy See, the thrones of Spain and Portugal, or the Order, he found his judgment reverting to the simplicities of childish liking, and he wanted Gabriel for a friend.

Each night they camped on a muddy bank. Altamirano's fine boots grew caked with mud, but he shaved his face scrupulously every morning in hot water, which Mendoza fetched for him without being told. It was also Mendoza who unpacked his things each night and packed them up again each morning, rendering the same service for Gabriel, too, unasked. He washed their clothes as well, but rarely spoke with them. He kept his conversation for the Guarani.

Hardship started when they disembarked at the rapids. The elemental smash of water over rock alarmed Altamirano. It was too wild. The canoes were dragged up the bank, turned upside down, and covered with branches. They camped for the night. In the morning Mendoza rolled Altamirano's bedding with his own and set off uphill with the bulky bundle, without a word, to lead the way. Altamirano followed. The rest of the party, Guarani included, followed after him. That day, and for several following days, from time to time an obstacle or incline compelled Altamirano to stop. He could not go on until Mendoza turned back to help him. On the fourth night, while Mendoza was spreading his bedding, the Jesuit asked, "Was it up here you carried all your weapons?"

"Yes, Reverenced Father."

"You must be very strong."

"I used to be, but I was rescued."

"By whom?"

"By him." He pointed at Hacugh. "Good night, and God be with you, Reverenced Father."

20

BEFORE NOON ON the seventh day they were back beside the river at a place where, on their journey to Asunción to attend the conference, the delegation from the Mission of San Sebastian had beached their raft. On this same raft they now resumed their voyage. Four days later, when they had camped for the night, Altamirano became aware that the darkness was filled with a low, dull, inescapable roar. "What's that?" he asked, although he knew what it must be, and it was only after a pause that Gabriel answered that it was the Falls of Iguaçú.

Throughout the next day's journey the roar grew louder and more ominous. After they had camped, Gabriel led the visitor to a high promontory from which the falls could be seen above the roof of the forest. Fascinated, Altamirano stayed there to gaze at the spectacle until it grew dark, and he kept waking throughout the night to hear the irresistible flow. By morning the sense of threatening catastrophe with which the din had first gripped him had given way to one of inevitability, so that next day he completed the ascent of the heights in a state of numbness, although his body trembled with the general vibration.

When they reached the top of the cliffs at last, Gabriel said, "If it please you, Reverenced Father, wait here for an hour."

As if in a dream, Altamirano watched the darkness gathering, stars coming out and rising from below to mount above the iridescent spray that changed from saffron to rose and finally, as it fell upon the forest below, to crimson.

Gabriel waited until it was completely dark before touching the Visitor General's sleeve and saying, "Now let us go. It is

time to sleep." That night the sound of falling water, behind
them now, was peaceful.

"Father," Gabriel announced the next morning, "you are
about to see the Garden of Eden." His taciturnity had gone. In
high good humor he pointed to a couple of dugout canoes,
each with a crew of two Guarani, that had come to fetch them.
Soon the sound of the falls died away, and all was silent as
they floated through the liquid calm, save for the pluck of the
paddles and the grunt of the prow. Long, bending branches
with dripping leaves stretched out like arms over the water.
There came a sudden shriek and splash at which Altamirano
sharply turned his head. A rotting branch had fallen under its
own weight into the stream.

Gabriel sensed his guest's uneasiness. "The Garden of
Eden is thinning itself out," he said cheerfully.

But it was not the strangeness or the silence or the unex-
pectedness that alarmed Altamirano. It was the absence of
anything within himself to set against these things, now that
he had left familiar surroundings.

The silence did not last all day, however. There had been
no sign of the boy when they awoke. Babuie had gone ahead
to prepare for their arrival.

Toward noon Gabriel suddenly raised his hand. "Ah,
Reverenced Father, hear!" and then he immediately fell silent,
himself listening.

There was no discernible change as yet in the view, but
faintly, like some hallucination conjured up in reaction to the
wilderness, the opening strains of the "Spem in Alium," could
be heard. Then the canoe rounded a bend in the river, and
Altamirano saw a complete tribe of Guarani standing motionless on the edge of a deep clearing, all joining in the chant.
Some were at the river's edge, others knee-deep in the water.
Those to the rear were stationed in the openings of the path-
ways between the huts of the village. Above it all rose a high
church tower on which a plain wooden cross had been
mounted.

They put in to land, while the chant swelled in magnifi-
cence and beauty. As he drew near, he could see the concen-

tration on the faces of the singers—men, women, and
gold-skinned children—and recognized a choir fit to grace
Saint Peter's. The chant soared to its conclusion. In the silence, Hacugh looked at him, and Altamirano acknowledged
to himself the justice of the pride he could see in the Guarani's
face. Then, without speaking, he signaled that he wished to be
alone, and followed a path into the forest.

Almost immediately the village was completely hidden
from him by foliage. There was no sign of human life. He had
cut himself off, as he intended, but the separation was alarming. He heard stealthy rustlings first in one direction, then in
another. There were sudden rattling sounds, harsh calls of unknown birds, and abrupt, eerie cries that seemed to mock one
another. At the foot of a sublime tree that rose straight and
true like a ceremonial pillar decorated with gold and ivory
flowers, he stumbled on the carcass of a monkey, swarming
with maggots. A six-inch spider glanced at him with lively
eyes from the summit of the fungus on which it was squatting,
while nearby orchids of the most intricate symmetry sprouted
on a moldering branch. A brilliant cloud of butterflies reveled
around a stagnant pool.

Altamirano had come away to seek strength and direction,
but now stood, confused, in a grotesque world where the
works of God and of the devil seemed to grow in and out of
one another. He sank to his knees. Once again, however,
prayer proved impossible. Nevertheless, it was a long time
before he rose to his feet in despair. From now on he would be
resolute enough. He would do what he had always known he
would have to do.

That night he told them. He was sitting in the largest hut.
Outside, the tribe surrounded it in the deepening twilight. The
braves stood close. Behind them were the women and then the
children. Inside, the Jesuit fathers sat silently against the
walls. Hacugh, backed by two elders, was seated facing Altamirano. Beside him sat Gabriel, serving as interpreter.

"You must understand you have a new ruler—no longer
the King of Spain but the King of Portugal." As he spoke he
knew he would never forget the thoughtful eyes of Hacugh,

watching him from the flat, taut Guarani face, but he did not flinch. "Tell him," he said to Gabriel. "Make sure he understands."

Altamirano did not see Gabriel's expression, because, even when he translated Hacugh's answer, Gabriel kept staring straight ahead: "He wants to know what that means. 'What will we have to do?' he asks."

"Whatever the King of Portugal orders."

"And if he orders us to leave the mission, what do we do then?" was the next translation.

Altamirano wished Hacugh would look at Gabriel instead of at him, but still he did not flinch as he replied: "Obey."

At this Mendoza, seated against the wall with the other Jesuits, raised his head to watch and listen while Hacugh and the two old braves discussed it.

"This mission is our home now," came their answer. "We have no wish to go back to the forest."

To which the visitor's response was "Submit yourselves to the will of God." But he saw it did not suffice.

Hacugh replied without strong emphasis but with a connected flow of speech spelling out an argument: "It was by the will of God we left the forest and built this mission. For what reason has He now changed His mind?"

"I do not know God's reasons." Altamirano found comfort in the orthodoxy of his evasion. It was, he reflected, also Socratic. He did not know, and he knew he did not know.

But Hacugh's answer was "I do not believe you speak for God. It is the Portuguese you speak for."

"I speak for the Church."

"Then speak for the Church to the King of Portugal."

"I have already spoken, but he has not heard."

"Then make him listen."

"When a king will not listen, I cannot make him listen."

Hacugh looked satisfied. This time he nodded directly to Gabriel. "I, too, am a king, and I will not listen," he said. Courteously he waited for this final declaration to be translated and then, followed by his two advisers, left the building. They could hear him addressing the crowd outside. Then the whole tribe went down to the river and sat on the bank. One of

Hacugh's advisers started speaking to them in a low, thoughtful voice.

"What is happening?" asked Altamirano. "What will they do?"

"They are going to fight," Gabriel informed him. "They mean to defend themselves."

"Try to persuade them not to. Have you not the power?"

Gabriel said, "But I have already failed to persuade Your Reverence."

"To do what?"

"To fight for them, to fight on their behalf, Reverenced Father in God."

Without replying to this, Altamirano stood and addressed the assembled Jesuits. "If they do fight," he informed them, "for the sake of the Order you must make absolutely sure that nobody can say you encouraged them to do so." He avoided Gabriel's eye. He looked admonishingly toward Mendoza, but the latter was staring into a corner. "For this reason, you will all return with me tomorrow to Asunción." He was aware of Mendoza's eyes turned suddenly upon him, as if making sure he meant what he said. "Whoever disobeys will be cast off," he continued. "He will be cast out of the Order. He will lose the succor of the Blessed Sacrament. He will be expelled from the consecrated body of the Church. In short, he will be denied all hope of redemption. And so, may God be with you, my brethren! May he be with us all!"

"God be with thee," echoed the priests as they departed, but Mendoza did not so much as exchange a glance with any of them. Alone and silently he went to his hut and dropped the screen. But even beyond his screen, except for the irrepressible forest noises, he heard only silence.

In the cloisters of the church, however, Altamirano consulted with Father Gabriel, who calmly inquired, "Did you know that this would be your decision from the beginning?"

"Of course," said Altamirano. "Didn't you?"

"No," Gabriel admitted.

"The only reason I postponed it and came here first," Altamirano explained, "was to teach the captain general that he must never take the Church—take me, in fact—for granted."

"I see," said Gabriel. "I did not understand," he confessed.

That was all he said. To Altamirano it sounded like an accusation. "That is not completely true," the Visitor General admitted. He had not spoken to anyone like this since that distant childhood which his visit to America had unaccountably resurrected. "It came to me," he confessed, "at one time not so long ago—indeed, quite recently—that if I came here, God might speak to me. God speaks to some," he seemed to apologize, "but not to me. There was no answer. There was no answer at all."

"I see," said Gabriel. "Is it settled, then?"

In reply Altamirano explained what would become of the Order if Carvalho did not get his way.

"The annihilation of the Order!" Gabriel seemed to contemplate the catastrophe. "Yes," he concurred, "it would be grievous. But it is more grievous," he continued, "for the Order to join in the devil's work."

"But the death of the Order," said Altamirano. "Surely, that is the worst thing of all."

"Perhaps death is not as it seems to us," said Gabriel. "But the work of the devil is unmistakable, even to the damned."

"Father Gabriel," Altamirano told him, "they chose wisely who appointed you to guard these savages. Nevertheless, what I have said must be."

A crouching figure emerged from the shadows and flung itself at Gabriel's feet, clutching his robe. Altamirano recognized the boy who had sung at Asunción and who idolized Mendoza. Words poured from him in a passionate plea. There came a pause. Gabriel gave some sort of answer, but no sooner had it ceased than the plea was renewed.

"He is afraid," Gabriel explained. "He fears to be left alone. He wants our help. He says that the devil is waiting out there in the forest. He says he has seen him. He begs me not to abandon him. He begs me to stay, Reverenced Father."

"You know better than I do, Father Gabriel, what will become of anyone who stays here," Altamirano said.

"This is not what I brought them out of the forest for," Gabriel answered heavily. Then he spoke to Babuie, consolingly but not encouragingly, until at last the child obediently went away, pausing at the end of the pathway for a last look at Altamirano, who, in his own turn, said, "Father Gabriel, I beg to be remembered in your prayers."

But he had not forbidden him to stay.

"And much good may my prayers do you!" Gabriel muttered, when he had left his superior. But upon entering his cell, he found Mendoza waiting for him. "What do *you* want?" Gabriel growled.

"What do I lose," asked Mendoza, "if I break my vow of obedience?"

"Leave me" was Gabriel's answer. "Disobedience is a thing I will not discuss." But Mendoza made to speak to him again. "Get out!" he ordered. "Leave me! I refuse to hear." At the same time, without knowing why, he pulled off his cassock to reveal a nondescript, skinny body with grizzled pectoral hair. "Just you, by yourself?" he asked Mendoza. "What do you hope to achieve? Death with honor, is that it?"

"We undertook to protect the Guarani."

"Remember this, Mendoza," Gabriel said hoarsely, delivering each word like a blow. "If you die with new blood on your hands you will die a traitor. You swore to give your life to God, and God is Love."

Part
Five

21

THE BACK OF the captain general's residence in Asunción overlooked the parade ground where, in swirling rain that had been falling all day, the expeditionary force was mustered to the accompaniment of kettledrums. Through a window Altamirano watched in comfort as the soldiers were inspected by their commanders. He had deputied his secretary to pronounce the necessary final blessing on the lot of them—Spanish troops, Portuguese troops, mercenary musketeers, bands of adventurers, and a party of Chaco Guarani, lost and drunk.

One of the soldiers of fortune, a black man, had a racking cough, and the inspection party paused to question him about his condition before passing down the line to check the artillery train—cannon loaded onto mules. Last of all the joint commanders, one Spanish and one Portuguese, came to where Cabeza stood with Hontar, to report to the representatives of their royal masters.

Cabeza addressed the two leaders: "No more force is to be used than you find necessary to carry out your lawful duties. Is that understood?"

"Perfectly, Excellency."

On the parade ground a priest stepped forward, and all the assembled men of war, except the Chaco Guarani, fell to their knees. Altamirano, however, was no longer at the window to see this, or to watch his secretary invoke God's blessing on the enterprise. He had slipped away.

The boy was alone in the canoe. He paddled downstream, toward the falls, until he reached the legendary place. Every Guarani at the mission knew the story of how Mendoza had come to live among them, and how Hacugh had freed him

from his burden of steel. They also knew exactly where that
burden had disappeared into the water. Beaching his craft,
Babuie peered into the river. He dived and surfaced again and
again until at last, gasping and exhausted, he emerged dragging what looked like a weed-infested piece of sodden wood.

He crouched on the riverbank to scrape what he had found
until a scabbard was revealed. Then with a pull, he drew forth
the sword. He examined it carefully and fell to cleaning it
until it shone nakedly. Stowing it in his canoe, he went back
upstream.

Following Altamirano's instructions to the letter, Gabriel
told the tribe they must abandon the mission. God would go
with them, and so would he. Deep in the jungle they would
found another mission.

When he had finished, Hacugh stood up. "You are a man
of God," he said. "But now God has abandoned us, as he did
his Son. We will stay in the home that we have built, and we
will fight. That is my word." And it was evident that he spoke
for the rest of the tribe.

Lying awake later that night, Gabriel wondered at the cunning of the devil who had persuaded clever men in Europe that
greed, left to its own devices, brought prosperity and peace.
Staring up at the brushwood ceiling, he found that the old
impulse to bring his difficulties to Christ had left him.

Mendoza, too, kept to his cell. It was there the boy brought
him his sword. He knew it at once, stretching out his hand
instinctively to heft its familiar weight, but just in time withdrew before he had touched it. A bundle of faggots lay in the
corner of the room. He told the boy to lean the sword against
it and go away. Nevertheless, his eyes were fixed on the
weapon, and it never left his thoughts that night. Toward evening of the next day, a text began to repeat itself in his mind:
"Finally, my brethren, be strong in the Lord and the power of
His might. Put on the whole armor of God, that ye may be
able to stand against the wiles of the devil; for we wrestle not
against flesh and blood, but against principalities, against
powers, against the rulers of darkness of this world."

Calmly he stood up and took the sword, which once again felt like an extension of his body. He went to Hacugh with it in his hand. "I bring no message from Christ," he told him. "If you wish to hear from Christ, go to Father Gabriel. But I am joining you."

Hacugh thanked him, adding frankly, "For, of ourselves, we have no thought how to defend this place."

By this time, the expeditionary force was proceeding upriver on three barges. It was approaching the San Croce mission. Within striking distance they camped. They were irresistible; they were jaguars.

The next morning, as they sailed around the bend and the jetty hove into sight, they found the whole population of the San Croce Mission assembled to receive them, armed only with banners on which the last moments of dying martyrs were portrayed.

The soldiers and their two commanders, one Spanish and one Portuguese, swarmed ashore. The Guarani knelt and offered their pictures of the final moments of the dying martyrs. The soldiers fell upon them with fire and sword. By nightfall the leaping flames of the great church, stores, and dwelling places were already dying down. The glowing remains sputtered and crackled as if in protest. Corpses of Guarani littered the square where, not so long ago, Altamirano had arrived in procession.

Some of the Guarani had escaped into the forest. Enough, however, had been captured to make up six bargeloads of slaves. The mission's barges were used to carry them down to Asunción for sale. They were taken away, keening, under the minimum guard. For the soldiers and Chaco Guarani still had to ascend the falls and take the Mission of San Sebastian.

Above the falls, in his retreat close by the village, Tanretopra learned that the day he had long been promising them had come. The spirits themselves now summoned him. In a quiet place in his mind, he prepared himself for this. To stay close to them he went without sleep and food. He replaced the ornate feathers in his huge headdress so that, when the time came for him to die, he would pass on this symbol of more than earthly power to another living person.

Now he painted his face and body with the correct lines and marks and, carrying the headdress, returned to the people. He watched, and when Mendoza had gone out into the forest, he donned the headdress and revealed himself to them, standing on a heap of earth. Slowly they gathered around to hear what he had to say.

"See, what I have foretold has come to pass. You accept the men of Christ, and then you must yield to the men of rapine."

"It is so," one of the old braves said to Hacugh. "He foretold it. Now hear him."

"You have built a fine village for Christ," Tanretopra went on, "and behold, Christ has led the warriors to it."

"Oh, that is true. Hear him," said the white-haired old brave.

"You have insulted the spirits by your doings."

"Then tell us, what should we do?" said the old brave.

Hacugh looked at the earth and knitted his brow. He did not know what to do.

Now Gabriel, realizing from the sudden silence that something was occurring, emerged from his hut. Seeing the tribe gathered around the primitive shaman, he went down and said, "No, no, now hear me."

"They do not hear you," said Tanretopra with a shake of his head. "You are a man of Christ. A man with the goodness of Christ. But where is that power with the unchastised parts of the forest?" And he turned to the tribe. "Let Christ depart. Let you return the spirits."

"Yes, yes," cried the elderly brave. "It is true, Hacugh."

Mendoza stepped out of the forest, having heard Tanretopra's question, and the tribe grew utterly quiet. With long, slow strides, he went up to the shaman and paused. He could see the wild eyes peering out of the headpiece as Tanretopra leaned on the stick he had cut from the forest. "What you speak is a lie," Mendoza said, and he passed his own staff to the boy and stepped still closer to the shaman, so close that he could feel the breath coming out of the headpiece. "Give me that," he said, taking the shaman's stick, but Tanretopra took a spear from the white-haired brave and leveled it at Mendoza's face, leaning back, poised for the thrust.

Mendoza moved to the left and forward and seized the spear, with a wrench that sent his assailant sprawling. Now it was Tanretopra's turn to gaze up into his opponent's face. The point of the spear descended and levered off the headpiece, revealing a man whose head was painted in red and yellow stripes. The shaman rose to his feet, looked at the tribe, and then turned about and was swallowed up into the forest.

The boy gave a catcall, which was taken up by several, but they were rebuked by Mendoza, who was watching Gabriel. Then the priest turned, went back into his hut, and shut the door.

"My ways are not the ways of Christ," Mendoza said to Hacugh. "If you want the ways of Christ, go to Father Gabriel."

"I have spoken: We follow you."

"Then," said Mendoza, taking the staff from the little boy and showing it, "you can get me three logs of this wood, as thick as your chest, as long as this. They must be of hardwood, like this."

Hacugh took the staff. "Of copperwood; yes, we can do it, but why?"

"Perhaps we shall be able to return the fire of their cannons."

"Good. But where shall you get the cannonballs and gunpowder?"

"Down there," he answered.

"I see," and the Guarani went, and presently they brought him three large logs from the forest. He made them split the logs in two, and then they bored a tunnel through each of them.

Down at the foot of the falls, the Spanish and Portuguese commanders stood gazing upward. Their forces were strung out behind them farther than a day's march. "Have you been here before?" asked the Portuguese commander.

"No," said the Spaniard. He was a man who had acquired the new taste for the picturesque. "What a spectacle. It is sublime."

"Yes? Possibly. We have to go up there"—he indicated the ascending spiral of water vapor—"to hunt down a tribe of half-tamed Guarani and a couple of priests?"

"To prove that we can."

Tanretopra stood on a jutting rock at the head of the falls facing the darkening water. He took from the grasses at his feet the headpiece. He flung it far above the surface of the river to float quietly toward the falls. For a long time he stood there, naked. Then he picked up three spears and vanished in the direction of the path that led to the place where the invaders were encamped. He made no effort to conceal his approach. A sergeant saw the painted, naked figure coming toward him. With an oath he cocked his gun and fired. Tanretopra fell, then rose to his feet again and began to throw his spears.

"Fire," screamed the sergeant, panic-stricken. "Fire, damn you, fire."

The whole camp came to see the exotic corpse. "It was a noble savage," said the Spanish commander. "Look at it. The proportions are truly classical."

Above, in the village, the Guarani bound the cannon with lengths of running root to minimize the chances of their bursting. They were mounted on wooden blocks. Mendoza said to Hacugh, "I want six men to come with me below the falls to fetch the powder and the balls."

Hacugh chose five. "I will be the sixth," he declared.

"No. You must stay here. You are the commander in chief; you must lead your people if we fail to return."

"I understand." He appointed the old white-haired brave to stand in for him.

The two sentries, half asleep, did not notice the seven figures who cautiously made their way among the rocks in the early hours of the following morning. Picking his way from one group to the other, Mendoza came at last upon the ammunition train. Cannonballs, kegs of powder, ramrods, wads, and bundles of fuse were strewn all anyhow upon the ground, with the sleeping forms of tired men scattered among them, wherever they had succeeded in finding comfort among the rocks. Mendoza could see everything he wanted within twelve paces of where he crouched, with the others pressing behind him, but a soldier with a cough that kept him half awake was huddled in the midst of it.

With his knife ready in his hand, Mendoza crawled toward the coughing man. When he was almost on top of him, a cough roused the sleeper. He raised his head, and Mendoza saw he was a Negro. The next second, as his knife pricked his victim's throat, he recognized Gaspachio's face staring up at him. They stared across the knife. Then, cautiously, the veteran soldier shook his head, to signify that he would make no sound, then let his head drop, waiting.

Mendoza was bewildered. Had it been anybody else, he would have pressed his knife home, on behalf of his Guarani brothers, but this man was his private enemy. Removing the knife, Mendoza signaled him to get to his feet and accompany him. With a mute gesture, Gaspachio inquired whether he should bring his weapons with him. Mendoza shook his head and then, turning to the Guarani, pointed out to them what they were to take—some small cannonballs, three kegs of powder, ramrods, and wads. They vanished as silently as they had come, only now they were eight.

When they reached the shadow of the falls, the white-haired brave asked, "Why have you brought this man? Why did you not kill him?"

"He is an enemy of mine from the old days."

"So?"

"I cannot do it."

"Then I will do it for you."

"No," Mendoza said, stretching his arm to protect Gaspachio.

And then Gaspachio smiled. *"Ola,* Father."

"Do not call me father."

"I am forgiven, is that it?"

Mendoza looked at him and took his decision. "Yes," he said.

"Poco del mundo," came the reply. "When I heard about

your conversion, I told the others it would be complete."

"You have only to raise your voice a little to see how in-complete it was."

Apart from his coughing, Gaspachio made the ascent with-out a sound.

As soon as they reached the mission, Mendoza widened the cannon holes to take the cannonballs with the crosswoods run-ning the other way and, with the twine, bound them up. He made the braves stand well back and fired one of the cannons. The explosion was impressive, and to the jubilation of the onlookers the cannonball went whizzing among the trees on the far side of the clearing.

Mendoza reloaded it and fired again. The second shot barely cleared the open space. At the third shot the cannon disintegrated, sending slivers of wood over their heads. "Now we know," said Mendoza, "what to expect. Two rounds from each cannon. After that we are back to the weapons we are used to."

"Yes," Hacugh said. He went and examined the powder. "It is a trick."

"Yes, but a trick of a terrible kind."

"Good," observed Gaspachio. "You could start an empire of your own now."

Mendoza looked at him keenly and said to the Guarani who had put him in charge, "Keep a close watch on this one; he is tricky. Kill him if you think fit."

He positioned the cannons, loaded them up, and placed pieces of matting over their holes.

22

FILTHY AND STINKING, the ragged army of the Spanish and Portuguese was assembled at the top of the cliffs. The Spaniard took his stand above the falls and exclaimed at the view. The men fitted together the barrels and the wheels of the two large and four small guns, and they made rafts on which they tied the two large guns, as well as a couple of rafts for the Portuguese soldiers.

Mendoza saw all this from the forest where the scouts he had posted came to report.

Toward the close of that day, Gabriel repaired to his hut. He would not speak a single word to Mendoza. But on this evening he looked for a long time at the shaft of sunlight that slanted in through the tiles, and when it turned red and then disappeared, he received a message from the braves—a high-pitched war cry, taken up by the others, a word of caution and a laugh. That night he said no prayers; the morning found him on his bed without having slept.

There was a knock at the door. He issued an invitation to enter. Mendoza opened the door and stood there like a shadow in the sunlight, carrying his sword in his hand and wearing a knife in his belt, which kilted up his cassock. He shut the door behind him and knelt at Gabriel's feet.

"Well," Gabriel asked, "what is it?"

"Bless me, Father."

The pale ghost of a smile flickered on Gabriel's lips. "No," he said. "If you are right, God's blessing will be on you. But if you are wrong, my blessing isn't needed." He paused for a long moment. "If might is right, love has nothing to do in the world. And it may be so," he reflected heavily. "It may be so.

But I haven't the fortitude to live in a world like that, Mendoza. No, I won't bless you."

Mendoza rose and was turning away impassively when suddenly Gabriel called him back and gave him the blue cross that Father Julien had worn, from his own neck to Mendoza's, then embraced and kissed him.

Shortly after this, Mendoza's scouts brought him word that the enemy had begun the advance on the mission. The Portuguese detachment was approaching on rafts along the river. The Spanish contingent—the Chaco Guarani and the soldiers —was coming through the forest, dragging three pieces of light artillery.

Mendoza turned to Hacugh. "Go, and may Christ go with you."

Hacugh led the archers at a trot to a place three miles nearer to the falls, where they had hidden their canoes in a backwater. When the Portuguese poled their rafts laboriously past them, they shot out into midstream and sped their first volley of arrows on them, hitting five. The Portuguese commander cursed and ordered his men to fire. The Guarani slewed their little dugouts to the right and the left so that only two of them were hit. Then they discharged another flight of arrows. The Portuguese had to leave off poling their rafts and reply while the current got hold of their rafts and began to carry them toward the falls.

The Spanish hacked their way through the jungle and came out on the open glade that lay between them and the mission. They were halfway across when the first flight of arrows struck them. They turned and fled back into the undergrowth, leaving a quarter of their number wounded or dead in the open.

The sight of the Spaniards fleeing from them was overwhelming to Mendoza's Guarani. They broke cover, ignoring Mendoza's command to stay where they were. The Spanish commander waited till the yelling men were in the mouths of the muskets, then gave the order to fire. A third of Mendoza's force was obliterated; the rest did what they all ought to have done, and took refuge in the undergrowth. The Spanish kept silence, save for the groans from the wounded, for twenty minutes, and their commander signaled to two of his soldiers to cross the clearing. When they had crossed and found no sign of the Guarani there, he sent the rest across in twos and threes, then formed them up and resumed his advance on the village.

In the church of the village Gabriel had gathered the women, children, and elderly. They waited passively, eyes fixed on Gabriel, who read to them about Christ in his mercy, seated at the right hand of God, who would, upon the Last Day of Judgment, rectify all the miscarriages of justice. After a while, Gabriel got up and went to the porch. Never before had he seen the clearing totally empty.

On the river the Guarani acquitted themselves well. Those who remained aimed their arrows truly, and many of the uniformed soldiers were dead. Other soldiers had poled their rafts up to the riverbank, where they waited for orders. These were not given by the Portuguese commander, who was dead, as was Hacugh. On the surface of the water floated a mantle of dugout canoes, their occupants dead or wounded, and two rafts flowing after them, toward the distant thunder of the falls.

Mendoza's cannons were placed in a thicket, where the enemy must come. He made the Guarani stand back again, and again Gaspachio's face wore that thoughtful expression, watching him. Mendoza could sense the Spaniards reaching the target area, and he thrust the glowing wick into the touch hole of the cannon at his side. He leaped away. The cannon roared. He glimpsed the havoc it had caused and went to stand beside the other cannon. Another roar and the mangled shapes of the Spaniards fell at the far side of the clearing. He reloaded the first cannon and set it up. It fired and then collapsed outward, sending its splinters among the Guarani.

The dugout canoes were crewed by dead men now, and the men on the rafts were working desperately to reach the side of the river. One raft did, and one didn't; it followed the dugout canoes, with their dead men, over the falls, its three soldiers flung far into the cavernous upsurge of water.

The Spanish commander spied the thatched roof of the mission church. The Chaco Guarani got down on their haunches, and he commanded them to tie strips of cotton to their arrows and set them on fire. Then, from a prone position, they fired.

Smoke began to billow from the church roof, and the sound of crackling flames filled the air. The old and young wailed at Gabriel, who seized the ciborium and pushed open the door.

As soon as he reached the top of the steps, he began to chant: "In thee, O Lord, have I put my trust; let me never be ashamed; deliver me, in my righteousness."

The Guarani poured out of the church after him, clinging to his cassock, and began to chant, "Bow down thine ear to me; deliver me speedily; be thou a strong house of defense for me." Unhurriedly he led them out of the shadow of the church, toward the Spanish soldiers.

Babuie was choked by the fumes and by fear; he left the hubbub around Gabriel and dashed to the far side of the clearing. There he saw Mendoza, and he went gladly toward him.

With the remaining gunpowder, Mendoza had mined the bridge over which the Spaniards would have to come, and he was bending over to light the long fuse of the explosives.

"Look," said Gaspachio, and Mendoza saw the boy.

"Go back," he yelled desperately. "Go back." Babuie came to a halt in full view of the Spanish commander. Mendoza ran to him and turned him around and pushed him. "Now, go," he yelled and the boy started at a jog and then went hurtling into the forest.

Mendoza turned and saw Gaspachio standing in the middle of the bridge, by the kegs, holding the end of the fuse in his hands as if to tear it out. He looked at Mendoza and then slowly shook his head.

Mendoza drew his sword and rushed at Gaspachio, who fled to the other side of the bridge. Mendoza, following him, was met by the Spanish musketeers. He attacked them fiendishly, as in his old soldiering days. It was then that the Spanish commander, astounded, drew his pistol and shot him.

As he fell, Mendoza thought, How are Philippo and my mother? Then he turned his misty eyes toward Gabriel, who was coming toward him amid the Guarani, leading them on, chanting, "Pull me out of the net that they have laid privily for me; for thou art my strength."

The sergeant major took careful aim and executed Gabriel, for that, as he never grew tired of telling, was a priest who had made the Garden of Eden in his mission. Gabriel had a swift dream of the coast of Kerry—"Father, forgive me"— and through this he could see the set face of Mendoza—"my son."

With a pale face Altamirano read the three-page report that the Spanish commander had prepared for him. It was night, and huge moths were flying in and out the windows of the captain general's residence.

Cabeza looked at his other guest and shrugged, but Hontar looked away.

"Have you the effrontery to call this slaughter necessary?" Altamirano asked in a low voice.

Cabeza stared back at him. "Given our legitimate purpose, duly sanctioned by the Reverenced Visitor General, yes."

Altamirano made no reply. He walked to the window and looked out at the cool night sky.

Hontar gave a cough. "You had no choice, Visitor General. You must work in the real world. And the real world is thus."

"Oh, no," said Altamirano. "Thus have we made it."

New York Times bestsellers— _Berkley Books at their best!_